Ariel Rising

Ariel Between Two Worlds: Episode 1

BY A.J. AND C.S. SPARBER

Table of Contents

iii

Web site: http://www.ajsparber.com/

Published by: Mind's Eye Press
ISBN-10: 0692543074
ISBN-13: 978-0692543078

Edited by Barb Terry-Howe. Cover design by Mae I Design.

Dedicated to those who wonder…

"What if ?"

Warning...

The following story might be hard to put down.

Acknowledgements

We'd like to thank our beta readers: Michelle LaPointe, Lisa Firke, Alexis Masters, Linda Rathgeber, Donna Cangelosi, Linda Spitzer, and Stephen Sidler. There are simply no words we can find to express the gratitude we feel. Thank you, one and all. And a special thank you goes to each and every one of our children, who, without a single threat, willingly read our story. Your interest in our little labor of love, as well as your valuable feedback, will be remembered for eons. Thank you Brian, Marc, Ryan, Jessica, and Melanie.

Chapter 1

I lock the front door behind me, do some quick stretches in the driveway, and then hit the street running.

There's nothing like a good, brisk afternoon run. It's a transcendent time. A time when I can breathe deeply and be alone in my thoughts.

My love of running comes from my mom, Dr. Andi (Andrea) Worthington—a pediatric surgeon and serious fitness advocate. She trained me well because, by ninth grade, I could run like a doe—probably faster than any girl on the track team. But committing my time and energy to a team sport is not my thing. Getting good grades and going to the right college is far more important in the grand scheme of things. In life, it's all about return on investment.

My regular route takes me into the Shenandoah Valley National Park—Virginia's own version of paradise. As I run, the afternoon sun wraps me in its warm caress, and my mind drifts.

Here I am, three weeks removed from my eighteenth birthday, graduation just a couple of months away, and then the countdown to college. My life will have meaning. I can make a difference. I *will* make a difference. And although it was not specifically mentioned in Bryce Institute's marketing brochures, there is a very good chance the Institute will have a decent inventory of men with fully functioning minds—and in full command of their hormones. How good will that be?

The sound of a car door closing brings me back to reality, and I look up to see a large shape barreling toward me from across the road. As his face comes into focus, I groan. It's Luke Blanton—star of the

Edgewood high school football team, and my idiot ex-boyfriend. We dated for six months, and it was not a good relationship. I wanted to take things slow. He wanted it all. And that was not going to happen. I never loved him. I hardly even liked him. I tolerated him. And, ultimately, I told him to get lost.

He's been trying to get me back for months and it's really getting annoying.

"Hey, Ari," he says through a crooked grin. "You look really hot."

He is leering like a bear in heat. I remember that leer.

"Well, I've been running for half an hour and it's kind of warm out. Yeah, I'm hot." I roll my eyes. "What are you doing around here, anyway? Are you lost?"

Luke lives at the other end of town. He's stalking me.

"Can we talk?" As he asks, he nudges me off the road and down toward the forest trail.

Alone in the woods with Luke—this is *not* going to end well. I begin to assess my escape options when, without warning, he grabs me around the waist and pulls me into him.

"Let me go!" I growl.

Luke is six foot two and well over two hundred pounds. I'm five inches shorter and tip the scales at just over a hundred and thirty—soaking wet.

"Chill. Hear me out, Okay?"

"Let go of me and maybe I'll listen." I'm trying really hard to suppress the dread that's building up inside me.

He loosens his hold, but is still very much in violation of my personal space. "Listen, I was a jerk last year."

"Uh-huh. Talk about understatements."

"I should've given you more time to warm up to me. But that's all water under the dam. I think we can move past that."

"Move past what? Attempted date rape?" I probably should be less confrontational, but Luke is playing me, and I'm getting seriously cranked. "By the way, Einstein, it's water *over* the dam—or *under* the bridge," I add with a scowl.

"Whatever. But date rape? That's a little extreme, Ari. I really do care about you, and I just want a chance to show it. How about we start over. Let's kiss and make up and we'll—"

"Damn it, Blanton!" I snap. "We've had this conversation before. There is nothing between us." I may wind up being the last virgin in Virginia, but I want more out of life. Much more. "Read my lips, meathead. I—"

"Meathead? What the hell is that supposed to mean?"

"*All in the Family.* TVLand. Classic sitcom. It means dead from the neck up."

I realize, probably too late, that antagonizing him is not a tactically sound approach. He leans into me, his lips dangerously close to mine, and whispers, "You got spirit. Makes me want you even more."

Oh great, he's trying to sound romantic.

Then he kisses me. Hard.

I manage to disengage my mouth from his, grab a breath, and tear into him. "I don't want you. I don't like you. And if you don't take your hands off of me I'm going to hurt you."

Can I hurt him?

"I'll get my hands off you after we settle up," he says with a sneer.

"Exactly *what* are we settling, Luke?"

"I want us to go to the prom."

"I'm not going to the prom with you."

"Are you going with that college dude…Gale?"

"His name is Galen, and what goes on between us is none of your damn business."

"I'm making it my business, Ari. We belong together."

3

"We do not belong together, and you're really starting to aggravate me. You need to leave me alone. Go home, Luke."

He's beginning to scare me a little. And then something strange happens. My scalp begins to tingle. The tingle turns into a buzz that reaches the middle of my chest. It's as if a fuse were lit. I feel charged, coiled, and ready to spring. Anger and fear is displaced by focus. My mind yields command to my body.

Luke leans in for another kiss.

Target acquired.

Before I can think, my left arm shoots out like a piston, and the heel of my hand connects with his nose.

He yelps like a puppy and staggers backwards. Blood gushes. And he looks extremely pissed off.

"You're dead meat," he says, glaring at me, as he struggles to regain his balance. Then, without warning, he charges.

Luke's expression is pure evil, and I know I'm in serious trouble. But something is off. Really off...

The world around me slows down. Luke seems as if he's moving in slow motion.

I dip to the left, easily avoiding his punch, as my right hand explodes into his jaw. Luke crumples to the ground in a heap. His eyes are shut tight. He isn't moving.

What did I do? Will he get up and attack again? Will he *ever* get up?

I turn and dart into the woods, accelerating at a frightening rate, as my body maneuvers over and around obstacles—like a guided missile.

Before I know it, I'm standing beside the Falls. My chest is heaving and I'm sweating profusely.

A nervous chuckle escapes me, because Renegade Falls is over a mile from where I left Luke. It doesn't make sense. Sure, I can run a mile. Easily. But not at a full-out sprint. Nobody can do that. But...

I shake my head rapidly, trying to force myself to think clearly. But I can't, because every muscle and nerve in my body is on fire, and my eyes won't focus. And then my head begins to spin.

I gingerly lower myself to a seat on a large rock and play back my confrontation with Luke. When I get to the last scene, I shiver.

"Did I k-kill him?" I ask myself.

A man's voice, deep and clear, answers, "He'll be okay."

I turn toward the voice, and a tall stranger steps into view. He's dressed for a run in black training pants and a sleeveless black tee. His neatly-trimmed hair is black as night; his eyes a vivid shade of green. He looks to be in his early twenties. He is strikingly handsome.

"Who are—?"

Before I can complete the question, a wave of nausea hits me, and I treat Whatshisname to a Broadway-quality puke show.

He crouches beside me, pulling the hair away from my face as he gently rubs a hand over my back. I heave again and again until everything I've ever eaten spews out—at least it feels that way.

"I'm Davin Andersen," he says softly.

"Oh, I'm so embarrassed, I—"

"It's okay. I saw what happened. There's nothing to be embarrassed about. Here, drink some water," he says, handing me a bottle.

I want to crawl into a hole and die.

"How much did you see?" I ask in a small voice, as I take a drink.

"Pretty much the important parts. He grabbed you, you told him to let go, he wouldn't, so you hit him."

"How did you happen to be there in the first place?"

Is he friend or foe?

"You're Ariel Worthington. Right?"

"You know me?" I turn to face him. He is watching me intently, with a look that seems to express compassion and concern. "I don't believe we've ever met."

"I know *of* you." His eyes lock onto mine, and he smiles, showing off a pair of dimples that are impossibly cute.

"And how is that? I'm not very famous."

"I'm your new neighbor. Your mom stopped by earlier this afternoon to welcome us. When she saw that I was dressed for a run, she told me what an avid runner you are. So, when my aunt saw you leave for a run, she suggested I go make friends with our new neighbor. The rest, as they say, is history."

"Oh. Well, that's a unique way to meet people," I say in a teasing tone.

"It's not easy to meet nice people these days. I guess I jumped at the chance. Or ran at the chance. Anyway, you were maybe two hundred yards ahead when your friend showed up. I stopped where you and he entered the park, and it occurred to me that he was probably your boyfriend, so—"

I cut him off.

"He's my ex-boyfriend. I ended our relationship last year."

Davin is tall, taller than Luke. And while Luke is built like a grizzly bear, Davin is more like a large cat—lithe, lissome, and imposing.

"I see," he says, giving me an appraising look. "I was about to turn back when I heard yelling. So I headed toward the voices to make sure you were safe. Before I could react, he was on the ground. I started to call out to you, but you took off like a missile."

"Yes, I was really moving pretty fast."

"Extremely fast. I'm surprised I was able to catch up with you."

"You look like a fast runner," I say. "Why did you follow me up here?"

"I wanted to make sure you were okay."

Maybe chivalry isn't dead, after all. "Thank you, Davin."

He nods. "The boy who attacked you…Luke?"

"Yes."

"Has he harassed you before?"

"Not like this. Ever since I broke up with him he's been trying to get me back. He's a hotshot football player and he thinks all females should grovel at his feet. He's…"

"An ass?"

"That works," I say with a little smile.

"Well, I'm glad you were not injured."

"I appreciate your concern." I am genuinely grateful.

"You could have been seriously hurt, Ariel."

"I know…and please, call me Ari.

"Alright, *Ari*."

I smile.

"So, you moved in today?" I ask, trying to be neighborly.

"Early this morning."

"Did you move here for work?"

"School, actually. I'm transferring from UC Santa Barbara to Bryce Institute. They were gracious enough to offer me a masters scholarship, which could have something to do with my aunt being recruited to head their genetics lab. Hopefully, I won't embarrass her."

"Well, that's a coincidence. I'll be going to the Institute, too. And to tell you the truth, I'm a little worried that I'll embarrass myself."

"If my first impression of you is accurate, I think you'll do just fine."

"Thank you, Davin. And I have a feeling you will do your aunt proud. What's your degree in?"

"Military history. And your major will be?"

"I'll be studying paleoanthropology," I say, feeling a little more geeky than I would like.

"Ah, a fascinating field," he says with an adorable smile. "Perhaps you will one day discover how mankind really evolved."

Usually I get a really blank stare at the mention of the word *paleoanthropology*. Davin actually knows what it means. I'm impressed.

"That's the plan. The Institute has a phenomenal program."

Bryce Institute is a very exclusive college, run by the Bryce Foundation, which is part think tank, part research facility, and conveniently located right here in the Valley, at the foot of Mt. Evan. Ostensibly, the best scientists and engineers in the world work there. You don't apply to the Institute—they recruit you. I'd been planning on going to Virginia Tech when I received an offer from Bryce—a full-ride scholarship. It was an offer I couldn't refuse.

"Have you taken the campus tour yet?" Davin asks.

"Uh-huh. Last week, actually. I'm really amped up. The place is awesome. What about you? Have you taken the tour?"

"Not yet. But according to my aunt, it's a remarkable place."

"So is Santa Barbara, I think."

"It's okay."

Southern California. I imagine him balanced on a surfboard, rippling muscles glistening in the sun, shorts riding low on his hips, abs tensed. My cheeks begin to heat up and I know it's time to leave the beach.

"It's kind of quiet around here. Hope you don't get bored."

"I'll survive."

"That's good," I say with a coy smile. "Oh, my! I almost forgot—do you think Luke is still back there?"

"He woke up a few seconds after you ran off. Looked really embarrassed when he saw me. I'd say he's going to need a nose job."

"I thought I hurt him badly."

"You defended yourself, Ari. How do *you* feel?"

"Better. So, did Luke say anything before he left?"

"We had a little chat. The notion of being defeated by a woman did not sit well with him. He wanted to go after you, but I told him that would be extremely ill-advised—and possibly painful."

"You really said that?" I am moved. Davin is my knight in black running clothes.

"I did."

"*Then* what happened?"

"He came at me swinging, so I hit him…in the ribs. As he knelt, doubled over, I informed him that I saw what happened—all of it—and that if you wanted to press charges, I would gladly volunteer my services as an eyewitness."

I chuckle. "I like your style."

"Thank you," he says with an unassuming smile.

I feel comfortable with him. At ease.

"I'm going to call a friend to pick me up," I say. "Would you like a ride or would you rather finish your run?"

I really hope he'll stay with me.

"I don't think I should leave you here alone."

Good answer.

I call Ella and give her a shortened version of what happened. She's an hour away—give or take. Frankly, if it means more time alone with Davin, I kind of hope traffic is seriously backed up.

"She'll be here in about an hour. You really don't have to wait with me if you've got things to do."

"Are you trying to get rid of me?"

"Nah. I just wanted to give you an option in case you really want to leave."

"I'll stay. Besides, it's really pretty up here," he says, giving me an appraising glance.

9

Is he flirting with me?

"This is one of my favorite places," I remark.

"Perhaps you could show me around someday? You know, give me a tour?"

"I'd love to," I say, because I really would.

"So you don't have a current boyfriend?"

He *is* flirting with me.

A blush spreads across my cheeks, and all I can do is stare, because my voice refuses to work.

He looks apologetic. "I didn't mean to pry—"

I cut him off because his question is not out of line and I really want him to know that I'm unattached. Mostly.

"It's okay," I say with a shy smile. "And it was a fair question. I date occasionally, but I am not in an exclusive relationship."

"I see," he replies, politely. "May I call you later?"

"Yes," I say, as I remove my phone from the porta-pocket strapped to my upper left arm.

We exchange numbers and stroll back toward the road—at a leisurely pace.

Davin is just what I need after my encounter with Luke. He has a calming effect on me.

Curious. *Very curious.*

Chapter 2

Davin looks surprised when he sees the bright red Jeep Wrangler bouncing down the path toward us. "Your friend?"

"Yes, that would be Ella."

"She drives a very capable vehicle," he remarks.

"She is a very capable driver."

Ella pulls up in front of us, gets out of the Jeep, and rushes to my side. "Are you okay, sweetie? Luke didn't hurt you, did he?"

"I'm fine, Ella. Not a scratch." I place my hand on Davin's arm. "This is Davin Andersen—my new neighbor."

She's gawking. Guess I can't blame her. "Howdy, neighbor! Nice to meet you. Did you scare Luke off? You look as if you could," she says, offering her hand.

Davin smiles and shakes her hand. "It's nice to meet you, Ella. I'm not sure if I scared Luke away. Let's just say I helped him to decide that hanging around would not be in his best interests."

Ella chuckles. "I like your attitude, Davin. Confidence without arrogance. It's a real skill."

"You should know," I say with a wink.

She gives me a big smile. Ella and I have been friends since we were toddlers. She's classically pretty—tall and graceful, with wavy, straw-colored hair, hazel eyes, a fabulous figure, and a perpetually impish grin that masks a razor-sharp mind. And she probably knows me better than I know myself.

"Let's go folks," Ella says, as she slides into the Jeep.

Davin hops in back, and I ride shotgun.

Ella puts the Jeep in gear and we bounce up the rocky path toward the road as if we were shot out of a cannon. Had I asked Ella to slow down, she'd have sped up—so I hold my tongue *and* the large grab handle on the Jeep's dashboard.

As we speed along Valley Road, toward home, I tell her what happened. But I sense that Ella is not buying it.

"Come on, Davin administered the beating. Right?"

Davin shakes his head. "It was all Ari."

"It was," I say. "Perhaps I had an adrenaline surge?"

She gives me a strange look, so I try again.

"Hysterical strength?"

Ella wrinkles her brow. "You hit him in the nose? Then you hit him in the jaw…and knocked him out?"

I nod.

"Okay, sweetie. If you say so."

Nope, she's not buying it at all.

There are issues I cannot explain. Issues that defy explanation. When Luke attacked me, he seemed to be moving in slow motion. There was no way I could have missed hitting him. And how was I able to run so far, so fast? Did I lose track of time? There is no logical explanation.

But if I did run that fast, *Davin must have, too.* Oh, man.

Davin's house is just across the road from mine. Ella drops him off, makes a quick U-turn, then pulls into my driveway.

"He's really hot, sweetie. Let me know right now if you want him, or he's mine," she says with an exaggerated drawl.

"For heaven's sake, I just met the guy today."

"Yeah, me too," she says with a smirk.

"Stop it!" I say, as I roll my eyes. "You already have a boyfriend."

"So you *do* want him. I knew it! But you've got Galen. What about Galen, huh? He's pretty dang hot, too."

"There is nothing serious between Galen and me." Did I just say that? Where did that come from?

"Well, I've heard he's totally into you. You better tell him you just met the man of your dreams, sweetie, because the way you just watched Davin walk away from this car was very PG-13, in my humble opinion."

"Ella, you don't have humble opinions. Why don't we go inside so we can start planning the wedding. Okay?"

"Nice!" Ella exclaims. She's grinning from ear to ear.

But I'm not grinning, because I can't figure out what changed. This morning I liked Galen. A lot. Now? Not so much. It's as if Davin entered my consciousness and made himself right at home. I can't stop thinking about him, which frightens me, because I never obsess over guys. *Never.*

"Hi, Ari. Hi, Ella," Mom calls out from the kitchen, as we walk inside the house. "Come here. I need to tell you something."

Mom is in full gourmet chef mode. The scent of her famous roasted chicken hovers in the air like ambrosia.

"Hi, Mom," I say.

"Hi, Doc. Something smells fabulous," Ella says.

Mom turns and raises an eyebrow as she looks me up and down.

"What happened to you? You look...are you okay?"

"It's a long story, Mom. I'm perfectly fine. I just got into a little tussle with Luke."

"Sit down and define exactly what you mean by 'a little tussle,' young lady."

Mom sits across from me and folds her arms, awaiting my report. She has that special look in her eyes that tells me there is absolutely no escape until she gets full disclosure.

I take a deep breath and begin...

"I was running along Valley Road when a car pulled over and stopped, just ahead of me. It was Luke. He nudged me down the trail, and then we argued. It seems he would like to rekindle our romance. You can imagine how that went."

"I imagine he hasn't gotten any smarter since I last talked to him?"

"He's worse. He kept trying to kiss me. When I told him to stop, he wouldn't. I was somewhere between mad as a hornet and scared—and I snapped. I hit him in the nose..."

Mom cuts in. "You hit Luke? Really?"

"As crazy as it sounds, I did. And then he charged, and I hit him again, and he kind of got knocked out."

"Honey, people either get knocked out or they don't. There is no *kind of*—at least from a clinical perspective. What exactly makes you believe he was unconscious?"

"Well, his eyes were closed tight and he didn't move."

"Ari, where is Luke now? Was he still lying there when you left?"

"No. After I hit him, I panicked and bolted up to the Falls. I didn't know it, but our new neighbor, Davin Andersen, saw it all—the kiss, the hit, and my running away. Davin stopped to make sure Luke was okay, but Luke went after him. Davin punched him in the stomach and watched him stumble away."

"So Luke was gone when you left the park?"

"Yes."

Mom grabs her phone and makes a call.

"Janice, this is Andi...

"Yes, I know. Are you feeling better?…

"That's good.…

"I have a favor to ask…

"Thanks. A close friend of Ari's was injured today, and we wanted to make sure he was okay…

"I know…

"His name is Luke Blanton. Is he still in the ER?"

Dr. Janice Ellison runs the ER at Edgewood Memorial Hospital. She and Mom attended medical school together and are very good friends. They are probably breaking a few patient disclosure rules, but...

Mom ends the call and looks at me. "You seem to have had quite an impact on Luke. His nose is broken, and he has a grade three concussion, which means no sports for at least a month. But he should be fine."

"Oh, wow." I grab the sides of my head and moan. "How could I have done that to him?"

"You're a strong healthy girl, honey. Noses are not all that difficult to fracture—especially if you struck him just right. Give me the blow-by-blow. Tell me exactly what happened. And please stop staring at *my* nose."

I explain as best as I can. When I finish, Mom rests her chin in her hands and pauses for a moment before responding.

"A direct blow to the bridge of the nose could easily cause a fracture. I think you have the strength to do that. As for the concussion, the fact that he was running toward you enabled you to generate significantly more power than if he'd been a stationary target—enough power to cause a concussion—especially if you consider that he probably hit his head when he fell…" She pauses, covering my hand with hers. "And I do not want you to feel any remorse. Had you not incapacitated him, it could have been far worse."

I shudder as I think about what could have happened. "Yes, it definitely could have been worse."

"What I don't understand is how an accomplished athlete could let someone so much smaller get the upper hand. We'll have to do a superpower scan on you." She gives me a crooked grin and continues. "I'll call Sheriff Johnson and let him know what happened. I don't think we need to press charges, but I do want to make sure we have this on record. You might need to meet with a deputy and fill out a report." Mom scowls and looks pissed. "I never liked that boy, Ari. He's out of control. If he comes near you, I want you to call 911 immediately. Okay?"

I nod. "Did Dr. Ellison mention Luke's ribs?"

She suppresses a chuckle. "Yes. He suffered a nondisplaced fracture of the seventh rib. It's not serious."

"Davin must have hit him pretty hard, huh?"

Mom raises an eyebrow. "It would seem that he did. Why don't you get cleaned up. Davin and his aunt will be our guests for dinner—in about one hour. If you are still interested in how hard he hit Luke, you can ask him yourself. Better get busy." She smiles as if she's just discovered a cure for the common cold.

"Oh no! I'm a mess!" I exclaim, turning toward Ella, who seems to be thoroughly enjoying herself...at my expense.

"Sweetie," Ella says, "I'll make sure you clean up real good...because I think—

"Please don't think. Not now. Can you just help me get ready? Please?"

"Of course, sweetie."

"Honey," Mom says, straight-faced, "I've met him. I know he's gorgeous. Now go get ready for dinner." Then she turns with a flourish...and giggles. She actually giggles.

After a much-needed hot shower, I feel invigorated, as Ella goes to work on me. It's truly amazing what that girl can do with a makeup kit and a curling iron in less than thirty minutes. Of course, she also picks out my clothes—black skinny jeans, a red V-neck top, and black ballet flats.

I feel chic.

Ella stands behind me as I look in the mirror. "You look hot, sweetie."

"Thanks Ella. You really can work wonders."

"You've got the assets to work with—silky black hair, hypnotic gray eyes, a million-dollar smile, and an amazing figure—when you're not hiding it under running clothes."

I'm such a tomboy. If it wasn't for Mom and Ella, my entire wardrobe would consist of running clothes, jeans, and casual tops. Practical? Yes. But I have this sudden urge to take a more hands-on role in my appearance.

"Thanks, Ella. I don't know what I'd do without you. We'll have to go shopping. I think it's time my wardrobe grew up. You know?"

"That's my girl," she says, smiling proudly.

I'm about to say something, when I feel a tingle. It starts along my scalp and works its way down my entire body. And then the doorbell rings.

Ella looks at me and laughs. "Remember, he's just a guy. Okay?"

"Got it."

"Shall we go?"

"Sure. No biggie. He's just a guy, after all."

"Just don't forget it between here and the front door."

I'm in serious trouble because Davin is not *just* a guy. Nope.

Chapter 3

After introductions, Ella leaves for a dinner date with her boyfriend Tom—but not before telling Davin and me what an adorable couple we make.

Much to my relief, dinner goes without a hitch. Davin's Aunt Thalia is charming and down to earth—and insists I call her Thalia. Actually, Davin calls her Thalia, too, which seems a little *strange* to me—except when you consider that she looks far too young to be his aunt. She could easily pass for his sister. Or his girlfriend.

Her chocolate-colored hair is tightly wound into a bun, making her look a bit matronly. But she is *very* pretty. And she looks really nice in jeans and a sweater—a blue sweater that matches her eyes.

Mom is in top social form, while Davin is charming and engaging. And a sight to behold in a muscle-hugging polo shirt over faded jeans.

As it turns out, Thalia is a molecular biologist, so she and Mom have a lot in common. After dinner, they talk shop. It sounds interesting, but I really want to socialize with Davin, so I invite him on a tour of the backyard, the highlight of the Worthington homestead.

The house has been in Dad's family for several generations and is situated on one hundred very beautiful acres comprised of pine forest, woodland paths, a ten-acre spring-fed lake, a large expanse of lawn, and a formal garden near the house—which is Mom's domain. Gardening is her favorite hobby. She does planting and pruning, while I take care of weeding, feeding, and mulching.

As Davin and I walk toward the lake, a nearly-full moon illuminates our path. "This is really beautiful," he says. "How large is your property?"

"A little over a hundred acres."

"That's a lot of land. It must be difficult to take care of."

"Most of it is natural. The lawn area is manageable, and I'm an expert tractor pilot," I say, smiling.

"Do you swim in the lake?"

"When it's really hot. But the water snakes and snapping turtles creep me out, especially since I can't see to the bottom. Mostly, I like to sit beside the lake and contemplate life."

"So, this is your personal Walden Pond." Half his face is bathed in soft moonlight, making him look angelic.

"It is. Oh, and Renegade Falls is only about a mile through the woods." I point in the general direction. "The scenery along the way is spectacular."

"Are you still willing to take me there?"

"Sure. If you still want to go," I say, trying to hide my excitement.

His right eye twitches slightly. "I do." Then he pulls out his phone and starts to type.

I chuckle. "Important call?"

He holds out a hand, motioning me to wait. "Weather looks perfect for Saturday. Sunny and mid-eighties. You like picnics?"

"I love picnics. And it would be a shame to waste the warm weather. It's usually in the sixties this time of year."

"Then it's a date," he says.

"Yeah, I guess it is," I reply, suppressing a sudden impulse to jump up and down.

"Saturday at eleven?"

"Perfect."

"Great. I'll take care of the supplies. We'll meet here and take the scenic route to the Falls. Okay?"

"I'm in." Then a thought flits into my head. "Wear a swimsuit so we can go behind the Falls. It's totally cool."

He arches his brow and nods, which causes me to blush. I'm curious. I've never reacted like this before. Then I realize. I've never met a guy like Davin before.

"So, are there usually a lot of hikers at the Falls on weekends?"

"Actually, no. It's one of many waterfalls in the park and it's not all that accessible. It's small, intimate, and the closest parking is at least a two-mile hike. Ella and I go there a lot and we rarely, if ever, see another soul. I'm afraid you're probably going to be alone with me," I say with a raised brow.

Davin gazes into my eyes. I hold his gaze, refusing to blink.

"Ari, you have the most interesting eyes I've ever seen. They are like pools of liquid silver. I…"

He pauses and places his hands on my shoulders, which causes my heart to race. I don't know where to put my hands. Should I hug him? Should I…

"Ari…?"

I shake my head rapidly. "Sorry. Mom says I have my dad's eyes. He died when I was a little girl. I…"

His smile fades. "I'm sorry. I hope I didn't upset you."

"You didn't. It's just been a very long and trying day."

I want to melt into his arms. I really do.

"That it has," he says.

And with that little exchange, all hope for a romantic interlude dissolves.

When we arrive back at the house, Thalia and Mom are talking as if they've been friends and colleagues for years. "So you see, Andi, the key to eliminating genetic issues starts with mtDNA. My approach is to intervene, preventing transmission of bad DNA from parent to child."

"Your approach is brilliant, Thalia," Mom says, just as Davin and I enter the room.

"We're back," I say cheerfully.

"Did you have a nice walk?" Thalia asks.

"Yes," Davin answers, smiling.

Thalia smiles back. "It's getting late and Ari has school tomorrow. We should go." She turns to Mom. "Andi, dinner was delicious, and I thoroughly enjoyed your company. Perhaps when I get settled in at the Institute we can meet and discuss my research."

"I would like that very much, Thalia," Mom replies.

"Excellent," Thalia says. "I will call you soon."

"Your chicken was magnificent, Dr. Worthington," Davin remarks. "And Ari, I really enjoyed our time together. I cannot wait until Saturday."

Thalia and Mom seem to raise their brows in unison, which makes me smile.

"Goodnight," I say, as Davin and Thalia leave.

Mom places a steaming pot of tea on the table and motions me over to sit with her. As she fills our cups, a warm smile spreads across her face. She looks as if she is about to say something, but thinks better of it as her lips squeeze into a thin line. Then her smile returns and she speaks. "I guess Galen won't be coming around anymore?"

"What makes you say that?"

"You're attracted to Davin. Aren't you?"

"I'm a little surprised you'd think I was attracted to him. Was it obvious?"

"Very much so—in both directions, actually. The looks you exchanged were precious." She looks at me with a motherly smile.

"Precious?"

"Yes. I thought that sounded more mature than *googly-eyed*."

I laugh. "You're pretty precious yourself, Mom."

"I like him, Ari. He seems really nice."

"You do? You don't think he's too old for me?"

How old **is** he? I completely forgot to ask.

"You are a very mature eighteen. No, I don't think a four-year age differential is an issue at all."

"Actually, I thought he was a little older. Did you ask Thalia how old he is?"

"Of course."

I chuckle. "So how did you and Thalia get along?"

"Like old friends. She is absolutely brilliant, and I'm dying to learn more about her research." She pauses and smiles at me. "So, back to you and Davin. I assume he's asked you out?"

"He did. We're going on a picnic. Saturday. Renegade Falls."

"Oh, that's such a lovely spot. I'm sure you'll have a great time."

"Yeah. I think we will. You and Dad used to go there often. Right?"

"Yes. It was one of our favorite places," she says with a rueful gaze.

Dad was killed when his private plane crashed. I was eight. Mom and I were devastated. It was so sudden—and his body was not recovered—so the funeral was really hard on her. She'll go out with a guy every now and then, but things never get much past the first date. She's so gorgeous. Her chestnut-brown hair looks like fine silk, she has a face that belongs on Mt. Olympus, and a figure that can stop hearts. You'd never know she's in her early forties.

"You've never stopped loving him, have you?" I ask.

"I never will. We weren't just husband and wife. We were soul mates. What we had together doesn't go away. It's forever."

"Do you think you'll ever find a man to love again? Not like Dad…but—"

"Oh, I think it's possible. I'm not dead, you know," she says with a little grin. "Tell you what, if Davin has an unmarried uncle, make sure to let me know."

"I will," I reply. "I better head up to bed. Math quiz tomorrow."

"Sweet dreams. Oh, and Ari…"

"Yes, Mom?"

"Are you still going out with Galen tomorrow night?"

"Yeah, I guess so. Why?"

"I think he likes you a lot more than you like him. Be careful. He doesn't seem like the jealous type, but you never know. I don't want to see a replay of the Luke situation."

"You think I'm going to stop seeing him. Don't you?"

"Aren't you?"

Am I?

"I'm not exactly sure. I still like him and I've only known Davin a few hours. I don't want to act impulsively, and it's not like Galen and I are in love or anything. It's pretty casual, Mom."

At least that's the way I feel most of the time. But sometimes I'm just not sure how I feel.

Mom smiles. "You're a lot more levelheaded than I was at your age."

I smile back. "If I am, it's because of you. Goodnight, Mom. I love you."

"Love you, too, Ari."

"More than chocolate?"

"Much more."

23

Chapter 4

I steal a glance at him as he studies his menu intently. At a little over six feet tall, Galen is solidly built and moves with an athlete's grace. His dark blond hair is a little on the long side, framing an attractive face and giving him a casual, surfer-boy look. He pulls it off really well.

"What are you having?" I ask, as he notices me staring.

He smiles. "The aged porterhouse is calling to me. How about you?"

"I feel like prime rib tonight."

His eyebrows twitch and his blue eyes do a cute little dance. "Then perhaps I'll have you, instead."

I roll my eyes. "You have a one-track mind." And a really corny sense of humor sometimes, I think.

"You can't blame a guy for trying. Can you?"

"Only if he tries too hard," I answer, a little more sharply than I should have.

"I'm sorry, Ari. It's just that…"

I hold my hand up. "I know, Galen. We've had this discussion before. I'm just not ready for the level of intimacy you are looking for…and that's all there is to it. End of issue."

He lets out a long sigh. "I don't understand. This is the twenty-first century…"

"Don't ruin our date."

Galen clamps his mouth shut and pouts. He's spoiled. He's had everything handed to him his entire life and I'm not about to offer myself up to him on a silver platter or, worse, a set of silk sheets.

24

Thankfully, our server appears before I can say something I might regret, and I wonder why all of Galen's faults seem magnified tonight. I quickly push that thought out of my mind because I know where it will lead and I can't afford to go there. Not tonight.

"Good evening, I'm Anne. May I get you something to drink?" our server asks. She is attractive, forty-something, and seems very confident.

"I'd like a glass of the Ravenswood Zinfandel," Galen replies.

"Excellent choice, sir," Anne says with a polite smile. "And for the lady?"

"Perrier with a twist of lime, thank you," I say.

She nods and smiles at me. "I'll have those out in a moment."

Our server leaves and I chuckle. "How do you do that, Galen?"

"Do what?" he answers with a twinkle in his eyes.

"How do you manage to order wine, or beer, or the occasional cocktail, without getting carded?"

It's true. Galen is nineteen. And nearly every time we have dinner out, he orders an alcoholic beverage. And he's never been carded. It's so weird.

"Hmm. That's an excellent question. I'm not sure. Maybe I'm charming enough to be…disarming?"

I snort. "Maybe you're a warlock. Did you put spell on our nice server?"

"You figured me out," he says, just as our drinks are served.

We place our dinner orders and, as Anne walks away, Galen's expression grows serious.

"Are you still onboard with the Institute?"

"Of course. It's one of the most prestigious colleges in the world, and it's so close to home…"

Ever since I told Galen about my scholarship offer, he's been trying to talk me into going to the University of Virginia at Charlottesville, which happens to be the college *he* attends.

"You know my dad can get you a scholarship to UVC. It's not far…and we could be together on campus."

Is he nuts? I've never even met his parents and it's not like I'm leaving the country. He wants us to be together. He wants us to live together.

"You want me to move into your apartment, don't you?"

"Well…"

"I'm not ready for that. And I *am* going to the Institute." His eyes flash with rage, but he quickly recovers. The anger is gone, and now he looks hurt. I feel sorry for him. But if he really cares about me, he should respect my decisions and be supportive of them. It would be different if I were going to move hundreds of miles away. But that's not the case. This shouldn't be an issue. But it obviously is.

He reaches across the table and takes my hands in his. As we lock eyes, it occurs to me that he's trying to figure things out. Maybe it wouldn't be so bad going to UVC. Maybe I should be more open-minded about sex. Maybe…

Whoa! What am I thinking? That's not me! I break eye contact and shake my head, rapidly, as if I'm trying to evict a spider from my hair.

"Are you okay, Ari?" His smile is wide. What is he smiling about?

"I'm fine." Am I fine? I'm still reeling from my encounter with Luke. And for some strange reason, I'm really wishing that it was Davin Andersen sitting across from me right now. Strange. Very strange.

I'm saved by Anne, who comes sidling up to our table, a large tray adroitly balanced on a single upturned palm. The woman has some skills. She smiles as she sets our plates down. "How was the Zin?" she asks Galen.

"Excellent," he says.

I just shake my head. Whatever power Galen has over servers and bartenders could be marketed to teens. He could make a fortune.

After dinner, we head over to Galen's to watch a movie. His apartment is in an upscale development, not far from the UVC campus. Galen's parents, whom I've never met because they are constantly traveling, are quite wealthy, though sometimes I wonder if they actually exist. The apartment came fully furnished. He even has a maid.

We settle on *Mr. Magorium's Wonder Emporium*—a relaxing, happy little story. Of course, Galen hates it, which is fine with me. I get to tease him about it.

"Magic toys. Don't you think this is a little childish?" he asks.

"It's good exercise for your imagination. Don't you have one?"

"Have what?"

"An imagination."

He smirks. "I'm a realist."

"That's so boring. Reality is not all it's cracked up to be."

"Yeah, but it's all we have. Why waste time contemplating the impossible?" he asks, looking a little sad. A little resigned. Hmm...

"As I said, it's good exercise." I smile at him. "You look a little down, Galen. Are you contemplating something impossible?"

He twists on the sofa, turning to face me. "After a fashion."

"Really? Care to share?"

"Well, I was thinking how impossibly perceptive you are sometimes."

"Just sometimes?" I ask with a quirk of my brow.

He shakes his head. "You're amazing, Ari, and I'm..."

He clamps his mouth shut, mid-sentence, leaving me hanging. "You're what?" I ask with pursed lips, holding his stare.

He fidgets around, obviously uncomfortable with something.

"You can talk to me, Galen. It's not good to hold things inside. You know?"

"I'm in love with you, Ari."

Crap. I walked into that one. What do I say? Here I sit with the type of guy most girls my age would drool over…and he's just declared his love for me. I should be deliriously happy. I should be ecstatic. I should thank my lucky stars. But I don't, because right now my stars really suck. So I say the first thing that comes to mind…

"Oh, Galen…"

Whether it's the tone of my voice or the expression on my face, he takes my words the wrong way. Suddenly he's kissing me. And I kiss him back because…well, he's a very good kisser. And I do like him. And I want to kiss him. I just don't love him. Do I?

His hand wanders down my side, stopping at my hip, and I don't know why I'm not throwing him off of me. It's as if I can't think straight. Is it hormones? I want him. I want to touch him. I want him to touch me. Huh?

This is not right! I scream inside my head, commanding my brain to clear. And when it does, I'm immediately appalled. Our shirts are off, and I'm lying on my back, and Galen is about to unsnap…

What the…? I plant my palm against his chest and push hard.

"Ari, what's the matter?"

I draw a deep breath, gathering my wits, and my shirt. "I think you need to take me home before something happens that we might regret," I say as I pull my shirt on.

"But you seemed…"

"I don't feel right, Galen. This is not right. I'm confused…"

"I'm sorry," he says, sounding genuinely remorseful.

"It's okay, Galen. No harm, no foul." I breathe a sigh of relief, thankful that he is more of a gentleman than Luke. "And it's getting late. I really should be getting home."

He nods. "Are you busy tomorrow night?"

Should I tell him I have a date with someone else? I've made it perfectly clear that our relationship is not exclusive. I decide to take an ambiguous approach. "Actually, I am. I told my mom I'd take our new neighbor on a hiking tour of the valley. I'm not sure what time I'll be back, but I'm pretty sure I'm going to be tired."

I put on my poker face and pray that he doesn't ask for details…especially about the *neighbor*.

He stares deeply into my eyes, and it's really amazing how it affects me. It's as if I'm being played like a yo-yo. I want to wrap my arms around him. Then I don't. I want to kiss him, but I'm not sure why. It all becomes academic as he wraps his arms around my neck and pulls me close. "I'll miss you, then," he says, as his lips lock onto mine.

Our kiss is sweet and, like almost every other kiss we've shared, it leaves me confused. Do I really even know how I feel about him? And then it hits me. I don't know how I feel about him. I know I should, but I don't. It's as if…

"Ari, are you daydreaming?"

"Uh, no. Just tired."

"Are you ready to go?"

"Yep.

Galen drops me at my front door and gives me a quick hug and kiss.

"Let me know if you get home early tomorrow. Maybe we could get together?" he asks.

"I'll let you know."

"Text me one way or another. Okay?"

"You got it. Goodnight, Galen."

"Goodnight, Ari."

I'm relieved to be home. I lock the door behind me and look up to see Mom walking toward me from the kitchen.

"Hi Mom." My voice sounds a little shaky.

"Are you okay?"

"Yeah," I say with a little chuckle.

"Are you sure?" she asks with a tilt of her head and an appraising glance.

"Absolutely."

"How was your date?"

Uh-oh. "We had dinner and watched a movie. It was good. Relaxing."

"Did you tell him you don't want to see him again?"

"What? No."

"But you want to?"

Oh God. Do I? "I'm not sure, Mom. It's kind of confusing."

"I see. Wanna know what I think?"

I think so. "Of course," I say with a genuine smile.

"I think you're dying to get to know Davin better. And until you do, you are not going to be able to figure out what to do about Galen. They're both nice fellas. So, you've really got no choice. As torturous as it might be, you're going to have to spend some time with Davin."

"The same thought occurred to me earlier," I say with a big smile. "Life is never easy. Is it?"

"It's not that it's never easy. But sometimes a little complexity can make things more fun. Spend some time with Davin. I have a feeling everything will become crystal clear."

"Thanks, Mom."

She gives me her best smile. "If you need to talk, you let me know. Okay?"

"In a heartbeat. Goodnight, Mom."

"Goodnight sweetheart.

I'm suddenly feeling very anxious about tomorrow. But it's a good *anxious*…and I can't wait for morning.

Chapter 5

The doorbell rings at 11:05. Davin is right on time. He's standing in the doorway, attached to a backpack that would bring the average Navy SEAL to his knees. Maybe he packed a butler inside to serve us.

"Good morning, Davin," I say cheerfully.

He steps inside, barely fitting through the doorframe. "Morning," he says, with a radiant smile.

After just two days, I feel as if I've known him for years. I'm not sure why. It's strange, but I just know. It's as if we have some kind of connection. Does he feel it, too?

Ella, who came over bright and early to make sure I was properly primped and outfitted, glides by on her way to the kitchen. Upon seeing Davin, she pauses, executing a classic double-take. "Well, good morning, Davin. Don't you look like a model for the well-equipped hiker. Just don't lean backwards, sweetie." She turns and flashes an impish grin. "Y'all have a good time and be safe."

Davin smiles and nods. He doesn't know what to say. He hasn't figured Ella out.

"Bye Ella," I say, as I grab my normal-sized backpack and walk out the back door with Davin.

"Are you going to be able to hike with that thing on your back?" I ask.

"Not a problem. I'm a lot stronger than I look," he answers.

"Now that's a frightening thought," I reply, as I playfully squeeze his bicep.

Should I have touched him like that? It's a really nice bicep. Really nice. I can't take it back, and he doesn't seem upset, so...

We walk across the yard, past the lake, and into the woods. There isn't an actual path to follow, which Davin must have noticed because he asks, "How do you know where we're going?"

"Ella and I have walked the route a hundred times. I can probably do it in the dark. But just in case—" I pull a compass out of my pocket. "It's due east."

"You're pretty resourceful."

"I like to be prepared."

Davin smiles. "Have you and Ella been friends for a long time?"

"Since we were toddlers. She didn't offend you, did she?"

"Not at all. In fact, she impresses me. She is not afraid to say what she feels. That is a good trait."

I chuckle. "When they handed out that particular trait, she got an extra helping. But I love her like a sister."

Maintaining a brisk pace, we arrive at the Falls in about twenty minutes. Davin looks all around, then turns to me and says, "It's really beautiful here."

"It truly is." And being here with him makes it even more beautiful than ever.

"Need help detaching yourself from your pack?"

"I'm good," he says, as he adroitly undoes the harness and lowers his pack to the ground...effortlessly. "I'm kind of hungry. How about you?"

No one ever accused me of eating like a girl. I can really pack it away. Mom says I have a turbocharged metabolism.

"I'm starving. Could eat a small horse."

Davin digs into his pack. "Didn't bring one. Sorry." But he does manage to pull out a blanket, a jumbo pillow, and two large insulated bags, packed with ice. One contains a six-pack of juice drinks, several bottles of water, sliced veggies, and some sliced cheese. The other is loaded with what look like sandwich wraps.

"Impressive," I say. "So, in addition to being dashing and witty, you are a chef, too?"

"Not really. Thalia took care of the food. She's a great cook. I've been known to wreak havoc in the kitchen."

I chuckle. I can just see him—standing in a kitchen, wearing an apron, a look of sheer terror on his face.

I help him spread the blanket near the edge of the pond, between two large boulders. Positioning the pillow against one of the boulders, we create a comfy backrest.

"So what did you do in Santa Barbara?"

"I did a lot of sailing. And I used to surf a little."

"You look like a surfer," I say, recalling how I'd fantasized about him on a board.

"Thanks…I think," he says with a wry smile.

"You must miss your friends."

"I didn't have very many."

Hmm. He's handsome, witty, and personable. How can he not have tons of friends?

"Really? You seem very friendly."

"I was engrossed in my work…my studies. I really didn't leave myself much time for friends."

"Not even a girlfriend?"

"I did date someone, but we broke up before I left California."

"I'm sorry. What's her name?"

"Alex…Alexandra," he says matter-of-factly.

I wonder. Is she pretty? Smart? "Nice name. It's pretty."

"Not nearly as pretty as yours, *Ariel*." He speaks my name in a deep, sultry tone, lingering on the last syllable. He makes it sound pretty.

"Sometimes it makes me think of Ariel Sharon," I say.

"The former Israeli Prime Minister?"

"Yes."

"He's dead, you know. And you're a lot prettier than he was."

"Smart-ass."

"Well, you are," he says.

"Thank you. How about a swim?"

"I thought you'd never ask," Davin replies.

He rises and strips off his shirt, revealing a torso that would make Aphrodite blush.

I realize too late that I'm staring at him—at his chest.

"Ari…"

"Huh," I murmur.

"Are you checking me out?" He narrows his eyes and shoots me a crooked grin.

"I–uh–no, I was just thinking."

Yup. I'm thinking about running my hands across his chest and over his abs.

"You were thinking…about me?" His smile grows wider.

"I was thinking about something personal." Mm-Hmm. Like I was about to dig myself a hole all the way from Edgewood to Australia, which I know is theoretically possible, because Ella and I tried it once, with a map app.

"I'll bet you were." He smiles like the cat that got the mouse.

I stick my tongue out playfully before stepping out of my shorts. Of course, he is staring intently, with folded arms, and a smirk plastered across his face. I'm so glad I decided to wear a one-piece suit. Calling on my nerve reserve, I take a deep breath and pull off my tee. Davin's eyebrows arch slightly, and my face suddenly gets really warm.

"That's a really practical swimsuit, Ari." He smiles at me in a way that makes me feel naked.

Instinctively, I look down to make sure I'm not.

Davin turns, walks to the edge of the pond, and dives into the crystal clear water. His form is perfect, in every conceivable aspect—and from several different angles.

When he surfaces, it occurs to me that he looks as good wet as he does dry—and I want to get close to him.

"The water is warm," he says.

"It's fed by a hot spring. They're all over the area."

I take a small waterproof bag from my backpack and toss it into the pond. "Davin, would you grab that for me? There's a blanket and some towels inside. See if you can fling it onto the ledge near the waterfall."

He retrieves the bag and gently lobs it up and onto the ledge. I watch as it makes a perfect landing.

"Nice throw."

"Ari…" He is staring at me again and smiling warmly.

"Davin…" I parry back.

"You really look very nice." He gives me the sweetest grin.

The feeling is mutual. I smile from the inside out.

I dive in and swim in a playful circle around him. The water tickles me ever so slightly—as if it's carbonated. *Strange.*

"Are you stalking me?" Davin asks.

"Maybe."

I swim closer. He grabs my hand as I pass, and his touch sends a small shock up my arm. It is not unpleasant. "Thanks for a wonderful day."

"It's not over," he replies.

"Let's check out the waterfall. Follow me."

The pond is oval and about one hundred feet across at its widest point. The perimeter is ringed by natural rock formations, with the backside forming a wide ledge that runs beside and behind the waterfall. I swim toward the ledge, which is about eight feet above the water line, and carefully climb up the rocks. Davin follows me.

I turn to check his progress. "Careful, the rocks are sharp..." I don't need to say it because Davin is moving like a mountain goat. I'm the one who's moving tentatively. I'm actually slowing him down.

We walk along the ledge and duck behind the cascading water. Looking out through the spray is like peering through a shimmering curtain. I've always found this place magical and I was happy to be sharing it with Davin. "It's beautiful. Isn't it?"

"It is," he says, as he turns to face me and places his hands on my shoulders. "Ari, can we talk?"

His touch causes me to shudder. "Is there anything wrong?"

"No, nothing is wrong. I'd like to talk about what happened Thursday. Let's go sit in the sun. Okay?"

"Sure." My thoughts flash back to my adrenaline-fueled power surge with Luke. Does Davin think I'm weird...*or dangerous?*

We walk back out along the ledge and into the sunlight. The warmth feels good. I open my bag, take out my blanket, spread it out...and we sit. "So, let's talk."

Davin takes a deliberate breath and lets out a long sigh. "When you thought Luke was about to hurt you, how did you *feel?*" He draws out the last word for emphasis.

"I was afraid. Luke seemed different. I mean, he was never what I would call nice. But the look on his face...it was evil. Then I wasn't afraid anymore. I was angry—so angry that I was shaking and tingling."

"Stand up, Ari." He rises to his feet and helps me up.

We stand, facing each other, and Davin takes my hands in his. I feel tingly. I feel...

"What did you just feel?"

I let go of his hands and reach up, grasping his shoulders. The sensation gets stronger—a lot stronger. Is he doing this to me?

I stagger backwards, losing my balance, and my right foot slips off the edge. I can't stop myself from falling!

"ARI!" Davin lunges, trying to grab my hand.

He is too late. Using momentum to push off the ledge as far as I can, I manage to keep my feet under me. Just barely. But I can't see where I'm going and my right thigh scrapes hard against the rocks.

"*Ah!*" I hit the pond feet first and sink toward the bottom. The water actually feels good, but when I kick off the bottom, my leg feels numb.

I break the surface, grasp the rock wall below the ledge for support, and nearly puke, as a wave of intense pain shoots up my leg. I look down and the water is red with blood. *My blood.* It's gushing out in a steady stream. This is bad. Really bad.

"Davin, I need help!"

He is beside me in an instant. "I'm going to lift you out, Ari. It may hurt."

"Do it," I say, through gritted teeth.

Davin lifts me, as if I'm weightless, making sure to avoid touching my wound.

"How are you doing?" he asks, as he gently lays me down on the blanket.

"It hurts," I moan, as he positions a pillow beneath my head. "It hurts a *lot.*"

Davin grimaces, which doesn't seem very encouraging. Blood is everywhere and I'm getting woozy.

38

He grabs a towel and presses it down firmly on the wound, making me cry out.

"I'm sorry. Hang in there, Ari."

"We need to stop the bleeding—and I think I'm about to go into shock." I'm going to die here.

"Stay as still as you can. Please trust me, Ari."

"What…what are you going to do?" My voice is shaky. "I need a doctor."

He lifts the blood-soaked towel and places his hand on my leg. Warmth radiates through his fingers—and then I'm hit with a wave of excruciating pain. My insides are on fire.

I look down and his hands are covered in a shimmering blue light—and so is my leg. I refuse to scream. I have a thing about showing weakness, but I also don't want to attract every hiker in the park to the Falls. So I moan. Low, pitiful, mewing sounds. I'm not sure how much time has passed, but the pain slowly starts to fade, and everything gets fuzzy and blurry. I'm aware of my surroundings, but I can't move, I can't focus, I can't tell if I'm asleep or awake.

Looking up at Davin through a veil of tears, I whisper, "What did you do?"

He exhales sharply and lies beside me, staring skyward.

"Davin?" He looks really worn out and there are tears in his eyes. "You need to tell me what just happened. Okay?"

"Give me a minute, Ari." His breathing is labored.

For the second time in the past two days my ability to reason has been stretched to the breaking point. What happened was impossible. My leg looks horrible, but it isn't bleeding anymore, and the pain has diminished to a dull ache.

I try to make sense of what happened, breaking things down to the simplest causes and effects—

Leg sliced open to the bone; Davin touches me; blue light; warmth and pain; lots of pain; leg stops bleeding; pain stops. Dear God! I have to see it. I have to see my leg.

"Help me sit up, Davin," I say, holding my hand out.

Davin eases me into a sitting position and moves the pillow behind me.

"Help me clean my leg." The words come out raspy.

Without speaking, Davin reaches over and grabs a water bottle. He empties its contents over my leg, then uses a towel to gently clean the blood away. It hurts a little—sort of like how your skin feels after a scab has come off. I examine my leg. All I see is a line of pink, new skin. I have to stay calm. If I want answers, I need to remain calm.

"Davin, my leg is healed." I can't manage much more than a whisper. "How?"

"You would have bled to death before help arrived."

"The light. You healed me?"

"Yes."

"How?"

He just stares at me as if he's lost the ability to speak. I narrow my eyes and stare back. "Answer me, Davin."

"Ari, it's complicated."

I lean in close and poke him in the chest. "Complicated? Seriously? You just did something that should be impossible. I don't care if it's complicated. I want answers. Are you human?"

"I think it would be safe to assume that I'm not." He pauses to rub his temples. "But neither are you."

All the breath is sucked out of me. This can't be happening. Any minute, my alarm will go off and this whole day will start again, for real. "What?"

He just stares and shakes his head slowly.

Please don't be crazy. "Are you crazy, Davin?"

"Ari, please calm down."

"You're trying to tell me I'm not human, and you expect me to calm down? Well, excuse me if I don't."

He takes a deep breath. "You have the ability to heal yourself. You have to know this, Ari. When was the last time you were sick?"

I never get sick. And cuts and bruises that should take a week to heal are usually fine in a day or two. "I'm not sure. A long time…"

"How long, Ari?"

A chill runs down my spine. "Never," I say in a small voice.

"Your powers are not fully evolved. You would not have been able to heal yourself before you bled to death. I gave you my energy and you used it to heal your leg."

"Huh?" Words and ideas are spinning like a tornado inside my head, but I can't form a sentence.

"Ari?"

I hold my hand up, motioning for him to wait. "WHAT ARE YOU?" I wrap my arms around myself and stare straight ahead, holding back a torrent of tears.

Davin reaches out for my hand, and I unconsciously let him hold it. "Ari, please try to calm down. I'm not going to hurt you."

"Okay. I'll be okay." I take a deep breath. "Everything that's happened. It's all so strange. You need to tell me everything. Okay?"

He nods. "I was born on another planet. It is called Olympus."

My mind shouts *Nutcase*, while my heart really wants to believe him. "Seriously? How on Earth does an alien world wind up with an ancient Greek name?"

"I am quite serious," he says. "The mountain in Greece was named in our honor. We've been visiting Earth for a very, very long time."

This is not what I expect. Not even close. "You said *we* were not human. So what am I? I'm pretty sure I was born in Virginia."

"We're not exactly sure. We know that you radiate energy. Enough for us to have detected you. Enough that you are able to do things that mortals should not be able to do." He pauses to draw in a deep breath. "Ari, the Institute is run by my people. We detected you. We offered you a scholarship so we can keep you safe and learn more about you."

What a unique idea for a sci-fi story.

"This is really a lot to handle, Davin. Let me see if I've got this straight." I count off the points on my fingers. "I'm not human. I radiate energy. The Institute is run by aliens. They want to help me—hopefully without dissecting me…" I pause for a breath. "And, of course, we didn't meet by accident. Right?"

"I'm an Olympian Warrior. I was sent here to assess you. To determine if you were good or evil."

"What?" I grab my head and squeeze. "Were you sent here to take me out on a date or to kill me?"

"Excuse me?" Davin asks with more than a hint of confusion.

"Were you sent here to kill me?" I repeat.

"I was sent to *assess* you. And you are clearly not evil."

Why didn't he just ask me? "Well, I could have told you I wasn't evil if you'd asked."

"You did tell me—in a way. And besides, you don't smell evil."

I don't know how to respond. I want to shout and slap his face. Instead, I narrow my eyes and shoot him an icy stare. "You *smelled* me?"

"To a Warrior, evil has a disagreeable odor. Your scent is very *pleasant.*"

"Well, I'm glad I used deodorant this morning." I fold my arms across my chest and glare. "You're a Warrior? Who are you at war with?"

"With evil."

"Perfect. When you are done, could you take care of stupidity, too? Because I think that would be really useful. Then you could move on to lawyers and politicians. Of course there would be significant crossover because I know for a fact there are lots of evil lawyers and stupid politicians."

"As well as evil politicians and stupid lawyers?"

"Yeah."

He chuckles. "We are here to protect humans from some very evil people. People who should not be on Earth. Stupidity is another problem entirely." He takes my hand in his. "Ari, your intellect has allowed you to make it through the past two days without breaking down. Trust your mind. Trust me. Please."

"What would you have done if you had judged me to be evil?"

"You're not evil, so the question is irrelevant."

"Humor me. What would you have done if you had decided that I was evil?"

"I would have known it. You would have attacked me, or tried to run, and…"

"You would have killed me?"

"No. I couldn't…" He takes a deep breath. "I would have incapacitated you. Captured you."

For some crazy reason, I trust him. He's answered my questions in a reasoned way. He's given me no reason to doubt him.

"Why?"

"Because if you were evil, you would be dangerous—too dangerous for us to allow you to roam the Earth."

Chapter 6

"I would be dangerous? Me?"

"Yes, you are an enigma, Ari. You should not exist, yet you do." His expression softens. He must see the concern in my eyes. The fear. "But it's not a bad thing. It's more like discovering an exotic and beautiful new flower."

"So you want to put me in a vase and sit me on your kitchen counter?"

"I think you need to be free and wild."

"Ya think?"

Davin nods slowly, as a smile spreads across his face, reaching his eyes.

"So, show me something that only a Warrior can do." I need more evidence.

"That you can beat up football players and heal wounds is not enough?"

I fold my arms and glare at him. He has a point, but I'm not going to admit it.

Davin pulls a knife—a big one—out of his pack, unsheathes it, and holds it over his arm.

"WAIT! What are you doing?"

"I'm going to cut myself so you can watch my wound heal."

"Are you nuts? I don't want you to hurt yourself and, besides, I've seen more than enough blood today. Can you do something else? Something that doesn't involve self-mutilation?"

"I am not going to mutilate myself. It will be a small scratch. Would you like to do it?"

"No. Go ahead, but make sure it's just a scratch."

He smirks. "Just a scratch. But if I lopped off a finger, that would be more…"

"Stop it. That's disturbing."

Would his finger grow back? No. I'm not going there. I don't even want to know. But…

"Would it grow back?"

He laughs. "Yes. But it would take several minutes."

"Um, how about arms and legs?"

"That would require hospitalization and several days of rest."

"So, all your parts can regrow?"

He nods. "Everything except our heads."

Wow. I am not about to review all of his *parts*, but this is amazing. If it's true. "Alright, scratch yourself."

"But you've already witnessed a wound healing. Are you sure you want me to do this?"

"Yes. I was out of it before. And I really couldn't observe what happened because of all the blood. And the pain."

"As you wish."

The knife must be wicked-sharp because all it takes is a touch. The cut is about two inches long, on the inside of his left forearm. A very sinewy, studly forearm. As soon as he pulls the knife away, a thin line of blood appears.

"Wipe the blood away," he says, as he hands me a napkin.

I gently swab at the scratch, not wanting to hurt him. The blood is gone. The scratch is no longer bleeding.

"Watch carefully. Keep your eye on the wound."

"How long will it take?"

"Shh. Just watch."

I do. And then something truly remarkable happens. It's like watching a time-lapse video. The scratch fades. It takes no more than a minute. It's gone. No trace. I blow out the air I've been holding inside my lungs and lean back.

"So what did we prove, Ari?"

I smile, timidly. "Well, after I eliminate all which is impossible, nothing remains. So, either you are not human, or I am delusional. Tough choice, huh?"

He scratches his head and smiles. "Did you just paraphrase Sherlock Holmes?"

"Um, yes. I am very well-read for my age."

"So you believe me?"

"I'm working on it," I say. "But I'm curious. After my leg healed, I saw tears on your face. Were you crying for me?"

He puts his hand on my shoulder and gives me a gentle squeeze. He looks a little embarrassed. "Warriors can help each other to heal. I've done it many times before. It's a painful process. But this was different. I felt as if I was on fire. I felt your anguish as if it was mine. Warriors do not typically feel such intense emotion. Yet I did. I guess that makes me an enigma, too."

"You're making it easy for me, Davin."

He gives me a quizzical look.

I grin. "You're making it easy for me to believe you."

"That's good," he says.

"Yeah, it is." It's all good. "So how did you get a mountain in Greece named after your planet?"

"It's complicated. How about I give you the condensed story now, along with my word to fill in the details when we have more time? Unless, of course, you don't want to see me again." He looks at me with those gorgeous green eyes, and I know I want to see him again.

"Deal," I say.

He nods. "When it comes to human evolution, I'm afraid your scientists are on the wrong track. The truth is that we visited Earth nearly half a million years ago and enhanced the DNA of one particularly advanced primate species. That's how humans really evolved."

"Hmm. If that's true, then there really was a missing link," I say thoughtfully.

"More like a missing catalyst," Davin replies.

I frown. "But modern humans appeared much more recently than half a million years ago. At least that's what I've been taught. The most advanced hominin of that era would have been Homo heidelbergensis."

"I'm sure a budding paleoanthropologist must know that dating pre-human fossils is not an exact science. In fact, there are human fossils that have aged dramatically over the past hundred years," Davin says, smiling.

"I'm aware that dating methods can be a bit inexact. So, how much time passed between your DNA manipulations and the appearance of modern humans?"

"One generation."

"No way. That goes against everything I've learned. But…"

"You believe me."

"Yeah, I do. Weird, huh?"

"Actually, it's quite logical."

"Yeah," I say with a little smile. "So, did Olympians remain on Earth?"

"Yes. I guess you can say we acted as teachers."

I'm not sure why, but the idea that Davin's people observed the dawn of human civilization, that they played a role in human evolution, brings tears to my eyes. If what he told me is true, and I'm swiftly buying into the story, it changes everything. Human beings are neither random nor magically created. And ancient aliens are real. Oh, my…

"Ari, are you alright?"

"I'm fine, Davin. I'm overwhelmed, but not in a bad way. Maybe I'll be changing majors," I say with a tight smile.

"You know, sometimes there is a compulsion to adapt truth to suit theories, instead of theories to suit truth. Knowing the truth, in your case, might make for a boring, and possibly frustrating, career."

"Is that an Olympian adage?" I ask.

"Actually, I was paraphrasing Sherlock Holmes," he answers with a grin.

I throw my head back and laugh. "You're amazing, Davin. Do you know that?"

"Perhaps I am merely trying to impress you," he says with a raised brow.

I roll my eyes. "So what about Olympus? Did someone do a DNA alteration on your world, too?"

He nods.

"So humans and Olympians are genetically similar?"

"Mortal Olympians and humans are genetically identical."

"But Warriors are different?"

"Yes. Our DNA is more…advanced."

"But you look human."

"And so do you. But we are not. Our DNA is similar to that of humans, but it is more complex. I will explain more, but not now. Okay?"

I nod. "So, Olympians hung around Earth until the Greeks came along?"

"Yes. We stayed until human society stabilized, and then we faded into legend."

"Are all Olympians like you?" I imagine millions of beautiful people strolling through a futuristic city somewhere. *Nah*, Davin has to be one-of-a-kind. He's just too perfect.

"No. Among half a billion Olympians, there are only two thousand Warriors."

"And among seven billion humans there is only one me? That's why I'm an enigma?"

"Yes. You were born of mortal human parents, yet you exhibit the traits of a Warrior, which should not be possible."

"I certainly don't feel like a Warrior. Well, discounting the fact that I can beat up football players."

"It's more than your physical strength. Your body can sense the energy that only Warriors can sense. It caused the tingling you felt when you fought Luke. It's what you feel when you touch me. As your abilities awaken, the feeling will become normal, it won't frighten you."

"The shock I felt when I held you on the ledge, that was your energy?"

"Mm-hmm. When we held hands, I released a small amount of energy into you. When you placed your hands on my shoulders, you *absorbed* a rather large amount. It was similar to what happened when you fought Luke. Your body sensed the energy and your Warrior instinct took over, drawing it in."

"You helped me with Luke?"

"Yes. I made sure you had enough energy to defeat him…" He hesitates a moment, taking in a deep breath. "What happened between Luke and you convinced me that you were not evil. The way you handled the situation was impressive. You exhibited honor and courage."

My little escapade may have impressed Davin, but it scared the hell out of me. "What exactly is this energy—and will I learn to control it?"

"We call it Ousia."

"Oo-what?"

'OO-**ZEE**-AH. "It means *the Essence*. Once you are trained, you will be able to control it."

It sounds a lot like the Jedi Force. "Where does it come from?"

"It is all around us. Human scientists call it dark energy."

"Oh. I've read about that. But it's theoretical. It's never been seen."

"That's why they call it dark," he says with a tilt of his head.

"I see. So how long does it take to be trained?"

"Warriors begin training years before they awaken. But you are awakening now. You will see results quickly."

"If Warriors are not mortal, how long do they live? How old are you?"

"I'm older than I look."

"Twenty-five?"

"No." He looks at me with a crooked smile.

"Thirty?"

He shakes his head.

"Davin, please don't tell me you're as old as Yoda. You're not *that* old, are you?"

He grins. "Yoda from *Star Wars*?"

I nod slowly.

"That's one of my favorite movies. He was 900 when Luke Skywalker found him, right?"

"Yes. So, are you—"

He cuts me off. "Maybe we should have this discussion some other time."

"Davin." I use my motherly tone.

He sighs. "I am approximately one million years old."

And I thought twenty-two was a little old? A nervous chortle escapes my throat as I ponder aloud, "Seriously? I'm attracted to a guy who is older than dirt?"

Oops.

"That's a unique way of looking at it…" He narrows his eyes. "You are attracted to me?"

He noticed.

"I don't know. Yes, a little."

Oh, this is so crazy. I'm sitting next to a man who could have known Aristotle, Socrates, Moses, and Da Vinci—and I'm acting like a complete fool.

"Just a little?" he asks with a pout.

"Yeah, just a little," I reply. "So, what about my lifespan?"

"You are a Warrior."

"How long will I live?"

"Most likely until you are older than dirt."

My breath catches. "Will we always look like we do now?"

"Yes."

If this is true, I will watch my loved ones grow old and die, while I stay young. "Oh no. I have to tell Mom and Ella—"

"We have to be careful. I think it would be wise to wait until the shock of today has worn off a bit and we've had a chance to plan a strategy."

He's right. If I approach Mom now I'd probably fall apart, and she'll think I'm nuts. Besides, there's still a chance I'm dreaming—Ha!

"So, is that why Alex and you broke up? Because she is human and would age?"

"Yes. She had a crush on me, and I didn't want to hurt her. So I took her out a few times. We didn't have very much in common so our time together was a little…boring."

He says it with a hint of regret and it makes me think of Galen. I have to tell him I don't want to see him again. And I have to do it soon.

"Do I bore you, Davin?"

"No. You are definitely not boring."

I frown. "I'm not sure how to take that."

"I meant it as a compliment."

"Thank you."

"So, do Warriors marry? Do they have baby Warriors?"

His cheeks flush.

"You're blushing, Davin. I didn't know you had it in you. It's really cute."

He clears his throat. "Warriors and Sages marry—though we call it binding. We cannot make babies, though we can certainly..."

I hold up my hand. "I get it," I say, as my face begins to flush.

Davin smiles, his cheeks retaining a hint of pink.

"What is a Sage?" I ask, recovering my poise.

"Warriors and Sages are similar, but a Sage's talents tend more toward science, academics, and politics."

"Like your aunt?"

He nods.

"So, are you married or bound...or whatever you call it?"

He looks like he's about to crawl out of his skin. "No. I am not bound. I do not have a Promise."

"What do you mean by *Promise?*"

"In Olympian culture, a Promise is what you would call a spouse. It is like *husband* or *wife.*"

"I like that word. It conveys so much more than *spouse.* So, aren't you a little old to still be single?"

He has to be hiding a very juicy past.

Davin laughs out loud, which sounds like a very sexy symphony to me. "When we bind, we make a solemn oath. That's why we call each other Promise. When we fall in love, it is for eternity. Warriors can only bind with other Warriors or Sages. There are not a lot of *fish* in the pond."

"Have you ever dated another Warrior, or a Sage?"

Davin sighs and runs his fingers through his hair. I'm clearly beating him into submission with all the questions. "I've had a few relationships."

"Anything serious?"

I know I'm prying, but I really want to know.

He gives me a strange look. "I was almost committed."

"Committed?"

"When two Olympians wish to bind, they commit to each other. It is like the exchange of vows in a human marriage, except it is done privately. Within a year of the commitment, a public binding celebration takes place."

"So, a commitment is like a trial marriage?"

"A commitment is a real marriage, but it can be dissolved before the binding celebration occurs—though that rarely happens."

"I'm really sorry, Davin. I'm prying into your personal life and that's wrong, but…"

"But you would like to pry a little more?" he asks with a crooked grin.

I give him a shy smile and nod.

"I don't mind," he says. "Her name is Reyna. We were not very compatible. Things did not work out. I broke off the relationship."

"Did she love you?"

"Yes."

"If Warrior love is eternal, will she ache for you—*eternally?*"

"No. The grief born of unrequited love fades over time. Warriors, like humans, learn to move on. Do you understand?"

"I think so. I'm glad you realized that sooner, rather than later," I say, sounding relieved. "So, tell me about the evil people you mentioned earlier."

His focus seems to intensify and he sits up straight. "We call them Zon, which in ancient Olympian means *evil ones*."

I feel a disturbingly cold chill and my body trembles.

"Are you okay?" Davin asks.

"I'm fine. Please continue."

Davin nods and clears his throat. "The Zon arrived shortly after Olympians evolved. Their mission was to nurture and teach. But they grew weary of the work. They became evil."

"All of them?"

"Yes. They began to instigate violence. Then they sat idly by as Olympians slaughtered each other in war after war. Millions died and the survivors were enslaved. The Zon, who lived in palaces while mortals groveled for food and shelter, held dominion over Olympus until the Warriors defeated them. But some Zon were able to evade them. Eventually, they managed to escape through an Earth portal."

"What exactly is an Earth portal?"

"It is a gateway through space, connecting Olympus and Earth. Instead of traveling through light-years of empty space, we simply walk through the portal."

"Oh," I say. "So Olympus and Earth are not really close, huh?"

"No. They are a little over a thousand light-years apart. Olympus is in a galaxy that human astronomers call Lyra."

"That's really far away." I take in a deep breath and let it out slowly. "Will I ever get to visit Olympus? Would you take me?"

"You would not be afraid?"

"Heavens, no. Adventure is my middle name."

"Then I will take you. I will be your guide."

"I'd like that," I say. "Tell me more about the Zon. Are they as powerful as Warriors?"

"They are very powerful—but they are no match for a Warrior."

"Are they immortal?"

"Yes."

"Can they find me the same way you did? Can they hurt me?"

"You could be detected. And since you are not trained, they can hurt you. But you have nothing to fear. I will protect you."

"You'll protect me because you want to? Or because it's your job?"

"I wouldn't protect you if I didn't want to."

Excellent answer.

"Where did the Zon come from? They must have come from somewhere else. Right?"

"It's complicated. Let's save it for the next time we chat, okay?"

"Okay. But I won't let you off the hook."

"I'm sure you won't," he says with a little grin.

"I guess my life will never be the same," I say softly.

He reaches over and gently strokes my cheek.

I turn to face him. I feel warm, very warm, as I realize how much I want to touch him. I'm in serious trouble.

"How do you feel?" he asks, looking concerned.

"Just a little tired. No pain."

"And emotionally?"

"I'm good," I lie. My insides are tied in a huge knot.

"You are not being honest with me."

I'm not. I want to kiss him. I want...

"I—"

He cuts me off. "It's alright. Everything will work out, Ari. I promise."

I'm not sure if it's the look on his face, or the fact that his mouth is inches from mine, but I lose all sense of restraint. I lean over, pressing my upper body into his.

"What are you doing, Ari?"

"This," I whisper softly, as I brush my lips across his. He sighs and our kiss deepens to an intensity I can feel in my soul. I can feel every ripple in his muscular chest. I can feel his energy coursing through me. Every inch of me. Now that I know what it is, it doesn't frighten me. On the contrary, it feels wonderful, as if every nerve in my body possesses a heightened ability to register pleasure. It's a soul-wrenching, gut-clenching, nuclear explosion of a kiss. A kiss that rocks me to my core. A kiss I can't end. A kiss I never want to end.

And then he pulls away. Abruptly. He looks bothered. "Ari, we shouldn't be doing this…"

I jerk back, feeling as if I've been punched in the stomach. "What?"

He averts his eyes and sighs. "I think we should head back."

What was I thinking? I've *never* been so aggressive with a guy. What did I just do? I say the only thing I can think of. "I think you're right."

Davin gets up and starts packing our things. I don't help him. I won't. I can't.

He zips up his pack and straps it on. "Are you ready to go?"

I nod.

"Ari?"

I can't look at him.

"I will need to stay close to you for the time being."

"You still want to protect me?" I ask, sarcastically.

"Of course."

"What about school?"

He seems to ponder that.

"I will assign a team of Warriors to set up a perimeter around your school. Nothing bad will be able to get past them. We can discuss the details later. Can you come to my house later?"

"I'll think about it."

But all I can think about is how mortified I feel. He kissed me back. He kissed me like he meant to. What the hell happened?

"Ari, I didn't mean to offend…"

"Shut it, Davin. Just shut it."

And, obligingly, he does.

The walk back home is uncomfortably silent. My brain is not happy with what I'm asking of it. I'm not human and I'm attracted to an alien. And if that's not enough, two days after accusing my ex-boyfriend of attempted date rape, and one day after inexplicably finding myself in a compromising position with Galen, I've come dangerously close to molesting Davin. What in heaven's name is wrong with me?

But he responded to my kiss. He kissed me back, and no one has ever kissed me like that. No one. And for some crazy reason, I can't stop thinking about his lips.

As I unlock the front door, Davin breaks the silence.

"Ari, I know you are upset, but it is important that we speak with Thalia. Will you come over?"

I wheel around. His expression is soft. Almost sad.

If I'm really not human, if I'm one of *them*—then I need more information. I have to swallow my pride, what's left of it, and my fear, and meet with them. He did save my life. That has to count for something. Doesn't it?

"Do I have a choice?"

"Of course you do."

"I'll be there in ninety minutes."

I turn on my heels and walk inside, slamming the door behind me, not caring if it hits him in the face.

I run upstairs, into my bathroom, and strip off my clothes. I'm a simmering, smoking hot mess. At least Mom isn't home. She's working and won't be home for several hours...and that's good, because I really need to be alone.

Standing under the shower, the hissing spray mutes my pitiful sobs, but does nothing to dull the ache in my heart. I long to pour my heart out to the people I love the most, but I know I can't. I need to sort this on my own.

Chapter 7

I stand frozen on Davin's front porch, unable to ring the doorbell. There are two aliens inside, and no matter how nice they seem, I cannot discount the possibility that their intentions might be sinister.

The question of whether to ring or not becomes academic when the door swings open. I nearly jump out of my skin. Thalia stands in front of me, smiling. "Hello, Ari. I didn't mean to frighten you, but I could see you through the window and you looked as if you were having a problem with the doorbell."

"Sorry. I was momentarily distracted."

"It's quite alright, dear. Please come in." She pauses and offers a warm smile, while placing a hand on my shoulder. "There is nothing to be frightened of."

I take a step inside. "Thank you, I—"

"Ari, are you alright?"

Seriously? "No, I'm not alright," I say, as several tears escape, running down my cheeks. "I don't know what I am. I'm not human?"

Thalia shakes her head. "Come, let's get you something to drink."

She takes my hand and leads me farther inside—into the kitchen.

"They're lovely," I say, pointing to a vase of freshly-cut wildflowers.

She gazes at them and smiles. "All the flowers of all the tomorrows are in the seeds of today."

I can't help smiling back, as I take a seat at the table. "That's quite profound."

"It is an ancient human proverb. East Indian, I believe. Would you like tea, coffee, or something cold?"

"A cup of tea would be nice. Thank you."

Thalia fills a tea kettle with bottled water, places it on the stove, then takes the seat directly across from me. "Davin is showering and will be joining us shortly."

I wince and Thalia arches her brow as she gives me a questioning look. "Did something happen between you and Davin?"

Shit. "Um..." He wouldn't have told her about the kiss. He couldn't have. "It was just a very traumatic day..."

"I'm sure it was. I want you to know that while Davin can be a bit intimidating, he would never hurt you."

"Thanks. That's good to know." I gather my poise, give her a little smile, and change the subject. "So, did you rent this house to be close to me?"

She smiles. "Yes."

I get straight to the point. "Did Davin tell you what happened today?"

"He did."

"It was quite an interesting day," I say with a humorless chuckle.

Thalia leans forward, propping her elbows on the table. "Your injury was unfortunate. We did not intend for you to find out that way."

"How did you intend for me to find out?"

"Gradually...and on your terms. Given enough time, you would have come to certain conclusions. You would have questioned certain things."

"For instance?"

Thalia sits back and gazes into my eyes, looking completely relaxed. "How you defeated a boy nearly twice your size; how you managed to run as fast as a cheetah; why you never get sick; and why you are so much smarter than other girls your age. You would have pondered these things,

Ari. You would have concluded that you are so very much more than who you thought you were."

"And you would have been there for me? To make the puzzle pieces fit?"

"Davin and I will be there for you. We will not let you go through this alone."

"I—"

I don't know what to say. I'm touched. Really touched.

The kettle is whistling. Thalia stands, walks to the stove, and turns off the burner. "Green or Chai?"

"Green," I say.

She prepares our cups, sets them on the table to steep, then returns to her seat across from me.

"Everything will work out, dear," she says.

I squeeze some honey into my cup and stir. "You really think I'm like you and Davin? Not human?"

"All life is made from the same *stuff*. The same building blocks. Our DNA is simply more evolved."

"But I was born in Edgewood. Are my parents—"

"We don't know yet, Ari," she says. "Cream?"

"No thank you. So, I'm a Warrior?"

"I'm not sure, dear. Your situation is unique and we're going to need to run tests…"

"Tests?" I ask. "What kind of tests?"

A chill shoots down my spine. Am I going to be poked, prodded or…worse?

"Nothing invasive and not until we have earned your trust. It seems safe to assume that at least one of your parents is Olympian. Your father is deceased?"

"Yes. He died when his small plane crashed."

"I'm so sorry, dear."

"It was a long time ago. I was a little girl."

Thalia pats my hand and purses her lips. There is nothing about this woman that seems alien.

"Thalia, you detected me from my energy. Right?"

"Yes."

"What about my mom? Does she emit energy?"

"Well, she does. But you emit so much. I'm not certain if what I sensed was actually hers. It may well have been a residual trace of your energy."

"Oh. I guess that makes sense."

Thalia nods, as a freshened Davin enters the kitchen and sits. *Next to me.*

He's dressed in jeans and a black tee shirt, and smells of shampoo. I'm still pissed off. He made me feel like a fool. But…

"Hello, Ari. Are you feeling better?"

Is he referring to my sliced leg or my bruised ego? Probably both.

"I'm fine. Just a little tired."

He gives me a smile. It's awkward and doesn't reach his eyes. He seems a little tense. I look away from him.

"So, Thalia. where do we go from here?" I ask.

"Your abilities are rapidly awakening, Ari," she says. "Would you like us to teach you how to harness them?"

The sooner I learn, the sooner I'll be able to protect myself. "Yes, I would like that."

"Excellent," she says. "We can start on Tuesday. There is a secure Olympian facility beneath the Institute. When does your school day end?"

"I'm usually out the door by two-thirty. But spring break starts tomorrow."

Davin and Thalia look alarmed. "Are you going on vacation?" Davin asks.

"No, my mom is scheduled at the hospital. We're not going anywhere. Why the concerned looks?"

"If you were leaving, we would need to make special arrangements for your security," Davin says.

"Oh."

"Yes, well, the fact that you are not leaving the area makes things easier to manage," Thalia says. "You can train two hours a day during the week and then all day Saturday. Would you like me to talk to your mom? I can tell her that I've offered you a job as my lab assistant."

"Alright. She seems to like you."

"Very well. I'll get in touch with her tonight. Is ten dollars per hour an appropriate wage?"

"More than appropriate. I'll tell her you've offered me a job and to expect your call."

"Good. I've got some work to do now. Why don't you and Davin go get something to eat. There is a very nice restaurant at the Institute called *Destiny*. I'm sure you'll love the food. I've made reservations."

"I'm really tired, Thalia. I don't know." I don't know if I'm ready to be alone with him.

"You must be famished. Are you sure?"

"I really appreciate the offer, but I'm going to decline. I just want to close my eyes."

"Of course, dear. You've had quite a day."

For sure. "I guess I'll see you on Tuesday?"

She nods. "Tuesday. Davin will pick you up at eight in the morning."

"Okay," I say, as I walk toward the front hall. Just before I reach the door, a question pops into my head and I turn back toward Thalia. "Should I tell my mom about…everything?"

"Soon, but not yet. There is more you need to learn, and I would like to get to know your mom a little better. We will do it together. Davin and I will be by your side…" She pauses and takes my hand in hers. It feels so solid and warm. "I know a lot has happened, but you can trust us," she says in a warm and sincere tone.

"Thanks, Thalia. I'm trying really hard."

"Wait," Davin calls out. "I'll walk you home."

His eyes lock on mine. He looks contrite. Maybe I should cut him some slack. Maybe I should give him a chance to explain, to redeem himself. Maybe…

"Sure."

Chapter 8

Davin and I walk to my house in silence. In my mind, I keep seeing our kiss, the expression on his face when he pulled away, how humiliated I felt.

"Well, thank you for seeing me home safely," I say softly.

"Ari, can we talk?"

"I guess." I nod toward the swing chair on the front porch. "Let's sit. I'm really tired."

I sit down and turn sideways, pulling my knees up to my chin. Davin sits down next to me, keeping as much distance between us as he can.

"I hurt you," he says.

"What makes you say that?"

"I have a well-developed sense of perception." He manages a thin smile.

"I had no right to kiss you like that, Davin. It was inappropriate. I mean, we've only known each other for two days. I don't know what came over me. One minute I was looking into your eyes and the next thing I knew, I was kissing you…"

"And I kissed you back," he finishes.

"Obviously. But the way you reacted…it was hurtful."

"I didn't mean…"

"It's not your fault. I was the aggressor."

"And I was an accessory to the crime."

"Crime?"

"Perhaps that was a bad choice of words. The fact is, I could not let myself be distracted. We were in a vulnerable position and we were physically drained from the healing."

His eyes look sad. Conflicted. Can this impossibly old Warrior simply be socially awkward? "There are more tactful ways to end an ill-timed kiss."

"Ari," he says softly, "In times of extreme stress, emotions cannot always be trusted."

"Balderdash. So, you think I was looking for comfort? A quick kiss, a calming fix?" I practically spit the words out. He thinks I'm weak.

Davin shakes his head slowly. "That's not what I think at all..." A smile slowly forms on his lips. "Balderdash? I like that word."

I roll my eyes. "Tell me what you really think, Davin. I'm dying to know. Do you think I'm an emotional wreck?" I'm building up a head of steam. "Why did you kiss me back?"

"It's complicated."

"Bull! That's a copout."

"Ari..."

"If you want to help me...if you really want to keep me safe, you have to be honest with me. I kissed you because I like you, Davin. I'm attracted to you. Perhaps it's a reaction to stress, but I need to deal with it, not run from it." My tone softens as I continue. "I think you like me, too. In fact, I'm pretty damn sure of it."

The look on his face tells me all I need to know, and I smile inside.

He sighs deeply and nods. "The truth is, I seem to be drawn to you like a moth to moonlight and I'm not sure I understand why. But if I am to keep you safe, I cannot afford to be distracted. Not now. Not yet. Not here."

I don't know how to respond, so I stare at him, like an idiot.

"Ari, if I surrender to my emotions it could compromise my ability to protect you."

"I understand," I say, placing my hand on top of his. "But I think there's more to it. I don't think you were expecting to be attracted to me, and when you were, it surprised you."

I tilt my head and arch my brow, inviting a rejoinder. Instead, he just stares at me. I decide to back off and lighten things up a bit.

"Do you think I might be a siren? An evil seductress?" I ask.

"Ari, there is nothing evil about you."

"So you don't hate me? You don't find me repulsive?"

A warm smile spreads across his face, reaching his eyes, making them sparkle. "I do not hate you and you are most assuredly not repulsive."

I let out a deep sigh. "Life isn't supposed to be this complicated, Davin. I feel like I'm being irresistibly drawn to the edge of a deep chasm and I'm not sure I can keep myself from falling."

"I won't let you fall," he says. His tender tone surprises me.

"Really?"

"Yes."

"You are so hard to figure out. Do you know that?"

"Mm-hmm. But think how accomplished you will feel when you do," he says with a tilt of his head.

"Just when I think I'm close, you change direction on me, Davin. Is it a test?"

He grins. "No. It's just that it's hard for me to interact with you when I'm trying to keep you safe. My senses are much sharper than yours. I can see things and hear things that you cannot. I can hear the fish swimming in your pond. I can hear a deer huffing in the woods. Earlier, I heard what was probably a cat, or a fox, making a kill. I need to filter these sounds and determine if any of them pose a threat to you."

"Will I develop senses like yours?"

"You will."

"So what have I learned today?" I muse. "Let's see—I'm immortal. Aliens are real, and they come in both evil and non-evil models. And, oh yeah, I have this really strange urge to kiss a man I've known less than two whole days. Does that cover it, Davin?"

"Yes. But you left out the part about being strong and brilliant enough to find humor and irony in it," he says.

"I'm not sure about the brilliant part."

"Why not?"

"Well, I'm taking a lot of things on face value. There is always the chance that I'm aiding and abetting an alien race hell-bent on taking over my planet. So I could be a little naïve. Don't you think?"

"Not possible."

"Says you."

"There is only one solution I can see."

"And what would that be?"

"You and I will go out for dinner tomorrow night and I will prove to you that I come in peace."

"How will you do that?"

"Have dinner with me tomorrow night and I will show you."

"Is that the only way?"

"Yes."

"Okay, but this just adds credence to how naïve I am."

"You are not naïve. You have good instincts and you know that I mean you no harm."

"I've been wrong. Once or twice."

"I'm asking you to dine with me in a public restaurant on the Institute campus. Since the Institute is perfectly secure, we can be more relaxed. I will not need to be so focused on protecting you."

"If you attack me, I'll be really pissed off."

"Ari…"

"I'm just saying."

"I would never attack you."

"Can you sense how afraid I am?"

"Of me?"

"Of both of us. One minute I'm afraid of what you are, and the next minute I just want to hold your hand, because I really do like you, and I understand that if you really did want to hurt me..." I take a deep breath. "Well, you could have let me die today."

"Ari..."

"But you didn't."

"I think a night out will help both of us," he says.

"I don't know."

"I promise you will not regret going. Please?"

Why did he have to say 'please' so sweetly? "So, how dressy is this restaurant."

"I think a simple dress would be appropriate."

I look down at my leg to see if there are any telltale signs of my injury. It's almost completely healed. A dress will work.

"Is it an alien hangout?"

He makes a choking sound.

"Just kidding," I say. "We certainly have a lot to talk about. Okay. I'll go."

He looks really pleased. Happy. Excited? "I'll pick you up at seven. Is that alright?"

"Sure. So will I be under guard tonight?" I ask.

"Yes. A team of Warriors will patrol your property. At daybreak, another team will take its place."

"Are they here now?"

"Yes."

"Where?"

"They are hiding."

"Oh. I guess that's good," I remark. "What about tomorrow? What if I leave the house? Will they go with me?"

"If you need to leave your house, call me and I will accompany you. If you do not call, two Warriors will follow you."

"Geez. So much for privacy."

"I realize this is an imposition, but it's temporary, and it's for your safety."

"Do you really think the Zon are going to find me?"

"I don't know, Ari, and that's why we need to be vigilant. There are no Zon in the immediate area, but that can change quickly."

"That's encouraging."

"You'll get through this. I promise."

And I believe him.

Chapter 9

I sleep like a baby, and if Mom didn't drop a laundry basket down the stairs at eleven, I may have slept through my dinner date with Davin, which, to my surprise, I'm now looking forward to. A lot. Our talk helped. It really did.

After a very long shower, I root through my closet, assessing every single dress I own. No luck. Those that still fit are either too casual or too ugly. I call Ella, praying she's close to home. She picks up on the third ring.

"Ella," I say, "Davin is taking me to a really nice restaurant tonight. I need a dress. None of mine fit. Do you think I can borrow one?"

"No problem, sweetie. I'll be over by six with everything you'll need. Except shoes. Do you have black pumps?"

"Yes, I do."

"Good. That's all you'll need. I'll bring the rest. See ya later."

We end the call, and I wonder what I would ever do without her.

Ella arrives a little after six, equipped with her trusty makeup kit and an armful of dresses. She sits on my bed, chin resting in her hands, and carefully appraises each dress. Finally, she makes her decision. "This one, sweetie."

It's a little black dress—the one I actually would have chosen.

"It'll take him two weeks of cold showers to recover from seeing you in this little number. Put it on," she says, holding the dress out to me.

"Well, okay then." I slip out of my shorts and top, and into the dress.

Ella gives me a big smile and a thumbs-up. "Wow. I like the look on you, sweetie."

I step in front of a mirror. It looks nice. Really nice. The top is cut low enough to be alluring—in a classy way. The hem comes to just above my knees. The lines accentuate my figure. "I like it."

"Ok, so that's settled. Now tell me about the picnic."

"Sure. We ate, we swam, and then we talked," I say with a grin.

Ella glares at me.

I chuckle. "We had a very nice time."

"Is he a keeper?"

"Um, possibly," I say, holding a straight face.

She sizes me up. "Mm-hmm. Yup. You like him. But what's not to like? He's the closest thing I've ever seen to a Greek god."

"He's nice, too. And smart." And he's drawn to me like a moth to moonlight.

"Tell me about the lips. Are they as tasty as they look?"

Oh, they are much tastier than they look. And so soft. And warm...

"*My* lips are sealed."

"I really need to know, sweetie. Sooner or later you're going to ask me for advice, so I need to put a dossier together. Ya know?"

"No, I don't know. But *you* know I never kiss and tell." I give her a little smirk.

"I'll let you slide—but only because I'm on a tight schedule. Now let's do the face and the hair. Come. Sit," she says, motioning me to a straight-backed chair. As I sit, she drapes a towel across my shoulders.

"One of these days I really need to learn how to do makeup..."

"If you don't keep still, Davin is going to be having dinner tonight with Chuckles the Clown. Know what I mean?"

"Mm-hmm," I say, without moving my lips."

"That's better, sweetie. Almost done…"

I grunt, not wanting to cause an incident, as Ella applies some finishing touches to my eyes.

"Done. Go look in the mirror," she says.

I give myself the once-over. Then, just to be sure, I look again. She did a fabulous job. "You're amazing. I feel…transformed."

"Now put these on," Ella says, as she retrieves the black pumps from my closet and hands them to me.

I slide into the shoes and do my best impersonation of a model as I spin slowly around with a flourish. "Ella, do I look beautiful tonight?"

"Um, yes…you do." She gives me a funny look. "Why do you ask?"

"Just wondering."

She cocks her head, stares for a moment, and then smiles. "You're hot, you're exotic, and you're dazzling. Why, if I were a guy—"

"Okay, that's enough!" I chuckle. "I'm serious. You really think I look beautiful?"

She studies me for a moment. "You *are* serious. Ariel Worthington, you are more than beautiful enough for Davin." She gives me an innocent smile.

"I didn't say—"

"You didn't say this was about Davin? You're right—*you didn't*. But you didn't have to. Just like you didn't have to tell me you kissed him. You are *so* obvious sometimes, ya know?"

"Really?" God, she can read me like a book.

"Really," she replies. "Now cut this insecurity crap. It is so unlike you."

I give her a toothy smile. "What would I ever do without you, Ella?"

"Hmm. It would probably be devastating, so let's hope we never find out. Now, y'all have a fabulous time tonight, and I'll expect a complete report by tomorrow." She pauses for a moment, then goes back into my closet. She emerges with a lacy black wrap. "Take this with you in case it gets chilly."

"Good idea. Thanks. You going out with Tom tonight?"

"Yeah, we're going to dinner in Charlottesville, which reminds me—I best get my little butt in gear or the dimwit will get confused and go by himself." She grabs the remaining dresses and her makeup kit—then blows me kisses as she leaves, pirouetting out of my room.

Ella is way out of Tom's league—and I don't know why she even bothers with him. I guess it's a safe way to occupy her time until she leaves for college. She needs to find a guy closer to her intellectual level. A guy like Galen? Hmm.

Several minutes later Mom calls out to me. "Ari, Davin just pulled up and…oh wow…nice car. Are you ready, honey?"

"Yes Mom. Be right down."

I'm halfway down the stairs when the doorbell rings. Mom lets him in—and I freeze. He's dressed in an exquisitely tailored black blazer over gray dress slacks, and a crisp white shirt, open at the collar. It's not the kind of outfit a teenager would wear. It looks like something you'd find in James Bond's closet. His clean-shaven face is radiant. His black hair shines. And my arms long to hold him. Oh boy…I'm in serious trouble.

"Ari, you look…stunning."

"Thank you, Davin. You look quite stunning yourself."

I can't take my eyes off of him—and I want him to know it.

"Well," Mom says, "you two supermodels have a nice dinner."

I make my way down the stairs and give her a big hug as I whisper in her ear. "Love you, Mom. I'll be home by one. Okay?"

"I'll be at the hospital. Call me if you'll be later," she whispers back, as she kisses my cheek. "But don't be much later."

"Gotcha," I reply.

"Shall we go?" Davin holds his arm out.

I take his arm, and we walk outside.

"I like your car," I say, as we approach a slate gray Porsche Carrera with a very red interior.

"I'm glad you like it." Davin holds the passenger door open and I lower myself into the seat. It's firm, but very comfortable. The entire interior is swathed in fine leather and carbon fiber. The scent reminds me of Ember's Tannery, a stylish saddle shop in the Valley.

As he slides into the driver's seat, Davin smiles at me. "I appreciate fine cars. They are like rolling works of art."

"This is certainly a nice one," I reply. It really is.

We back out of the driveway and head toward the Institute. As we drive, I wonder what kinds of vehicles an advanced civilization has. Do Olympians even have cars?

"Are there cars on Olympus?"

"Yes," he replies. "We call them transports."

"What are they like?"

I imagine the flying cars in *Star Wars* movies.

He ponders my question for a moment. "In urban areas, we have public transports. They are connected to a computer network. They're comfortable, very fast, but quite boring—since computers do the driving. Every Olympian has access to this type of transport."

"So they don't own the cars?"

"No, they are available for use by anyone. Thousands are in service at all times. When you need to go somewhere, you enter the transport level and call for a vehicle. One usually appears within a minute or two."

"Are there personal vehicles, too?"

"Yes, some of us have the need to be able to travel long distances quickly. A personal transport gives us that ability. In the city, it operates on the public network. But when we need to travel between population centers, the vehicle is capable of running independently. It can travel over land, on the sea, or in the air."

"Seriously?"

"Mm-hmm."

How cool. "Will you take me for a ride someday?"

"Of course," he says.

"I'll hold you to it."

"I'm sure you will," he replies.

We enter the main campus and turn onto a service road. A couple of minutes later, we reach a security checkpoint. A man emerges from a small guardhouse and waves us through, giving Davin a formal nod. Obviously, they know each other.

"Is he a Warrior?" I ask.

"Yes."

"He seemed a little submissive. Do you outrank him? Do Warriors have ranks?"

"Yes, we have a hierarchy. A chain of command."

"What is your rank?"

"Lotani," he says.

"Oh, is that like a lieutenant?"

"Actually, it means *Master*."

"Like a Jedi Master?" I ask.

"In a way," he answers.

I imagine the young Anakin Skywalker tormenting his Jedi Master, Obi-Wan Kenobi. "Then I must be your *Padawan*," I say with a smirk.

Davin rolls his eyes. He does it really well, too—as if he's been practicing.

I put on a serious expression. "May the force be with you, Master."

He shakes his head slowly, but keeps his eyes on the road, as he mutters, "And may heaven help me."

Smart-ass.

We are several miles past the security gate. The road is completely deserted. "Where are we going?" I ask.

"We are almost there. I thought I'd give you a quick tour before we eat."

"Really? Or are you going to throw me into a dungeon, deep under the Institute?" I ask, playfully.

Davin stares at me for a moment.

"What?" I ask.

"I sense that you are still a little uncertain about *things*."

I shift in my seat to face him. "If I'm wrong about you and Thalia, it's too late. I am resigned to my fate, Davin. My life is in your hands."

"You couldn't be safer."

The road ends at the foot of Mt. Evan. We stop in front of a metallic garage-sized door. Davin opens his window and a blue light flashes, illuminating his face. The door opens and we drive in, and down, and around, and down some more. "We are here, Love."

"And where is *here*, Darling?" We are inside what looks like an underground parking garage. The area is huge, but I can only see about ten cars. All of them look very expensive.

"Shh, you'll ruin the surprise," he says, as he pulls into a numbered parking space.

Surprise? "What kind of surprise? Davin…?"

"Shh. Don't ask so many questions."

"But…"

"If I tell you, it won't be a surprise."

"I hate surprises."

"Impossible. You are female."

"What's that supposed to mean?"

"It is a universal law. Females like surprises. Everyone knows this."

I glare at him.

He turns off the engine and we get out of the car.

"This way," he says, taking my hand, as he leads me toward a metal door.

"It's kind of spooky down here," I say. "Is this garage for aliens only?"

"Yes," he says, as he lays his palm on a translucent black panel set into the door.

A female voice responds to his touch, in a language I've never heard before. I assume it's Olympian. It sounds like Mandarin spoken with a French accent. But some of the words sound Greek. Neat.

Davin answers in the same language, and the door slides open.

"Does she know I'm not human?"

"When I laid my hand on the door, a DNA scan was performed, and your Warrior DNA was detected. But since you are not programmed into the system, I was asked to override security protocols to allow for your entry. Only a Master or an official of the Governing Council can do that."

"I feel special."

"You are," Davin says, as he leads me inside.

We enter a small windowless lobby. The walls are polished stone and covered with elegant artwork—paintings of flowers, exquisitely detailed, deliciously abstract. They remind me of Georgia O'Keefe.

Two very imposing guards are stationed behind a counter in the center. They are dressed in white suits—probably body armor. Their faces are completely hidden behind black mesh masks. Hanging from each of their belts is a wicked-looking knife and what looks like a pistol. The taller guard speaks to Davin in Olympian. Davin answers in English, nodding in my direction.

"Ari, these are my friends, Tal and Seto."

"Ah, I am honored to meet you, Ariel. Enjoy your visit," Tal says.

Seto nods. "It is indeed an honor," he says cordially.

"I'm pleased to meet you both," I say, wondering what they look like.

Davin steers me past the guards. "Do they always dress like that?" I ask.

"Only when they're on guard duty. It's ceremonial. Warriors are dangerously lethal—with or without their uniforms."

"Oh."

Davin leads me toward a black door on the right side of the lobby. A light flashes in my eyes, startling me, and then the door slides open—revealing a small room, perhaps eight feet square. The walls are transparent, and the ceiling and floor are a polished black material. The only door is the one through which we entered.

"This is an elevator?"

"Yes. The Institute was built in 1938 atop an Olympian facility. This elevator travels within a shaft that was cut through the heart of Mt. Evan."

"I thought you said the Institute was an Olympian base. But the base is *beneath* the Institute? I'm confused."

"The Institute is a real college, Ari—with human students and faculty. It has to be authentic or we would call too much attention to ourselves. The base is fifteen hundred feet below the surface."

"No humans have ever discovered your little secret?"

"Unauthorized entry is not possible," he states with pride. "From the surface, there is only one way into the base. An interloper would be intercepted and redirected long before becoming a security threat."

"To the dungeon," I mutter to myself.

Davin keys a sequence of numbers into a panel on the elevator's wall. I hear a faint hum. "Hang on, next stop is the main dungeon level."

"Damn your super-hearing," I mumble.

"Your hearing is just as super. You just don't know how to use it. Yet."

"What?"

"Very funny."

I gasp as the elevator car begins to descend—*rapidly*—taking my breath with it. "Wow. That was like a Disney ride."

The door slides open and we emerge into a cavernous room. Dozens of people in white onesie suits buzz around like worker bees. The ceiling has to be a hundred feet high. The walls appear to be metal—without a visible seam—and are covered with large art deco posters, captioned in a language that is foreign, alien, *Olympian*. The floors are polished and stone-like, with a gray-black patterned texture.

"Is this the only level?" I ask.

"Yes."

Davin takes my hand and we walk toward an alcove in the far wall. The walls inside the alcove are lined with counters, divided into workstations. Four people sit in front of holographic displays, which are obviously computers—but unlike any computers I've ever seen. Images and words float in space above them. As we get closer, I can see what look like keyboards—suspended inside each of the displays. One of the operators is air-typing. How incredibly cool.

"I'll give you a quick tour of the facility and then we'll eat," Davin says. "Are you hungry?"

I nod absently as a tall young woman approaches us. "Davin, it's so nice to see you," she says in perfect English.

She gives him a friendly hug, then steps back to look at me. "You must be Ariel." She smiles warmly and squeezes my hand gently. "I am honored to meet you."

"Ari," Davin says to me, "this is Sage Eleni, an esteemed scientist and a dear friend of Thalia's and mine."

"I'm pleased to meet you, Eleni," I say with a polite smile. She is very attractive and looks to be in her early twenties. Of course she does. She's immortal.

"You two have a lovely dinner," Eleni says, while motioning us toward a large, vault-like door at the end of the alcove.

Davin gazes at me with a self-satisfied grin. Then it hits me. "Davin?" I gasp, looking from him to the vault.

"Ari?" he parries.

Eleni and her associates look like they're watching a tennis match as their heads whip back and forth between Davin and me. They're all smiling—as if everyone knows what's going on. Everyone, that is, *except me*.

"Davin!" I exclaim, "What's through that door?"

"I guess you'll find out when we go through it," he says with a roguish smile.

"It's the portal," I whisper. "We're having dinner on Olympus?"

Before I can react, he picks me up in a swift and gentle motion, holding me in his arms as you would a child. He looks into my eyes and speaks softly. "I wanted to dispel any doubts you may have had about me. Yes, we are having dinner on Olympus. Are you ready?"

"Oh, I'm ready. I'm very ready. Let's go!" I'm smiling so wide my cheeks hurt.

"Wait, please," Eleni says, as she walks over to us. "May I see your right ear, Ariel?"

"Huh?" I turn my head, and she clips something to the top of my ear. "What was that?"

"It's a translator. You will now understand Olympian. Translation is in real time, so if you look closely at my lips you should be able to tell that I am not speaking English—yet you understand me, yes?"

"Oh, this is very cool. Yes, I read you loud and clear. Thank you, Eleni."

The vault door opens with a hiss. I look at Davin. "Shall we go, Darling?"

"You really are fearless," he says with a warm smile.

"Yeah, but I have a good feeling about this. I'm not sure why, but I'm beginning to think you aren't a monster, after all."

"Well, let's hope you're right," he says, as we enter the vault.

It's as if we are passing through a veil. Energy courses through me. As we move forward, I see vibrating waves all around me, and the sides of the portal seem to be rushing by, impossibly fast. Yet Davin is walking at a normal pace. After little more than a minute, I see shapes in front of me—people. And then we emerge.

"Welcome to Portal City," Davin says as he puts me down.

"We're not in Virginia anymore," I say with wide-eyed wonder.

A lanky young man approaches us. "Greetings, Warriors," he says, with a slight, but formal bow. Davin nods. I do, too.

We are in a large and very beautiful concourse. The floors are polished stone and the wall covering looks like exotic wood. The artwork and décor are exquisite.

It was such a short walk. No more than two minutes. Yet we've traveled one thousand light-years into space. A hundred feet ahead of us is a staircase that leads up to a glass wall. Rays of light shine through. The light of another star. We walk toward it.

The door opens automatically and we walk outside. What I see takes my breath away and brings tears to my eyes. I look out on a vista of unimaginable beauty. Trees and shrubs that are perfectly shaped. Flowers in colors that do not even exist on Earth. Fragrances that are new and deliciously intoxicating. My senses are utterly overwhelmed.

"It's amazing, Davin."

He smiles and wraps an arm around my waist. "I'm glad you are pleased."

Incredibly beautiful birds—in a startling multiplicity of shapes, sizes, and colors—soar across the blue-green Olympian sky.

Large butterfly-like creatures hover in midair, feasting on nectar, hummingbird-style. Even the insects are beautiful.

In the distance, rock formations and snow-capped mountains rise to meet billowy white clouds. It's a scene only God could have painted.

All around us, people stroll about on stone paths. They're dressed like humans—but in clothes designed more like what you'd see in an old movie. A 1940s movie. Men are decked out in well-tailored suits and sport coats; women wear dresses or skirts. Everyone looks so elegant and chic. Even the children are dressed up.

I'm happy to see that Olympians do not all look alike. While they do seem healthier-looking than humans, they are not all supermodel-gorgeous—like Davin.

"Does Olympus have different races of people?"

"Not anymore. Time and interbreeding have led to a high degree of homogeneity."

"Of course." I sigh. I wonder if Earth will ever reach such a state.

No buildings are visible. Instead, small arched structures dot the landscape.

"Davin, are the arches entrances to underground buildings?"

"Yes. Building below the surface allows us to preserve and enjoy our natural beauty."

"It's all so lovely here, Davin. It's the kind of world Walt Disney would have designed. I think I'm suffering from planet envy."

I touch his arm compulsively. I haven't touched him in several minutes. Can I only go a set amount of time without touching him before I explode?

"Earth is beautiful, too. You have places like Renegade Falls that are *magical*." He holds me tighter.

I look at his beautiful face and feel the pull of our hearts. He took me to another galaxy—not just for a dinner date, but to allay my doubts; to eliminate the possibility, in my mind, that one or both of us were delusional—or worse. I want to lose myself in his embrace. I want…

"You seem lost in thought, Ari. What are you thinking about?" he asks.

"That I may be dreaming."

"Then let me make it a happy dream." He cups my face in his hands and slowly pulls me close. "A very happy dream," he says, as he brushes his lips against mine.

Our lips part, time stands still, and nothing exists except Davin and me.

"You kissed me," I say, while gazing into his eyes.

"You noticed?" he asks.

"I did. It was very obvious," I say with a playful smile. "Aren't you putting me at risk by giving in to your emotions?"

"There is no risk to you here. I am…"

"You are free to be yourself?"

"Something like that."

"And you don't think I'm a helpless female?"

"You have no idea just how strong you are, Ari. But you will find out soon."

"Mm-hmm. Well, I'm famished. Weren't you going to feed me?"

Davin smiles.

"The restaurant is a short walk in that direction," he says, pointing to his left.

Chapter 10

"What does the writing say?" I ask, as we stand in front of the restaurant entrance.

He pronounces the name slowly. "EE-STOYA OH-TA NAH-GEE. It means…"

I cut him off. "Nagi's Restaurant. The translator Eleni gave me really works," I say, as I tap the device affixed to my ear. "But *how* does it work?"

"The device on your ear is communicating directly with your brain. It is teaching you to understand Olympian. Over time, it will also teach you to read and speak our language. And then, you will no longer need it."

"That's unbelievable."

"Thalia will teach you how to use the device to its full capabilities. She will also teach you many other unbelievable things."

He looks at me and smiles. "Shall we dine, Padawan?"

"I thought you'd never ask."

He takes my hand and leads me through the entrance, and I smile as I dreamily ponder the enormity of what is taking place.

Nagi's is filled with smiling people—most of whom are engaged in animated conversation. "Why is everyone dressed like humans?" I ask

"Olympian clothing used to be boring—designed mainly for efficiency. In the 1930s, however, human cinema became popular.

Everyone wanted to look like Cary Grant or Katherine Hepburn. The trend did not fade away."

"You know, it's not as *alien* as I thought it would be," I remark.

"Hmm?"

"The clothes. The friendliness. The smell of coffee…"

"Alas, what would life be like without coffee? I believe our first encounter with it was during the European Renaissance. It was love at first sip. Olympians and humans are related, Ari. In ancient times, there was much contact between us. Humans observed our behavior as much as we observed theirs. The line between what is purely human and purely Olympian is considerably blurred. Wait until you taste the chocolate."

"Chocolate?"

"Yes. It is as popular on Olympus as it is on Earth."

"Chocolate is not popular on Earth, Davin. It is cherished. It is loved. It is revered. If the Zon threatened chocolate, instead of people, they would have been torn apart by crazed human women many years ago."

"I know a few Olympians who would have helped."

Davin and I chuckle, and it occurs to me that we are acting like two people on a date. Two people who like each other.

"So, what do you recommend for dinner?"

"Do you like beef steak?"

"I love it."

"I would recommend torik. It has the texture of beef tenderloin, and a flavor that is slightly sweet. It is my favorite."

"That sounds wonderful. I'll have the torik. Why don't you order for me. I trust you."

"You do?"

"With my life." My words surprise me. But they're true, and it brings a smile to my face.

Davin fixes me with a stare, as a smile slowly forms on his lips. "I think you are as hard to figure out as I am."

"Actually, I'm really easy to figure out, Davin. You just haven't been trying hard enough," I say, as I bat my lashes and pout.

His green eyes sparkle like precious gems. He is speechless and I'm loving it.

My torik is served with a medley of incredibly delicious—and bright blue—vegetables. I'm like a young child experiencing new flavors for the first time. Every bite is an adventure.

"Tell me about torik. Are they raised for their meat?" I ask.

"No," Davin explains. "They used to be. Now they are happy and free. We manufacture torik meat from a genetic profile. Not a single living beast is ever harmed."

"That's so awesome," I say, because no creature had to give up its life for my meal. My delicious meal. "Are all foods manufactured that way?"

"Yes. Everything we need is fabricated on-site and delivered within minutes. There's never a need to stock an inventory. Our homes also have systems that prepare food and dispense it—ready to eat. You don't need appliances unless you really want to cook, in which case, you have access to any ingredient—so long as its molecular and genetic profiles are programmed into the system."

"Incredible!"

"Vegetables, grains, and fruits are also produced by Olympian food prep systems. And they are exact replicas of their natural counterparts."

"Wow. This is so amazing!"

"I guess it is. Did you enjoy your dinner?"

"It was scrumptious, Davin. You chose well."

"Roast torik is a favorite of mine. I thought you'd like it."

"I did. I really did."

Davin looks at his phone. "It's almost nine. Would you like to skip dessert and take a walk?"

As much as I'd love to try an Olympian dessert, especially one made with chocolate, I want to see more of this remarkable city. I want to immerse myself in its beauty. "Let's walk, Davin."

He smiles and stands, moving behind my chair. "Let's go, then."

"Don't we have to pay?"

"Things work a little differently here, Ari. There is a scanner on the table. The amount of our meal has been deducted from my personal account."

"Oh. I must have missed that. When we have some time, I would like to learn all about your economy," I say. Then I realize that nature is beckoning. "Uh, I need to find a—"

He points down a hallway and says, "First door on the right," as he tries to stifle a laugh.

"Does it, um, *work* the same way as on Earth?"

He bends down and whispers the instructions in my ear. "Red light means occupied. Blue light means you can enter. What's inside should be very familiar to you. Nothing will hurt you."

"Smart-ass." I roll my eyes, then head for the ladies room, calling back over my shoulder, "Meet you by the door in a few minutes."

As we stroll outside, the early evening air is warm and fragrant. The sun is low in the sky and a soft orange glow hugs the horizon. Gosh, this is amazing.

"Davin, does the portal affect time? I mean, if we spend four hours here, how much time will have passed on Earth?"

"Four hours," he replies. "We have yet to master time travel," he adds, with a smile.

I look at my phone and gasp. Nine o'clock. What the…

"How is my phone able to display the time?"

"Ah, fascinating. Is it not?"

"How is it even possible?"

"Cellular signals are captured at the Institute and routed through a special network that runs along the portal. Your phone is fully operational. You can place a call to Earth and it will go through."

"Wow. So, right now it's nine o'clock in Virginia and here, too?"

"Pretty much. We could be a minute or two apart."

"Really?"

He nods and smiles. "Imagine Olympus and Earth are two cookies, glued to opposite ends of a paper plate, six inches apart. If we fold the plate in half, the cookies can be made to touch. The portal bends space. It creates a shortcut. It's actually more stressful traveling between Virginia and California, than between Virginia and Olympus."

"Okay. No portal lag. But my head is starting to throb."

"It's a lot to ponder. You'll get used to things."

I sigh. There will be a lot of things I'll need to get used to. "Is all of Olympus this beautiful, Davin? Are there *bad* areas? Are there slums?"

"We've had eons to get things right. There are no slums, no bad areas. Everyone has what they need."

"How can that be? Is your government socialist?"

"No. There is no Earthly counterpart to our form of government. At least, not yet."

"Are there nation-states on Olympus?"

"Our government is planet-wide. Every Olympian is guaranteed food, shelter, an education, and medical care. Everyone works and compensation is merit-based. The incentives are much as they are in America—a nicer house, a personal transport, more upscale restaurants. Even a master underachiever has everything he or she needs—it's just a little less fancy."

"What is the crime rate on Olympus?"

"Violent crime is very rare. Theft, in its various forms, is almost nonexistent. Property crimes are a little more common and typically committed by young ones. Mostly, they are nothing more than pranks."

Young ones. Davin said that half a billion people live on Olympus. "How do you keep your population from growing out of control?"

"Olympus has evolved to the point where common sense is the common wisdom. Once an Olympian boy reaches puberty, he is genetically altered. He is made sterile."

I gasp.

Davin smiles. "It's not as bad as it sounds, and it is reversible. When a bound couple wants to have a child, they meet with a Sage, who provides counsel. The process is very enlightening, and the couple usually winds up learning more about themselves. In most cases, the process ends with the couple and their counselor in complete agreement. If it is decided that a child should be conceived, the male is made fertile for one year. Upon conception, the male is rendered sterile again. The process is totally safe and completely painless."

"And you don't think it's a violation of personal freedom?"

"Olympian birth control is not a law. It's a tradition. It is also the most logical way to manage population, while ensuring that all children are wanted, loved, and cared for."

"So there are no unwanted pregnancies? No abortions? No unloved kids?"

"We are not perfect," Davin replies. "Most children are looked upon as gifts to be cherished. But there are exceptions. And we deal with the exceptions very effectively—usually through counseling and education.

If all else fails, unwanted children are placed in homes where they will be loved."

"Adoption?" I ask.

"Yes."

He's right. It's perfectly logical. Compared to Olympus, Earth is still so primitive. "Do only bound couples have babies?"

"With rare exceptions, yes."

"You must think humans are savages."

"Not at all. They are still learning and evolving. We consider humans to be our children. We had our growing pains, too." He gives me a warm, parental smile.

"Okay, Pops. How about prisons—do you have any of those?"

"Prisons no longer exist on Olympus. Instead, we have remediation facilities, which are more like schools."

"Do you think humans will ever learn to play as nicely as Olympians do? I am not as confident as you seem to be. I'm not sure that we can ever become like Olympians. We are so obsessed with talking about personal freedom that we fail to realize how little of it we actually have."

Davin scratches his chin. "Humans will eventually evolve to a higher level of social enlightenment. At least I hope so."

"Considering the sheer number of people on Earth, it really seems hopeless. I mean, look at Washington. Just a few blocks from where the President lives, people are living in squalor." I feel exasperated. It's so hopeless. "Where do you even begin?"

He smiles. "How do you eat an elephant?"

"Yes. One bite at a time. But there are seven billion people on Earth. How many do you think are living in poverty?"

"Too many. And since we are talking about pachyderms, wouldn't you agree that population growth is the elephant in the room—the one that your leaders have been reluctant to acknowledge?"

"Oh, yes. Mom and I talk about that all the time."

"But it is a topic that is gaining traction. It's just going to take time, Ari. Olympians have gone through the process. It's painful and it takes a very long time. Human life expectancy has risen dramatically during the past seventy years, without a correlative decrease in reproductive rates. It's a simple concept, but difficult and delicate to implement."

"I hope I'm around to see it implemented," I sigh, as I realize how far humans have to go.

"There's a very good chance you will."

"Oh, yes. Immortality."

Davin grins. "Yes, you will have time to observe the process. We will observe it together. It should make for interesting conversation."

"Olympus is so amazing. Low crime rates, no slums, a world government. How can a world government even work? Who protects the people? Who keeps the government from becoming corrupt or tyrannical?"

"We do, Love. The Warriors do."

"I don't understand. Soldiers run this world?"

"We are not really soldiers, Ari."

"I forgot. We're more like *Star Wars* Jedi," I say with a wink.

"Let's walk down to the promenade. The sunsets are beautiful there."

As we walk, I immerse myself in the beauty that surrounds me. Portal City is so pristine, so idyllic, so…

A small furry animal darts in front of me, pauses for a second, and then scurries away. It's no larger than a squirrel, but it looks like a monkey. Its little face is adorable.

"What was that, Davin?" I ask excitedly.

"A vorkin. They are the smallest primates on Olympus and as abundant as squirrels on Earth."

"They're so cute!"

"I guess they are. But they can be a nuisance, too. Don't ever feed one, or you'll never get rid of it."

"Do you have zoos and museums on Olympus?"

"We have many museums, but no zoos. Some museums are equipped with virtual reality devices that allow you to see, feel, and smell Olympian wildlife—without being eaten. Of course, you can also explore the wilderness, see animals in their natural habitats—but then you could be eaten," he says with a smile.

"Oh." I gaze at the distant mountains. What kinds of ferocious critters are lurking out there?

"Will you take me to the museums. I would love to see them. All of them!"

"I would be delighted to, Ari."

It strikes me that I may be the only human to ever walk on the surface of an alien planet. Then again, I'm not actually human. "Am I the first human to visit Olympus?"

"You are not human."

"Yeah. Um, you know what I mean."

"You are the first person born on Earth to visit Olympus."

"Have you never wanted to share your technology? Couldn't Olympian science help humans?"

"It could. But in the wrong hands, our technology could cause mass suffering."

"Do the Zon have scientists?"

"No. Their role on Olympus did not involve science. And even if it did, they would never share technology with humans. Their raison d'être is to cause suffering, not to cure cancer."

"I see. So, there is only one portal. Right?"

"Yes."

"Is there any other way to travel between Earth and Olympus?"

"No."

"So Olympus is safe from the Zon. They can't sneak in and they don't have the smarts to create their own portal. Is that right?"

"Yes."

My head is spinning. There is so much I have to learn. So very much.

Chapter 11

Ahead of us, I can see water, and my excitement meter rises. "Is that an ocean, Davin?"

"Yes. It's called the Promethean Sea."

"The Greek thing again, huh?"

He nods. "And this is the promenade," he says, pointing to a lovely expanse of blue lawn in front of us.

It's beautiful. Davin and I sit down on a bench overlooking the sea and I snuggle close to him. The breeze blowing in is warm and smells of salt.

"How big is the sea?" I ask.

"The Promethean is our only ocean. It is about twenty-five percent larger than all of the oceans of Earth combined."

"Is Olympus that much larger than Earth or do you have less land mass?"

"Olympus and Earth are close in size, but our land mass is smaller."

"I see. Olympus is so amazing, Davin. And the Warriors really run the government?"

"It's more like we keep the balance. Olympus is administered by Sages—like Thalia. We work alongside them. We complement each other."

"Thalia is a big shot then?" I ask.

"She is our most powerful Sage and the most influential member of the Governing Council."

"She's like the Prime Minister, then?"

"In a way. Whatever she decides, the Council will usually agree to."

"If Thalia is the most powerful Sage, who is the most powerful Warrior?"

He looks at me and arches his brow—but doesn't answer.

"You?" I ask.

"I am one of six Warrior Masters. We work as a team."

"That's impressive." I wonder if it's considered appropriate for a Master to fraternize with a newbie.

"Will being with me cause you any problems?"

"Absolutely not. You're stuck with me, little Padawan."

I smile as I inch closer to him.

"I guess there could be worse things than being stuck with you," I say, as I stroke his cheek.

As my fingers near his lips, he captures them, kissing each one, and causing little shivers to run down my spine. If fingers could smile, mine would be grinning from knuckle to knuckle.

"Tell me a story, Master. Tell me about the Warriors." I stare at him, doing my best impression of wide-eyed wonder.

"Sometimes you make it very hard for me to be serious, you know?" He massages his temple.

I hope I haven't given him a headache. "Sorry."

"What would you like to know?" he asks.

"How did the Warriors defeat the Zon?"

"Do you remember what I said about the Zon yesterday?"

"Yes," I say. "They helped to nurture Olympian society, but then they got tired of their mission, and they turned evil."

"Right. A little over a million years ago, the Zon had basically enslaved the entire planet. Things were very bad. Then, on an island called Aegia, in the middle of the Promethean Sea, scores of men and women with remarkable powers appeared—"

97

"Wait," I say. "They appeared? Where did they come from?"

"I will get to that," he replies. "Be patient."

"Sorry. Go ahead."

"They were the Warrior Elders. Their leader, Damas, acquired a ship, and the Warriors set sail for Xandra—the main Zon stronghold. The Zon were used to being the most powerful creatures on Olympus. When the Warriors appeared, the Zon did not take them seriously. Within a few hours, thousands of Zon lay dead."

"And then what happened?"

"The Zon had outposts all over Olympus. Damas and his Warriors spent nearly a year going from outpost to outpost. The results were the same. The Zon were defeated and the Warriors established a new Olympian government, which they oversaw—and continue to oversee to this day."

Incredible. If I wasn't sitting on a bench, a thousand light-years from home, I'd find this very hard to believe. "But some hid and then escaped to Earth?"

"The Elders were not aware that any of the Zon had eluded them. When the first Earth portal was completed, the surviving Zon attacked. Hundreds of them. Most were killed, but a large number managed to escape through the portal."

"And they hid on Earth? Did you try to find them?"

"Yes. Several Warrior teams were dispatched, but by the time we arrived, the Zon were well-hidden."

"Couldn't you detect them?"

"Earth has a lot of hiding places. We need to be in close physical proximity in order to detect them. They remained underground until human civilization began to flourish."

"And then they came out of hiding and found a bunch of helpless, hapless victims?"

"Yes. They derive pleasure from the pain and suffering of innocent mortals. Through the ages, they have been responsible for mass killings, human bondage, and unspeakable acts of terror. They are truly evil beings."

"So you have hunted them all these years, yet they still thrive?"

"They are not easy to find among billions of humans."

"But sometimes you do. Right?"

"Yes, but we must be careful. We are not permitted to reveal ourselves to humans."

"The prime directive?" I ask.

"Excuse me?"

I chuckle. "From the old *Star Trek* show. Starfleet was prohibited from interfering in the natural development of alien societies. At all costs."

Davin smiles. "Good analogy. We *could* affect the natural course of things. And there is always the risk that revealing ourselves could cause mass hysteria. The Zon have been recruiting humans for millennia. There are politicians, journalists, celebrities, and other influential humans under Zon control. We could easily be made to appear as the villains."

"Good point. So how have you avoided detection all these years?"

"We strike with stealth. But we have not gone totally unnoticed. Thankfully, human nature works to our advantage. Those who witness our powers are written off as unbalanced, paranoid, or delusional. In ancient times, we were described as demigods, heroes, or angels."

"So, we *are* mythological creatures. I knew it!"

"Ari, I'm trying to be serious."

"Sorry." I pretend to wipe the smile off my face. "So, how many Zon are there on Earth?"

"The number could be in the hundreds. We are not really certain."

"You told me that Warriors cannot reproduce. What about the Zon?"

"There is no evidence they can."

"That's good. Do the Zon have an endgame in mind? Do they want to exterminate the human race?"

"We don't think so. It would not be in their interest to destroy humanity. That would eliminate the source of their pleasure. And it would allow us to hunt them with impunity. The Zon seem to be more interested in controlling and influencing human leaders. Not replacing them."

"Davin, were the Zon instrumental in starting World War II?"

"Yes. They were very instrumental."

"And didn't over fifty million people die during that war?"

"Yes."

"How bad do you think it would be if humans found out about you? Relatively speaking, of course."

"Some of us would agree with you."

"Would *you*?"

"Yes. But it would take a lot of planning and a total commitment to the cause."

I sigh. "Maybe someday we can make it happen. Or maybe we can rehabilitate the Zon. Can they be reformed?"

"No. They are pure evil. They cannot be changed."

"Can we be turned evil? Can the Zon corrupt us?"

"A Zon can trick a Warrior into letting his or her defenses down. But a Warrior cannot become evil unless he or she chooses to."

"Has that ever happened? Do evil Warriors exist?"

"Yes. Several Warrior Elders joined the Zon rebellion."

"Davin...?"

"Ari?"

"We're angels, aren't we?" He doesn't need to answer, because I know it. I feel it in my soul.

He arches his brow. "Do you think we are?"

I lock eyes with him. "I do."

"I guess it's possible," he says with pursed lips and the barest hint of a smile.

"You're holding back."

"Really?"

"Absolutely. It is a very logical assumption. Don't you think?"

"It is plausible."

"It is *probable*. Are you going to give me a straight answer?"

"Eventually."

"That was not a straight answer. I'll let you slide for a few moments. But be forewarned...I will hound you incessantly until I get one."

"A straight answer?"

"Yes."

"Fair enough."

I sigh. He is playing with me. He's having a good time. But so am I.

"So what happened to the Elders?"

"They watched over Olympus for several centuries. And they bore children. When those children had grown into mature Warriors and Sages, the Elders left."

"Where did they go?"

"It is written in the Gia, the sacred book of Olympus, that the Elders went home. Damas requested an audience with the Governing Council. He informed them that he, along with the other Elders, had been called home. Their work was finished and they would be leaving. The councilors were dismayed. When they asked Damas who would protect them, he said that the children would. He said that the young ones were powerful Warriors and wise Sages. Damas told the council that they would be in capable hands."

"You are a child of the Elders?"

"Yes. All Warriors and Sages are."

"And you knew your parents?"

"Of course. They raised me."

"And they told you where they came from?"

He nodded.

"Davin, I'm not afraid to hear the truth."

He places his chin on my head. "No matter how outlandish it sounds?"

"Outlandish? I am sitting on a bench a thousand light-years from home. I have a very open mind right now, Darling."

Davin clears his throat, and his expression becomes serious. "Very well. Let's revisit the Zon for a moment. They grew weary of their work on Olympus because they felt abandoned, so they rebelled. They renounced their allegiance to Paradise."

I gasp. "Paradise?"

"Yes."

"Did all of them rebel?"

"In the end, yes."

"And the Warriors were sent from Paradise to set things right?"

"Yes."

"But some Warriors rebelled too. Right?"

"A few."

"So we *are* angels, and the rebels are *fallen* angels," I say, barely above a whisper.

Davin nods.

"I'll be damned." I chuckle inside at my choice of invective, and my mind begins to wander. What are the odds? I imagine myself born into an impoverished family living on the African savannah; or to Chinese peasants barely able to feed me; or to the leader of a drug cartel. My life could have taken so many different paths. But…I'm an angel. Absently I look up into the sky and smile as I mouth the words 'thank you'.

"No," Davin says with a smile. "You will never be damned. *Never.*"

I smile back. I guess he's right. But there is a price to pay. My humanity. My dreams, hopes, and goals are no longer relevant. I won't be a paleoanthropologist. I won't have a house in the country. And I'll never be able to...

"You have parents, yet you cannot make babies. Why?"

"Sometimes you change subjects so fast that I'm afraid I will get whiplash," he says, looking amused.

"Sorry."

"Humans are not immortal, yet there are seven billion of them. Imagine how many Warriors and Sages there would be if we were allowed to reproduce."

"Oh. Can't Warriors and Sages be made fertile?"

"Theoretically. No one has ever asked me that. It's an interesting question."

"That's why I asked," I say with pursed lips.

"Are you upset that you will not be able to have children?"

I imagine myself holding a baby. My baby. And I feel sad, because now I know it's never going to happen. "Yes, I am. I grew up on Earth, Davin. Most human girls want to be mothers."

"I'm sorry, Ari."

I'm sorry, too. If my parents were able to have me, maybe there's a way. "Why were the Elders allowed to have children?"

Davin runs his fingers through his hair. "The children replaced their parents, who were then allowed to return to Paradise. It was thought that since we were born and raised on Olympus, we would feel more bound to the mortal world, and less-inclined to rebel."

"Oh. But don't you feel abandoned by your parents?"

"Not really. It was not as if they left when we were children. My parents were here for several hundred years."

"Are they ever able to visit?"

"Occasionally."

"They check up on you, huh?"

"In a manner of speaking, I guess they do."

"Why didn't you tell me you were an angel when we were at the Falls?"

He sighs long and deep. "I didn't think you were ready to hear it. *Angel* is a human word, which has very specific implications. I think we are far more interesting than the angels of human lore—even if we don't have wings. Don't you agree?"

I think about it. Based on what I remember from the Bible, we are way more interesting. "Yes, I do. And I always thought the whole *wing thing* was absurd."

"They make lovely Christmas cards, though," Davin says.

"That they do. Is there an Olympian word for angel?"

"Angelos."

"That's the Greek word, too?"

"Yes."

"Something is really bothering me, Davin."

"And what is that?"

"The mortals on Olympus know we're angels. Right?"

"Yes."

"And they've known for a million years?"

He nods.

"It seems to me that Olympus has benefitted immensely from our influence…from the influence of angels. But Earth has kind of been left to fend for itself. It seems logical to assume that if humans knew we existed, that if we interacted with them, the quality of life on Earth might be a whole lot better."

"Your powers of perception are strong, Ari. And you are right. When we were initially sent to Earth, it was decided that we should not become as deeply involved in the affairs of man as the Zon were involved in the affairs of Olympians. Paradise wished to prevent a repeat of the Zon rebellion. In that sense, the strategy was successful. But the downside is that human progress has been stunted."

"The strategy is flawed, Davin. As long as the Zon exist, humans will be at risk."

"This is why many of us believe we should take a more proactive role in human society. Unfortunately, it is not our decision to make. Paradise must approve it, and to date, they have not."

"Do you think they ever will?"

He scratches his chin and appears to be pondering my question. "I hope so. I really do."

We sit quietly for a few moments—mainly because my incessant talking probably makes him very tired. Actually, it takes a lot out of me, too.

I think of all the questions I still have. It could take months to get answers. "Thalia is not your aunt, is she?"

"No."

"And since you rented the house in Edgewood to observe me, where do you and Thalia really live?"

"We live in Portal City—not far from here."

"Do you and Thalia live together?"

"Of course not. She is like a sister to me."

"Oh." I feel relieved. "And you are not from Santa Barbara?"

"Actually, I *was* posted there for nearly a year."

"I see. But your last name is not really Andersen, is it?"

"No. We really don't have last names on Olympus. In official records, I am identified by a code, which is indexed to an honorific—Davin of Genobli, Warrior Master, son of Lecco and Annia."

"Now, that's a mouthful." I chuckle. "So I would be Ariel of Edgewood, Warrior Newbie, daughter of Damian and Andrea."

105

"Damian?" He says the name slowly.

"Yes. Why do you ask?"

"The name has ancient Greek roots. It's a fine name. Are your father's parents still alive?"

"Dad's parents and grandparents died before I was born."

"I see."

"Do you think my dad could be an angel?"

"The thought did cross my mind."

"Wow. That would explain a lot of things," I say.

"It would. Perhaps Thalia can come up with something. Don't worry about it just yet. Okay?"

I nod, and then my mind drifts to Davin's youth. "Did you have a happy childhood? Did you get along with your parents?"

"We were very close."

"I'm glad," I say.

I look up. The moons are rising in the evening sky. The moons? "I see two moons, Davin."

"Beautiful, aren't they?"

I nod and gaze at Davin, mesmerized by his beauty. "You seem more at ease. More comfortable."

"You are safe here, and that puts me at ease."

"I always feel safe when I'm near you." I squeeze closer, laying my head on his shoulder. "You know what I like about you, Davin?"

He shakes his head slowly and arches his brow, as I ramble on. "You speak really well. When we first met, you made some awkward attempts to sound like a teenager. It wasn't *you*. I love listening to you now. You're..." I pause as I search for the right word. "You're a classic."

"That's about the nicest thing anyone has ever said to me," he replies, with what has become my most favorite of his smiles. "And do you know what I like about you?"

"No. Tell me."

"I like the sound of your voice. It exudes intelligence, conveys an almost-perpetual sense of wonderment, and sings to me with the barest hint of southern accent. I can listen to you speak for hours on end, which is something you seem to enjoy doing...*immensely*. You are a classic in your own right."

I crinkle my nose. "You make me think, which makes me talk. In fact, whenever I'm with you all I want to do is think and talk. Like, right now I want to talk about us."

"I thought we were doing that already."

"I want to talk about why you feel drawn to me like..."

"A moth to moonlight?"

"Yeah, that's it."

"I'm not entirely sure. Perhaps it's because I've never met a woman quite like you."

"I'm not sure how to take that. Care to elaborate?"

"It's as if we were meant to meet. As if fate has brought us together. And now we get to see what fate has in store for us."

"It's kind of like an adventure, huh?"

He smiles and tilts his head. "Adventure, journey, escapade. It can be anything we want it to be. Anything at all. We get to define it."

The way he says it causes my heart to leap. I turn and gaze into his eyes. "You know, for some strange and amazing reason, it feels as though I've known you for a very long time. I sense a connection between us. It's so hard to explain, but so wonderful to feel."

"I feel it, too," he says.

"Thank you for sharing. I was beginning to think you were one of those angels who keeps his feelings inside."

"You should never stereotype a person. Especially not an angel."

Cute.

Chapter 12

I awake on Monday feeling refreshed and a little giddy from my otherworldly adventure. I'm an angel. A living, breathing, celestial being. But it doesn't frighten me. It's beginning to feel natural—as if this is what I'm meant to be. I feel elated, which surprises me.

Without thinking, I reach for my phone and call Davin. He answers on the second ring. "Good morning, Ari. Is everything okay?"

"Yes!" I answer. "I just need to verify that what happened last night was real. We actually had dinner on Olympus, right?"

"Affirmative," Davin says with a smile in his voice.

"Um, the government can't listen in to our calls. Can they?"

Davin chuckles. "No one can monitor this call."

"I thought the NSA monitored all cell phone calls?"

"Our phones are secure. Your phone is routed through our system. We can talk about anything."

"Really?"

"Yes. Actually, your mom's phone is also secure."

"Cool! So, I'm really an angel?"

"You most certainly are."

"And you kissed me last night?"

"I did."

"I thought I imagined it, Davin. I thought it had to be a dream."

"Which part?"

"Everything!" I exclaim.

"You sound happy."

"I am. Taking me to dinner on Olympus was a stroke of genius."

"I've been known to have an occasional outburst of brilliance."

"And a few spells of angel attitude," I add with a playful tone. "Um, I forgot to tell you that I need to be at school today. I volunteered to help set up for the annual library book sale."

"What is your schedule?"

"I need to be there at nine. We should be finished by three in the afternoon."

"I'll alert my team. They will follow you and set up positions around the school. You won't even know they are there."

"Okay. Sorry about the short notice."

"It's not a problem. Thank you for letting me know."

"Training is still on for tomorrow?"

"Yes. I will pick you up between seven-thirty and eight."

"Will I see you later?" I ask.

"If you'd like. Was there something you wanted to do?"

"I'm probably going to be tired and we do need to get up early. Would you like to come over to my house and talk? I still have a ton of questions."

"Sure. What time?"

"Seven-thirty?"

"Perfect. I'll see you later, then. Enjoy your day."

"You, too, Davin," I say, ending the call.

I hop up off the bed and glide to the bathroom, still in a dreamlike state, as I wonder—how in the name of all that's holy can Davin make me tingle through my phone?

As I back out of my driveway, I cast a glance at Davin's house to see if I can spot my entourage of guards. I half-expect to see a black Chevy Tahoe, but there's nothing in sight. Either they are really good at this or someone dropped the ball.

As I turn onto Valley Road, I check my rear-view mirror and see the imposing grill of a black Range Rover. Just past Miller Road, the Range Rover slows down, allowing a silver Audi sedan to pull in behind me. The two men in the Audi are young and attractive—and they sport very dark glasses. Okay, they are really good at this.

I turn into the school parking lot and, glancing back, notice the Audi has stopped and is backing into a parking space on the street. The Range Rover is no longer behind me. It must have turned onto Emory Lane, which runs along the east side of the school. These guys are pros.

Since school is not in session, I park in front of the main door, next to Ella's Jeep. As I scan the row of cars, I glimpse Galen's Camaro, parked at the end. My mood darkens and I slap the steering wheel. I told him about the book sale weeks ago and he offered to help. How could I have forgotten?

I enter the school and make my way toward the library. Maybe Galen being here is for the best. I can't put off the inevitable. He's human, I'm not, and our relationship has to end before things get really, really complicated. I may as well get it over with today.

Taking a deep breath, I open the library door.

"Good morning, sweetie," Ella calls, much too cheerfully. She walks closer and whispers, "So how was dinner?"

"Wonderful," I reply, smiling. "Um, have you seen Galen?"

"Yeah. He's in the back, packing boxes and fighting off Becky Whittaker."

"Becky?"

"Yeah. Apparently she has this thing about hot college guys. Go figure," she says with a giggle. "Do you need to talk to him privately?"

Oh God, I am so dreading this. "Yes."

"Are you going to tell him you don't want to see him anymore?"

"Mm-hmm."

"Are you sure?"

I nod, feeling a little sad.

"Sweetie, what's wrong? Did your date with Davin go okay?"

"It was amazing."

"Then what is it? You look so sad."

"I–I'm not sure." I can't tell Ella everything, and that frustrates me. I can't tell her that being with Galen is simply not possible because he's human.

"Come with me," she says, taking my hand and leading me out of the library. "We need to talk."

"Where are we going?"

"The gym."

The only light in the gym comes from the skylights and the glass doors along the back wall. It feels a little eerie. We sit on the bottom row of the bleachers and Ella turns to face me, straddling the seat. "Ok, tell me what's wrong, sweetie."

"I'm not sure."

"How do you feel about Galen?"

"I like him, Ella. He's a really good guy."

"And Davin?"

"Well, I've only know him a short time, but…" I can't put into words what I feel.

She narrows her eyes and stares. "Spill it, Ari."

"I'm really not sure. He makes me feel so alive. More alive than I've ever felt before. And whenever I'm near him I just want to—"

"Jump on him?"

"Yeah, something like that. It's like animal magnetism. I can't explain it. He makes me want to do things that make me want to blush."

"And the fact that he makes Brad Pitt look like a nerd has nothing to do with it?"

"I guess it doesn't hurt," I say with a smile. "Galen is pretty handsome, too. But he flaunts it. And sometimes I think he's obsessed with me. Davin is different. He's handsome, but he's almost a little defensive about it. It's as if he doesn't want his looks to define him. Do you understand what I mean?"

"Yeah. I do. He doesn't seem to have an arrogant bone in his adorable body."

I laugh. "Leave his adorable body out of this before you make me hyperventilate. I'm pretty sure I would still want him, even if he looked ordinary, *like Brad Pitt.*"

Ella laughs out loud. "It sounds like you're falling for him, sweetie."

"Ya think?"

"Yeah. And does Galen make you feel anything special?"

"Not really. He makes me feel comfortable. But there's no spark. Even when we kiss, it's more peaceful than sensual. Davin makes me feel like…like the Fourth of July."

"Ari, you have a kind heart. I think the problem is that you don't want to hurt Galen. If what you're saying is true, and I have no reason to doubt you, breaking things off with Galen is the kindhearted thing to do. Agreed?"

"Yeah, but it doesn't make it any easier."

Ella looks into my eyes and smiles. "I've heard it's not about finding someone you can live *with*; it's about finding someone you *can't live without*. I have a feeling your 'someone' is Davin. Follow your heart, sweetie."

"You are wise beyond your years," I say, smiling, because she makes me feel so much better.

"Not really. Well, maybe a little. But the fact is, I've never seen you so smitten before. When you talk about Davin, when I even mention his name, you light all up. It's a sight to behold. I'm not saying you should start shopping for a wedding dress, but you have to give this a chance. You have to see where it leads you. Fourth of July kisses are nothing to sneeze at. Ya know?"

"Yeah, I do."

"Good. You should talk to Galen during our lunch break. Okay?"

I nod.

"Okay. Let's go before they call out a search party," Ella says.

The Ladies Club arranged for pizza delivery, which is set up in the main lunch area—a large, open atrium in the middle of the first floor.

"Just one slice, Ari?" Galen asks, as he comes up behind me.

"I'm not very hungry today," I reply, as I watch him pile four slices onto his plate.

"Wanna grab a corner table?" he asks. His deep blue eyes are dancing.

Perfect. "Sure."

The seating area wraps around one side of the lunch counter, creating a relatively private niche. Galen chooses the very last table, sitting down next to me. A glass wall behind us overlooks a nicely-landscaped courtyard. On school days, it's not unusual to see several teachers out there reading, or talking, or perhaps escaping from the chaos of the student lunch room.

"How was the rest of your weekend?" I ask

"Depressing. I missed you," he says with puppy-dog eyes.

He looks vulnerable. Does he sense I am about to drop the hammer on our relationship?

"I'm sorry, Galen."

"Ari, we've known each other for months and..." He pauses, looking a little anxious. "You're the only girl I want to be with."

I don't answer. Instead, I play with my pizza, avoiding eye contact. This is not going to be easy at all. Nope.

He turns his chair to face me. "Ari, please look at me."

I turn my chair, and Galen leans toward me, placing his hands on my knees. "I'd like you to spend spring break with me, in Bermuda. We can drive to DC and catch a flight in the morning."

My brow shoots up and I chuckle. "Bermuda? Seriously?"

"Yes. My family has a villa there. What do you say?"

I'm stunned. What do I say to that? Before I can answer, he pulls me close and kisses me.

"Galen..."

"I can't resist you," he replies, with a cute smile, as he cups my face in his hands. Then he kisses me again.

I know it's wrong. I know I should resist. But I can't. And for some insane and inexplicable reason, I decide to see if Galen can rock me the way Davin does. I throw caution to the wind, and focus on all that's good in Galen. Our kiss is sweet, but there are no fireworks. I pull back, tears welling up in my eyes, and I know. He can never be *the one*. He's a good person, a thoughtful person, but I need to set him free.

"Ari, what's wrong?"

"*This* is wrong," I whisper.

He gently turns my chin so that I have no choice but to look at him. "What?"

"Us," I say. "We're wrong, Galen. I'm so sorry, but we shouldn't be together."

"I love you, Ari, and nothing feels wrong about it."

"What? No. You don't understand. I don't love you the way you want me to."

"But you just kissed me."

"I shouldn't have. It was a goodbye kiss—"

He looks crushed. "Are you saying you don't want to see me anymore?"

I nod. "You're everything most girls could ever hope for. But I'm just not ready to fall in love. I'm so…"

Before I can say more, the door between the lunchroom and the courtyard opens, and two of my Warrior guards walk through, followed by Davin. Did they see us kiss?

"What's going on?" I ask.

He stares at me for a second, then whispers to one of the other Warriors, who promptly grasps Galen's right arm, forcing him to stand. "You will come with us," the Warrior says softly, but sternly. "If you attempt to escape, it will not end well for you."

Galen groans, but does not protest, which I find awfully strange. He simply casts me a sad glance, as he slowly walks away with the two Warriors, leaving me alone with Davin.

I'm dumbstruck. Where are they taking him? And why?

"Davin?"

"Let's walk outside, Ari."

I nod absently and follow him. Davin points to a bench in front of the main entrance and we sit.

My mind races. What just happened? Can an angel arrest a human? For kissing? I'm confused.

"What's going on? Why did you take him away?"

"We need to interrogate him."

"For what?" I ask.

"He is an angel."

"WHAT?" This can't be true.

"You did not know?" There is no emotion in Davin's voice.

"No."

His eyes close for a moment. When he opens them, his gaze is distant. He looks hurt. "Are you in love with him?"

"No. I was in the process of telling him that I don't want to see him anymore when you arrived."

"Do you always end your relationships with a kiss? I think there are better ways," he says with a raised brow.

He saw the kiss. Crap. Crap. Crap. Damn. I'm such an idiot.

"It's not what it seems, Davin."

"I don't want to discuss it now."

"Davin, please. Let me explain."

"Not now."

"Is he evil?"

"He is not Fallen. But there is no record of his existence, which means he is probably bound to Earth."

"What does that mean?"

"It means he was sent from Paradise to live and work on Earth."

"If he's not Fallen, why are you treating him like a prisoner? I don't understand."

"He should not have approached you without permission. We need to discover his motives."

His motives? What could he possibly have wanted? "He never hurt me."

"That's why he's still alive."

A shiver runs down my spine. Am I a target? Will they beat the truth out of Galen? Will he be...

"Will he be tortured?"

"No. We do not torture."

"I'm sorry Davin. I didn't—"

"Not now, Ari."

"Why not?"

"I need to leave. I must be present when Galen is interrogated."

"You're going to Olympus?"

"Yes."

"When will you be back?"

"Tonight."

"Can we talk later?"

"I will come to your house."

"What time?"

"Between eight and nine."

"Okay."

I want to apologize, but I think it'll make things worse, so I bite my tongue.

He grasps my shoulders and turns me to face him. His expression is fierce. His gaze intense. "You need to be extremely cautious. There are three Warriors still here. They will follow you home. Another team will secure your property. Stay home until I get back. I shouldn't leave you..."

"You have your duty. Be careful, Davin," I say, while choking back a sob.

He doesn't respond. He simply turns and jogs across the lawn.

I fight a powerful urge to run after him, to touch him, to tell him my stupid reason for kissing Galen. "It's you I want, Davin," I whisper to myself. "It's you…"

"There you are, sweetie."

"Oh, hi Ella," I say mindlessly.

"Was that Davin I just saw running off?"

I sigh. "Yeah."

She sits beside me on the bench and puts her hand on my shoulder. "Is everything alright? Where's Galen?"

"Um, he went home," I lie.

"Did you tell him you don't want to see him anymore?"

"Yes."

"How did he take it?"

"He looked a little sad. But all things considered, I guess he took it pretty well."

Yeah, he took it really well—considering he was being hauled off to an interrogation by two ferocious-looking Warriors.

"That's good, sweetie. So what was Davin doing here?"

"Well, now that's an interesting little story…"

Ella groans. "You messed up?"

"Oh yeah."

"How bad?"

"Really bad. I was about to tell Galen that it was over between us, when he kissed me."

"Galen kissed you?"

"Mm-hmm."

"And what did you do when he kissed you?"

"I–I sort of kissed him back."

Ella's eyes widen and her eyebrows disappear into her bangs. "Please tell me you didn't do that. Tell me you're joking."

I hide my face in my hands and mumble, "Not joking."

"ARE YOU NUTS?" Ella asks, loud enough to be heard in the next county.

"It gets worse," I say in a very small voice.

She gives me a little hand motion, imploring me to continue.

"Davin walked into the lunchroom."

"He saw the kiss?"

I nod slowly.

"Oh, Ari. What were you thinking, sweetie?"

"I guess you could say it was an experiment."

"Seriously? An Experiment?"

"Yeah. I wanted to see how kissing Galen compared with kissing Davin."

"That wasn't very smart. So Davin is pissed off?"

"I'm not sure. I told him I can explain why I kissed Galen. He's coming over tonight."

"Galen is coming over?" she asks with a little chuckle.

"Don't make fun of me. I need to get out of this. *Davin* is coming over. Do you have any suggestions?"

"Yeah. Tell him the truth. And do not, under any circumstances, get defensive or unreasonable. And make sure you maintain eye contact. It's not like you and Davin are engaged. I have a feeling everything will work out."

"Thanks," I say.

"Yeah, well, just don't do anything dumb."

"I won't. Do you mind covering for me? I really want to go home."

"No problem. Kick back and don't overthink things. Remember, just tell him the truth. Okay?"

"Yeah. I got it. The truth."

"Call me if you need me, sweetie."

"Will do," I say, as we stand.

I give Ella a hug and head toward my car, wishing I could have told her everything. I feel so alone, so vulnerable. What else could possibly go wrong?

The thought makes me shudder.

Chapter 13

I pull into my driveway and glance down the street. The Range Rover parks in front of Davin's. Three guys exit the vehicle and enter the house, their movements graceful and synchronized. My Secret Service detail. My personal Swiss Guard. I roll my eyes.

I pull into the garage, close the overhead door, and shuffle into the quiet house. Mom is working a late shift and won't be home until the morning. I kick off my shoes, grab a water bottle from the fridge, and wobble into the family room, feeling emotionally drained.

Curling up on the sofa, I turn on the TV, which is tuned to *TVLand*—my never-failing secret sleep sauce. The last thing I remember is the theme song from *Bonanza*, and then a distant voice calls my name.

"Ari, are you sleeping?"

Mom?

"Not anymore, Mom," I say, yawning.

"Sorry, sweetheart."

"It's okay. I needed to wake up. What time is it?"

"Five-forty."

"How long have you been home?"

"A couple of hours."

"Why didn't you wake me up earlier?"

"I tried," she says with a chuckle. "I figured you must have been very tired, and I really needed a hot shower."

"Are you going back to the hospital?"

"Yes," she says, sighing softly, as she grabs her purse.

"Nice seeing you," I tease.

"Things will be back to normal next week…" She pauses and smiles at me. "So how was your date?"

I give her a thumbs-up. "We had a good time. A really good time," I reply, returning her smile.

"How was the restaurant?"

"Out of this world."

"Thalia called me last night and told me she offered you a job. That was very nice of her. And it sounds like a terrific opportunity."

"Yes, I'm really excited about it." And a little terrified.

Mom pauses in front of the garage door and turns to face me. "Don't forget to set your alarm. You don't want to be late for your first day of work."

"Don't worry. I'll be on time. Goodnight, Mom. Love you."

"Goodnight, sweetheart. I Love you, too. See you tomorrow," she says, as she walks out into the garage.

Tomorrow. What will tomorrow bring? I am beginning to hate tomorrows. Actually, tonight is looking pretty damn scary.

I step out of the shower, towel off, then stand in front of the mirror, as I wave the blow dryer across my hair. If this is my last chance to be with Davin, I at least want to look good.

I apply some eyeliner and lip-gloss, then go to work on my hair, which looks more like a tangled mass of fur attached to my head. I look at the comb in my hand. I'm wielding it like a weapon.

I comb, brush, and beat my hair into submission. Then I twist it into a sloppy bun, as I study my reflection in the mirror. Not too bad.

I pull on a pair of black jeans and a teal V-neck sweater, slide into black flats, and head downstairs to wait for Davin. It's nearly seven, so I have at least an hour to kill. I fix myself a grilled cheddar sandwich with a side of sweet potato chips.

As I eat, my mind drifts to thoughts of Davin. I've known him for only five days, yet when I'm with him it feels so natural. It's as if we belong together. I can talk to him with a level of candor I've only been able to manage with Ella and my mom. He makes me smile—inside and out.

Considering how we met, I should be afraid of him. Intimidated by him. In awe of him. I should still be angry with him over what he did at the Falls. But I'm not. And it hurts me that I may have hurt him.

What is it that I feel? Am I actually falling for him? When did I let down my guard? When did I let him into my heart? What's happening to me?

I clean up the kitchen and head back toward the family room when the doorbell rings, making me jump. I peer through the peephole. It's Davin. I open the door and he stands there, looking stressed. "Are you alright?" I ask, ushering him inside.

"I'm fine," he replies. He is not smiling. He is not happy.

"Come into the kitchen and I'll get you something to drink."

He nods and follows me.

"Sit down," I say. "What would you like?"

"Water would be fine."

I pour him a tall glass of chilled water and sit down across from him. "How did the interrogation go?" I ask apprehensively.

Davin props his elbows on the table, runs his fingers through his hair, and sighs, deeply.

"That bad?" I ask.

"He was sent to seduce you; to persuade you to fall in love with him."

"Excuse me?"

His eyes meet mine. He looks distant.

"Apparently, there is a small group of Earth-bound angels who believe your existence is based upon a prophecy. By having one of their own bind with you, they hoped to control you, to keep you from the Fallen."

"Prophecy?"

"They believe you are a new kind of angel. The most powerful angel ever born."

I stare, incredulously, unable to speak.

His eyes meet mine and he locks on.

"Ari, I won't let anything bad happen to you."

"Oh geez. Am I in any danger, Davin?"

I look down at my hands, which are visibly trembling. I want to be a human girl again. I never asked for this.

"Don't be frightened." Davin looks concerned.

"I'm terrified." My voice is shaking, uncontrollably.

"Does your mom keep any spirits in the house?"

"Alcohol?"

"Yes."

"Yeah. I think so." I start to stand.

"Please, stay there. I'll get it," Davin says. "Where?"

"The louvered door next to the stove." I point.

Davin enters the pantry and I hear bottles gently clanging. He emerges, holding a pretty pear-shaped bottle containing a dark amber liquid. "Glasses?"

"In the cupboard above the sink."

Davin fetches a glass and sits back down at the table. "Courvoisier," he says, as he fills the glass. "Your mom has very good taste."

I have no idea what he's talking about. But if he needs a drink…

"What is it?"

"Cognac."

"Which is?"

"Distilled wine."

"It smells stronger than wine."

"It is."

Davin pours about an inch of Cognac into a juice glass, then places the glass in my hand. "Drink it slowly. Little sips. It will relax you."

"Are you sure? I'm underage, you know."

"You're an angel; you are not underage," he says.

"Yeah, a new kind of angel…" I pause, shaking my head. "What the hell does that even mean? Does Galen know what it means?"

"He doesn't. They could be wrong. It could be nothing."

"But it could be something," I argue. "Can you really protect me, Davin?"

I take a sip of Cognac. It feels really warm going down and it does relax me, once my throat stops burning.

"I will not allow any harm to come to you."

"You sound so confident."

"I will never fail you," he says with a fierceness in his eyes that is frightening, exhilarating, and kind of sexy—all at the same time. Then he reaches across the table and gently grasps my hands.

His hands are warm, strong, and his touch reassuring.

"Aren't you angry with me?" I ask, a little hesitantly, because I'm afraid he is.

"Why would I be angry with you?"

"Because you saw me kiss him."

"We've known each other less than a week, I can hardly claim you as my own."

"Don't you want to know why I kissed him?"

"I'm not sure. But you're going to tell me anyway. Aren't you?"

"Yes." I grab the edge of the table and squeeze, trying to compose myself. "My relationship with Galen was not exclusive—at least from my perspective. He was fun to be with, but I didn't love him. He was more of a friend than a…"

"Lover?"

"Yes. But he tried to be more. He tried really hard. But I'm not easily manipulated. And I'm still…" I pause, clearing my throat, because it suddenly feels really dry. "I'm still waiting for the right man."

"Did he ever try to force himself on you?"

"No. Never."

"So, why did you kiss him if you were breaking up with him?"

"He initiated the kiss. It kind of surprised me, actually. But then I wanted to see if he could make me feel the way you make me feel." I end in a whisper, as I try to keep my composure.

"I'm not sure I understand."

"Things are moving too fast. Sometimes I think I'm losing touch with the girl I used to be. It's scary, Davin."

"You have evolved, Ari. You are no longer a girl. You're an angel."

"Is this what it's supposed to be like? Did you evolve, too?"

"It's been so long, the memories are so distant, but I do remember one thing."

"What's that?"

"It kind of sneaks up on you. I remember my childhood, and you will always remember yours. You are not losing anything. But you are gaining much."

"It sure feels like I'm losing a whole lot."

"Did you kiss him because you thought he could help you hold on to your humanity?"

"In a way. I kind of hoped that he could make me feel the same way I felt when I kissed you. And that it would make me feel human. It was stupid, immature, and I wish I could take it back."

Davin shakes his head slowly, then smiles.

I smile back. "You're really not angry. Are you?" I ask.

"No."

"Did I hurt you?"

"No."

"I don't believe you. You may not be angry, but I know I hurt you."

"Ari…"

"Come with me." I take him by the hand and pull him into the family room.

"Sit," I say, pointing to the sofa.

He settles into the cushions, and I sit next to him, turning sideways to face him. "I'm fully evolved. Right?" I ask.

"From an emotional and cognitive perspective, you are. Your training will serve to awaken your physical capabilities."

"So my sense of perception is pretty strong?"

"Very strong."

"Then I'm fairly certain that when you walked into the lunchroom, and saw us kissing, you were hurt…"

"Ari…"

"Please let me finish," I say. "I would never intentionally hurt you, Davin. The look on your face has been haunting me all day."

"Ari, it's…"

"Hush," I say, as I pull him to me urgently. "I should have known."

"What should you have known?"

"That you are the only man I want to kiss."

"Ari…"

My lips find his and it's the Fourth of July again. Every kiss I've ever had before is immediately forgotten. Gone. Never even happened.

I don't end the kiss. I want it to last forever. Davin is the strong one. He gently separates our lips and then rests his forehead against mine.

"Thank you for putting up with me. I'm usually not so difficult."

"Your life has been turned upside down. Things will improve."

I let out a long sigh. "I suppose. So, we still have a lot to talk about."

"We do," he says, as he loosens his grip on me.

I turn so I'm facing him and clear my throat.

"Will they try again? Will Galen's friends send more suitors to court me?"

"It's unlikely. Since we were able to intercept Galen with relative ease, they will probably not be inclined to have more of their group captured, especially since we now know who they are."

"Are other angels frightened of Warriors?"

"Yes."

"How many types of angels are there?" I ask.

"There are four Orders. Stratóri are the most common. They are the eyes and ears of Paradise. Many are bound to Earth. The Zon belonged to this Order before they fell."

"Do Stratóri battle the Zon on Earth?"

"Sometimes. But their primary function is gathering intelligence. Their most powerful ability is persuasion. If a human inadvertently sees

128

something he should not see, Stratóri are called in, and the human is persuaded that what he witnessed was perfectly normal."

"Are there Stratóri on Olympus?"

"Not since the Zon rebellion. There is really no need for them since mortal Olympians are aware that angels exist. Most angels on Olympus belong to the Warrior Order."

"So what kind of angel is Galen?"

"He is Stratóri."

"Um, did he use persuasion on me?"

"Yes. But he said it was unsuccessful. He was very surprised you were able to resist."

"Son of a…"

My opinion of Galen takes a serious nosedive. I am seething. The strange feelings. I thought I was confused. But I wasn't. I was fighting his influence.

"Ari, angels are immune to the charms of Stratóri. What surprised him was that you were able to resist without the benefit of training. That fact alone has him convinced that the prophecy is real."

"I just can't believe he tried to do that. That's like slipping something into a girl's drink. I feel violated. And if I ever see him again, I'm going to kick his butt."

Davin smiles.

"What?" I ask.

"You have a Warrior's disposition."

"After what he did, I have every right to be angry."

"Let's just be thankful you were able to resist."

"Don't you understand?"

"Understand what?"

"All the time I was with him, I thought I was confused about my feelings. But I wasn't confused at all. I was resisting his efforts to persuade me! Ooh, I need to slap him, Davin. Will you take me to him?"

"That would not be a good idea. You could kill him, and then once you calmed down you would be distraught."

He's probably right.

"Is he a prisoner?"

"It's more like he's in protective custody."

"Will he ever be free again?"

"Eventually. This is for his own good, Ari. It would not be safe for him to return to Earth."

"Do you think he's held anything back from you?"

"No. Thalia is very thorough."

"Thorough is good. But Galen can be pretty slick, if you know what I mean." I recall some of his more creative seduction attempts. He was persistent.

"Don't worry, Ari. Nothing bad is going to happen. We will simply not allow it."

"I guess I'm going to have to trust you."

"You're family now. We protect our own."

"Oh, so I'm in the angel Mafia now?"

"Just keep your sense of humor and leave your safety in my hands."

I have to smile. He is so chivalrous. "I'll do that. So, what is the Second Order of angels?"

"They are called Apestáli, which means *messenger*. They serve as communication links between Paradise and the mortal worlds."

"Do they have a special ability?"

"They are very diplomatic...and extremely fast."

"In case someone tries to kill the messenger?" I ask with a smirk.

"Good one," he says with a grin.

"Do Warriors have any special abilities?"

"Our primary job is to hunt and destroy the Fallen. We are the apex predators of the angel community. The best fighters. We serve as a balancing force, keeping other angels in line. We are…"

"Badass?" I ask with a quirk of my brow.

"Something like that."

A thought suddenly occurs to me. "I believe you said that the Zon did not take Damas and his Warriors seriously. Can angels not sense another angel's rank or status?"

"Good question," Davin says. "The Zon surely knew what Damas was. There is no doubt. We can indeed sense other angels. But the Zon were confident that their superior numbers would provide a tactical advantage. You also must consider the era. Olympian technology was fairly primitive. There were no videos and precious few images. It's hard to discern the truth from what has become legend."

"Ah, I see. Then it's kind of like looking at human history prior to the advent of motion pictures and sound recording. There are a lot of assumptions. We can see photographs of Abraham Lincoln, for instance, but we cannot hear his voice. We cannot analyze his emotions. He is more legend than real."

"Exactly," he says, smiling with what looks like pride.

I smile back, proud of myself for impressing him.

"So, Warriors are the Third Order?" I ask.

"Yes."

"What is the Fourth Order called?"

"Serafeím. They are like princes and princesses, and they act the part," he says derisively.

"You mean they can be divas?" I ask.

"Yes. They can be quite arrogant and pompous. They are the politicians and the patricians of Paradise."

"And you don't like them very much?"

"There are Serafeím on Olympus. But because they are bound to Olympus, they are more…"

"Down-to-earth?" I suggest.

"Yes," Davin says with an eye roll, which makes me smile.

"You're getting really good at that."

"At what?"

"Rolling your eyes."

"Thank you. I have an excellent teacher."

I roll my eyes.

"Do the Serafeím have special abilities?"

"They are strong, like Warriors, but they lack our ferocity and fearlessness. They do not like getting their hands dirty. A small number of the most powerful Serafeím possess the ability to fly."

I gasp. "They have wings?"

"No, they use the Essence."

"Whoa. Jet Essence, huh?"

"In a manner of speaking."

"What about Sages? Are they an *Order*?"

"Sages are either Warriors or Serafeím. But they possess more specialized cognitive abilities that make them ideal administrators, teachers, scientists, counselors, and artists."

"Ah, the celestial cognoscenti?"

"Something like that," Davin says. "And there is one more group of angels. They are too few in number to be called an Order, but they are significant because of what they can do."

"And what can they do?"

"They are the ones who altered the paths of evolution on Olympus and Earth. They are called Prostáti. They are able to alter DNA through touch."

"Do they have other jobs?"

"Yes. They are highly skilled guardians, and are sometimes assigned to protect important humans, such as politicians and scientists, from the Fallen. Prostáti are able to fly. They can also bend light to make themselves virtually invisible. And they are nearly indestructible."

"Wow. Are there any Prostáti on Olympus?"

"No. They reside in Paradise and only visit the mortal worlds when they are assigned a mission."

"How many Prostáti are there?"

"Legend has it that there are twenty-four."

"How many angels are there in total?"

"There are many more angels in Paradise than are bound to the mortal worlds. I am not sure of the exact number."

"What do they do in Paradise?"

"Many things, but mostly they manage the afterlives of mortals."

"There are mortals in Paradise?"

"Yes."

"There is really an afterlife?"

"Of course."

"So every mortal who has ever lived and died now exists in Paradise?"

"Not all make it to Paradise, I'm afraid."

"So there is a hell, too?"

"Think in terms of a planetary system that exists in another dimension. The system includes many worlds, which together comprise what we call Paradise and Acheron."

"Acheron is hell?"

"Yes."

"So how many mortals exist between Paradise and Acheron?"

"I'm not sure of the exact number, but it is surely in the billions."

I blow out a long breath. "This is a lot of information to process."

"You don't need to do it in one sitting. Your training will be thorough, and Thalia is an excellent teacher."

"What about God? Have you, um, met him?"

"We've never been formally introduced. And what makes you think God is a 'he'?"

"Good point," I say. "A truly nurturing deity may well be a woman. So what about angels who've been to Paradise? Have your parents met God?"

"They do not speak of Paradise."

"Have you never asked them questions?"

"I have. But after several hundred years of not getting answers, I gave up. Those who have been to Paradise are simply not permitted to discuss it."

I smile. "What happens in Paradise stays in Paradise, eh?"

"Something like that," he replies.

I sigh and lean back, resting my head on the back of the sofa. "I think I have a headache, Davin."

"Then put it right here," he says, patting his shoulder.

"Are you coming on to me, Warrior?"

"No. I'm in a comforting mood."

"Sure," I say, as I lay my head on his shoulder. "Aren't you afraid you're going to get distracted?"

"We are surrounded by my best Warriors. You are perfectly safe."

"And that makes you comfortable?"

"Yes."

"I'd like you to stay with me tonight, Davin."

"I can't do that, Ari."

"Can't or won't?"

He sighs. "You've endured much these past several days. You need rest and I'm not sure…"

"My mom is working all night and I'm afraid to be alone in the house. You make me feel safe. Please?"

"Alright," he says, looking a little uncomfortable.

"Thank you, Davin."

"I need to contact my team leader and advise him that I'll be spending the night. I may never hear the end of this," he mutters.

"You mean they'll think we're…"

"They could."

"Davin, do you have a reputation as a player?" I ask with a playful gasp.

"Absolutely not," he says indignantly.

I toss my head back and laugh. "I'm sorry I've put you in such an awkward situation," I say, as he gets up and walks into the kitchen. "Where are you going?"

"I am going to make a call and I would like a little privacy."

Davin is so cute when he gets embarrassed. I try really hard to keep from laughing again, with little success.

"Why don't you go to your house? You can talk to your team and change into running pants, or something more comfortable than jeans."

He ponders my suggestion and nods. "I'll be back in about thirty minutes. I'm not entirely comfortable with this, but if you'll feel safer…"

I give his hand a quick squeeze. "I will. Thank you, Davin."

He gives me a shy smile and walks outside. I lock the door behind him and head upstairs to change.

"Did they understand?" I ask, when Davin returns.

"More or less."

"Hmm. I'll have to straighten them out tomorrow."

He shakes his head and sighs, and I smile, because it occurs to me that angels can sometimes be quite *human.*

I lead him into the family room and we sit on the sofa.

"Will you be involved in my training?" I ask.

"Yes. Thalia and I will be with you every step of the way."

"Davin?"

"Yes?"

"Do angels have souls?"

He looks at me as if I've grown a second head. "Of course. Yes. Why do you ask?"

I feel a little embarrassed. "Well, I've read a few books about angels…"

"Novels?"

"Yes," I answer, feeling a bit sheepish.

"We are not mythical creatures. We eat, we drink, we sleep, we love, and we have souls," he says with a warm smile.

"I'm glad we have souls. Mostly because that means we can have soul mates."

"I agree. But it's also good to have a soul because it means that a part of us will always be able to find its way home."

"That's so sweet. So profound. Sometimes you truly amaze me, Davin."

"Touché," he says, with a big grin.

There is a good chance that what I feel for Davin is due to stress and anxiety. Only time will tell, and I have to give it time. I have to know. I have to give us a chance. I pull an Afghan over us and lean my head on his shoulder. Gosh, he feels so good.

"Davin?"

"Yes?"

"Are you sure I won't forget what it's like to feel human."

"You won't. You were born and raised on Earth. You will never lose that part of yourself."

"Do you really remember what it was like to grow up on Olympus?"

"I do. It's part of me. I remember playing with my friends. I remember school. I remember sitting on my mother's knee. It won't go away, Ari. It is part of what defines us."

"Thank you."

"Everything will work out," he says, as he wraps me in a protective embrace.

"Davin?"

"Hmm?"

"You really weren't hurt? Not even a little?"

"Did you want me to be hurt?"

"No. But if you…"

"Ari?"

"Yes, Davin?"

"If I kiss you, will you stop asking me if I was hurt?"

"I'll try, but I think it could take more than one kiss."

"You think?"

"I do. I really do."

"Ari?"

"Yes, Davin?"

"Shh," he says, as his lips find mine.

I know I hurt him, but it's over, and we're back on good terms. And right now, that'll have to be good enough.

The sound of my phone's alarm gradually enters my consciousness and I begin to awaken. A warm breeze whispers across my cheek and I open my eyes. Davin's face is inches away. He looks so sweet. I can't resist stroking his cheek with my finger.

"Davin?"

His eyes open slowly and his lips curve into an adorable smile. "Good morning."

"Good morning," I say, returning his smile. "Did you sleep well?"

"Yes, your sofa is surprisingly comfortable. And did you sleep well?"

"Like a baby. I'm glad you stayed."

He just stares at me and smiles.

"What?"

"I'm glad I stayed, too," he says, which makes me smile.

I nod. "Thanks, Davin…for answering my silly questions last night."

"There was nothing silly about your questions, and I would love to spend the rest of the day answering many more, but we do need to start your training…and I need to clean up. Will you be alright while I'm gone?"

"Yeah. I need to get ready, too," I say. "Oh, what should I wear?"

"Dress casually. You will be issued appropriate clothing at the training center."

"Okay. I'll make us a quick breakfast. Hurry back."

"You might spoil me."

"Never," I tease, as I kiss his cheek.

Davin and I devour a six-egg omelet, several slices of toast, a half-pound of bacon, and a quart of orange juice. "I seem to have acquired your appetite. Do angels eat every meal as if it was their last?" I ask.

"We expend considerably more energy than mortals. We require more fuel."

"Are there any chubby angels?"

"I've never seen one," he says.

"Good," I reply, as I make a grab for the last two bacon slices.

"Hey, I wanted one of those," he says as he grabs one of the slices off my plate."

"Bacon thief. I'll let you slide, but don't ever try that with chocolate."

"I am not that stupid."

I feel so totally at ease with him. I can let my guard down and just be myself, which is something I've never been able to do with a guy before. "Good," I say, with a big grin. "I'd hate to have to kick your butt."

"Okay, killer. Duly noted."

Before I can respond, my mind drifts to a question I wanted to ask him last night. Somehow, I'd gotten off on a tangent and forgot. Until now. "Did you ever meet Moses, or Abraham, or Mohammed, or…Jesus?"

Davin stares at me for a moment. "How did we go from chubby angels and food fights, to religion?"

"Um, I meant to ask you last night."

"No, I never met those men. And, to answer your next question…" He pauses and gives me a crooked grin. "I do believe they existed."

"So, they weren't Olympian?"

"No. It is possible that the answers you seek are known to Paradise, but…"

"No one who's been to Paradise can speak of them."

"Correct."

I sigh. "I guess, in a way, that's good."

"Why is that?"

"Well, it preserves the mystery-aspect of faith."

"Excellent point. Perhaps it was meant to be. Perhaps someday we will reveal ourselves to humans and…"

"And we won't destroy the foundations of all that they believe in."

Davin smiles and places a hand over mine. "You have a beautiful mind."

But what about the mythological gods of Greece. If the Warriors spent so much time in ancient Greece, maybe…

"Do you know how the gods of Olympus came to be *invented?*"

"As a matter of fact, I have intimate knowledge of that."

"Wanna share?"

"Some Warriors and Serafeím have the ability to project energy, as a weapon—"

"And you have this ability?"

He nods. "I was assigned to a colony on the island of Crete. One night, I was standing on the beach…practicing. The ability was still relatively new to me and I was determined to master it. It was very late, and there was a full moon. I raised my arm and projected a magnificent blue beam that arced across the sky. Just before the beam left my fingers, I'd noticed two shapes approaching me from the west. One was my friend, Tal. The other was a Kritikí—a native. Tal knew what I was about to do and shouted for me to stop. He had warned me, on numerous occasions, that I should not be doing this on Earth, that a human might see me. So, in his anger and frustration, he shouted the most vile of Olympian obscenities— equivalent to the f-bomb. But I couldn't stop. As my beam lit the sky, the word echoed across the beach, and a connection between the word and my beam was formed in the native's mind…"

"And this vile word was?"

"Zeus."

I sit there, staring and pondering, wanting to laugh, but somehow holding it in.

"And the rest," he continues, "is…mythology."

The damn bursts and my laughter comes out in a roar that begins with a very unladylike snort. And I can't stop.

"Having fun?"

"Y-yes," I sputter.

"Ari…"

"Sorry," I say, as I slowly regain my composure. "That's the funniest story I've ever heard. And I did learn something."

Davin gives me a look that has 'this ought to be good' written all over it. "And what did you learn?"

"Oh, well…that I should never utter the word 'Zeus' in mixed company?"

Davin just shakes his head and smiles.

"Got any more funny stories?"

"Not today. I would hate to see you hurt yourself laughing."

I figure I should stop while I'm ahead, so I change the subject. "Well, you did put me in a very good mood and I'm ready to start training. Shall we go?"

"I am ready, but perhaps you should fix your face. Your makeup has…well, you look like a raccoon." His lips curl into an adorable smile, and he adds, "A very cute one."

Chapter 14

"Good morning, Sania," I say to Thalia's personal assistant.

"Good morning, Ariel," she replies, in perfect English. "It is good to see you. I hear your training has gone very well."

"Thank you. It's been an interesting eight weeks," I say with a smile. "Is she ready for me?"

"Yes…"

The door slides open, with a hiss, and Thalia stands there, beaming. "Ari, come in, please." She motions for me to enter her office.

I walk inside and wait for her. The door closes and I turn. She is smiling. She looks happy.

"Sit, please," she says, motioning to the small conference table in the corner of her office.

She sits across from me and points to a tray. "There is fresh coffee."

I pour myself a cup. Thalia's office is comfortable, but unpretentious. The walls are covered with colorful abstract prints, and the virtual window makes me feel as if we're at the seashore. It's serene and peaceful. Like Thalia.

"You've made extraordinary strides, Ari. I am very proud of you."

"Thanks. I've had extraordinary teachers."

"Considering the circumstances, it is quite remarkable. It's been nearly one million years since an angel has been trained. None of us has ever done this before."

"There's no manual, is there?"

She laughs. "No, I'm afraid not."

"So, is this my official debriefing?"

"In a sense. But it's also a meeting between friends."

"I'm glad we're friends. It's made everything a lot easier to bear."

She smiles. "Tal and Seto tell me that you are faster than any Warrior they know. And Davin tells me you are nearly as strong as he is."

"So, I'm a freak, huh?"

"Hardly. I've awarded you official status."

"You mean I'm a Warrior? Officially?"

"No. Your genetic makeup is hard to define. I've classified you as Serafeím."

"Are you still analyzing my DNA?"

"I have an entire team devoted to it."

"Have they discovered anything? Anything at all?"

"Based on your DNA, you are more than Warrior, more than Serafeím. Much more."

I wrinkle my brow. "How much more?"

"The word that comes to mind is *godlike*."

I take in a deep breath and hold it for a beat. "Excuse me?"

"Your ability to generate a defensive shield is off the charts. My best engineers have done some advanced modeling. It seems that you are virtually indestructible, and I do not think this is a genetic anomaly. I believe your existence has a deeper meaning."

Existentially Ari. That's me. Maybe I need a team of philosophers to work alongside Thalia's engineers.

"Can your models be wrong?"

"That would be highly unlikely. Your body contains many times the number of amplification clusters found in a typical Warrior or Serafeím. The strength of your shield would be nearly impossible to penetrate."

"Am I more powerful than the Prostáti?"

"We do not have a profile on record. They are rather hard to pin down," she says with a wry smile.

"You're scaring me, Thalia. What does this mean?"

"It could mean that the prophecy Galen mentioned is right. At least partially."

"I could be the most powerful angel ever born?"

"Yes."

"And you have no idea why?"

"I can only speculate."

"Then go ahead, Thalia. Speculate…"

She smiles, and I have a feeling that I'm about to hear something truly bizarre.

"You are neither a freak nor an accident. You are purposefully designed—the most perfect being I have ever encountered. But what purpose can you possibly have? Why do you exist?"

"Well, I've been trying to figure that out since I discovered I'm an angel."

"When Olympus faced its darkest hour, Paradise sent the Warriors…"

"So you think something is going to happen, and I'm the solution?"

"I do."

"You think Earth is in danger. Don't you?"

She nods. "The Zon have been getting rather bold. I think a crisis is imminent. And I think you are destined to play a major role in stopping them. Paradise has erred. Humans should never have been left to fend for themselves."

"You think I'm supposed to save mankind?"

"I think it's quite possible you are."

"Geez. Like I needed more pressure?"

"You asked me to speculate."

"Yeah. I did."

"And you shouldn't worry. If Paradise sent you, then you will be capable of handling the situation." She pauses and smiles. "You don't understand how truly powerful you are. But you will."

"I've heard that before." I shake my head and sigh. "More training?"

"There is little left that we can teach you beyond offensive energy projection."

"I'm not familiar with the term, but it sounds a little frightening."

"A few angels have the ability to direct a concentrated beam of energy along a controlled path. As a weapon."

"Oh, right. Davin mentioned something about that to me before I started training."

"Ah, so you know that he is truly a Greek god?" she asks with a wide grin.

"Yes," I say with an involuntary giggle.

"He is extremely skilled in that area. He will be teaching you."

I smile. Of course. "I guess I should have known."

Thalia smiles back. "How are you and he getting along?"

"Um, very well. We are…"

"A couple?"

A choking sound escapes my throat.

"It's pretty obvious, Ari."

I'm suddenly worried. "Are we breaking any rules?"

"Heavens, no. In fact, I have not seen Davin so happy in…eons."

"You don't think I'm too young for him?"

"Of course not. Once an angel awakens, age is irrelevant. For all intents and purposes, we are all the same age."

I let out a sigh of relief.

"Ari, you are the best thing to ever happen to him."

"You really think so?"

"I've known him for a few years." She gives me a wink. "May I ask you a personal question?"

"You want to know how I feel about him. Don't you?"

"If you are willing to confide in me. Yes, I would like to know."

"We've become good friends. I care about him. A lot."

"Are you in love with him?"

Oh, man. She's as bad as Ella.

"I'm not going to think about it until my life settles down. There's too much going on right now."

"I understand," she says.

She tries to suppress a smile, but fails miserably. She thinks I love him. Do I?

"Have you discussed this with Davin?"

"No."

"But you know how he feels about *me*?"

"I have my suspicions."

"Would you care to share them with me?"

"He cares deeply for you, Ari. He is like my brother. I know him so well…"

She seems worried. Is she concerned I might hurt him?

"You think he loves me?"

"I cannot answer for him."

"No, you can't. It was unfair of me to ask."

"Telling, perhaps. But not unfair," she says with a little smile. She looks bemused.

I smile back. We played each other perfectly. And we both know it. Davin and I love each other. But are we *in love* with each other? Am I ready to be in love? Life just keeps getting more and more interesting.

"Oh, before I forget…we've scheduled a mock battle for Monday."

"Who with?" I ask.

"Three Warriors. We want to see how you do against multiple opponents."

Great.

"How do *you* think I'll do?"

"I don't think you'll break a sweat."

"Against three Warriors? Did you tell them to go easy on me?"

"Of course not," she says with a grin. "Their orders are to hold nothing back."

Great. I wonder how long it would take to heal from a broken neck.

Thank heaven for free medical care.

The practice arena is the size of a football field. A domed ceiling looms a hundred feet overhead. It's an antiseptic version of the Pantheon.

We wear body armor and head gear, which is connected to a computer network. The system is programmed to determine the lethality of each strike. Thalia, ever the impish rogue, has synchronized the computer to a *Pac-Man* soundtrack. When a killing blow is struck, the *Pac-Man dies* sound effect plays. It's really cute.

I face off against three imposing Warriors. One of them is no taller than me—but he's nearly as wide as he is tall. The second one is built like Davin—a little over six feet tall and very muscular. The third one makes my breath catch. He's at least six and a half feet tall and seriously ripped. Thalia

148

calls them Shrek, Thor, and the Ripper. I know she's kidding, but it doesn't matter. They look seriously dangerous.

I know from my lessons with Davin that real combat, against multiple opponents, bears little resemblance to staged movie fights. Your opponents don't wait in line. If you're outnumbered, you have to carefully calculate each offensive move to ensure that a strike against one will not leave you vulnerable to another. Superhuman speed helps a lot.

The *Pac-Man* theme begins and I know we are ready to rumble. Davin, Thalia, and Tal stand off to the side—each looking a bit apprehensive. Davin's deep voice booms over the music, "Ready, positions, fight!"

Shrek and Thor run off in opposite directions—Shrek to my left and Thor to my right. They are setting up a flanking maneuver. The Ripper charges me head on—snarling, huffing, and moving like a wild animal. The Essence surges inside me. My movements are automatic and lightning-quick. Just before the Ripper reaches me, I somersault over him. As he turns to face me, I land a wicked roundhouse kick to the side of his neck. My foot meets no resistance. It's as if his energy shield is made of paper. He grunts and stumbles backwards, landing on his butt. Out of the game. *Pac-Man* dead.

I turn my attention to Thor and Shrek, who are closing in from either side—planning to pancake me. I wait until the last second—until it's too late for them to change direction or stop—then dart toward the far wall. When they reach the spot where they expect me to be, they collide like rutting bucks, and the force of their collision sends them sprawling.

I hit the wall at full speed, race thirty feet up, kick off hard, and launch myself up and out. Landing twenty feet in front of Thor, I charge straight at him—letting Shrek, who is moving in from my right, believe that I don't notice him. As Thor prepares to engage me, I spin quickly to the right—just as Shrek arrives. He curses and tries to stop, but it's too late. I find his throat with a vicious straight left hand. He's history. *Pac-Man* dead.

I continue my spin toward Thor. As I punch, he jumps, but he's too late. He should have kept his feet on the ground because, instead of getting hit in the face, he takes my best shot, south of the border.

"Sorry," I say, remorsefully. He tries to answer, but whatever he says is unintelligible.

"Game over," Davin calls out, invoking the Warrior version of the mercy rule.

Everyone is shouting and clapping, as if the home team has won the Super Bowl. Shrek and the Ripper pull off their head coverings and pat me on the back. The Ripper is actually kind of cute, on a gigantic scale. Shrek looks like a teddy bear. I avert my eyes from Thor, feeling embarrassed about where I hit him. I guess he's gotten his wind back because he grins and says, "Well done." I smile and give him a little wave.

I turn toward Davin. "So how'd I do, boss?"

"You are the sexiest killer I've ever seen," he says, as he grasps my waist and lifts me off the ground.

Before he can put me down, I wrap my legs around his waist and my arms around his neck. "I'm a killa kisser, too," I say, as I playfully nibble on his bottom lip.

"Get a room!" Tal says.

Like Davin, Tal is a Warrior Master. His Norse features are dominated by longish blonde hair and startling blue eyes. He's a little taller than Davin, but less muscular. He's the greyhound of our little circle.

"Ya wanna?" I ask Davin, as I shoot him a devilish grin. I imagine what it would be like to share a room with him, and my cheeks get really hot.

"And what would you do if I said yes?" His eyes are shimmering and I'm ready to melt.

"Um, I guess I'd make you marry me first," I say, trying to sound nonchalant.

"I should have seen that coming," he says with an exaggerated pout.

"Alright, children, you can go and get cleaned up now. It's beginning to smell a bit musty in here," Thalia says.

I unlatch myself from Davin, and we walk toward the Warrior lounge. "How do you think I'd do in a fight with a Zon?"

"Physically, no Zon would stand a chance against you. But until you've had a real fight, it's hard to say how you would react emotionally."

"Care to elaborate?"

"You're very lethal, Ari." He stops and turns to face me before continuing. "Training is not the same as a real battle—a battle to the death. Are you ready to kill for real? Could you look a snarling Zon in the eye and destroy him without hesitation?"

When he puts it that way, I don't know. Why does my life have to be so damn complicated? Can I really kill someone?

"I don't know, Davin. I really don't know. Ya gonna kick me off the team?" I give him a half-hearted smile.

"You have a lifetime membership." He squeezes my arm gently as we enter the lounge area.

The training center doesn't have locker rooms or communal showers. Instead, there is a large anteroom with a refreshment area, a lounge, sitting areas, and individual changing rooms equipped with high-tech showers.

I take a quick shower, change into jeans and a tee, and walk out to the lounge. Davin is standing in the corner, smiling at me. "Hey, you look refreshed," I say.

"I like those jeans."

"Thank you, Davin."

He motions to a sofa. "Come and sit with me."

I sit next to him and place my head on his shoulder. "I'm not feeling all that great right now, Davin." The past two months have been a whirlwind, and I don't know where the winds will carry me next. "I really like happy endings. Is there one in the cards for me?" My voice catches, and I feel a tear trickle down my cheek.

He gently takes my face in his hands, and whispers in my ear. "The happiest endings are *never-endings*."

Does he mean us? Does he want us to be never-ending? I want to tell him that I'm his. That I'll be his forever. I open my mouth, but I can't say it. I want to slap myself, but then I'll look as foolish as I feel.

"Ari, are you alright?"

"I'm better," I say.

"Are you sure?"

No. I am not sure at all. "There's a lot going on in my life in case you hadn't noticed. I'll be fine. I just get a little overwhelmed sometimes."

"Given the events of the past two months, I think you are more than entitled to feel a little overwhelmed. And I know for a fact that you have earned the highest respect of every Warrior who's met you. I don't think you know how extraordinary you are, Ari."

As a human girl, I *am* kind of extraordinary. As an angel, I'm just a baby—and I'm craving respect. Desperately. "Have I earned your respect, Davin?"

"You earned my respect the first day I met you."

"That really means a lot to me. Being a part of your team means a lot to me, too."

"I know it does. How about a latte before I take you home?"

"That sounds delicious."

We walk over to the café and place our orders. I smile as I remember the first cup of coffee I ever had. It was just three years ago. Mom had taken me with her to a medical conference in California. It was the farthest from home I'd ever been.

Now look how far I've come.

Chapter 15

Fridays are usually pretty sedate, but Davin talks me into a quick sparring session. He thinks I'm holding back, that I can generate significantly more hand speed. So he gets on my case, like a drill sergeant. It's totally out of character for him, and it throws me completely off-guard.

"Come on, Serafeím, you can do better than that!"

I'm afraid of hurting him, so I'm holding back.

I jab at his facemask, adding a little more speed.

"That was really pathetic. This session does not end until I see real speed."

Okay, he asked for it. It's not like I'll kill him. If I hurt him, he'll heal in a few minutes.

I focus on Davin, circling him slowly. His instincts might be better, but I'm faster. I imagine he is a Zon. I'm suddenly filled with a concentration of energy I've never felt before. It's as if a balloon is being inflated—inside my chest. It feels dangerous. I see an opening, and as I prepare to strike, a bolt of energy surges down my arm. I divert the angle of my strike away from Davin's head at the last possible second and scream as energy explodes from my fingertips. Holy crap!

There's a smoking hole in the wall behind Davin. Tal is standing nearby, wide-eyed. He stares first at the hole, then at me, and then back to the hole. He doesn't say a word.

Davin gathers himself quickly. "Ari, that was incredible."

"Incredible? I could have killed you, Davin." I'm shaking like a leaf. "That's it!" I scream. "You're fired! I'm not doing this with you anymore." I end in a whisper, as tears flow down my cheeks.

"I'm sorry, Ari." He moves closer and reaches out to take me in his arms.

"Stay back," I warn. "What the hell did I just do?"

"You projected energy."

"I didn't try to. It just happened. How…?"

I feel like a loose cannon. Literally.

"Thalia was right. She had a feeling you could," Davin says.

He actually looks proud of me.

Tal jogs over, followed by Thalia and Seto—my agility trainer. Concern is etched on their faces.

"Are you alright, dear?" Thalia asks, as she wraps me in a protective hug.

"I feel drained," I say weakly.

"What you just did was remarkable, Ari," Thalia says, rubbing my back.

"The problem is I have no idea how I did it."

"If you did it once, you can do it again. You just need practice. Davin will work with you."

She looks excited, but I'm not sure I can handle any more surprises.

"Okay," I reply, as I begin to feel my composure returning.

I look at Davin with remorse in my eyes. "Come here, Warrior," I say with outstretched arms. I hug him close and whisper, "I'm sorry."

"I'm sorry, too," he says.

"I just need to stay calm until I can figure out how to control this new *feature* of mine. I would hate to sneeze and take out half the mall. You know?"

I wish the new me came with an operating manual.

"We'll work on this next week, dear. Go clean up and relax," Thalia says, smiling warmly.

Davin and I walk toward the lounge area. Thalia is the most powerful Sage on Olympus. She and I have become good friends. "She's special."

"Thalia?"

I nod.

"You have no idea." He sighs. "Thalia is to Olympians what an amalgamation of Einstein, Gandhi, and Mother Teresa would be to humans."

"She's a peaceful brainiac-altruist, huh?" It's reassuring to me that the woman I'm becoming so reliant on—and attached to—is important to Davin, too.

"Those are excellent analogies."

"How come she looks older than you?"

"She dresses older," he says with a smile. "She can look quite young when she wants to."

"How come she's not bound?"

"She *was* bound once," he says.

"What happened?"

"Her Promise is Fallen."

"Is he alive?"

"Yes. He is on Earth."

"That's horrible. I feel so sorry for her."

"It's been a very long time. But yes, it is very sad. When bad things happen to good people, it…" He pauses and takes a deep breath. "She is like a sister. I love her very much."

"That's sweet, Davin."

"I'm known for my sweetness, Love." He shoots me a little grin. An adorable, dimply little grin.

I crinkle my nose. "Better take a shower then, Darling. You don't smell all that sweet right now."

"I am deeply offended. I am crushed. I am…"

"Going to take a shower?"

"Yes."

The shower feels wonderful. I towel off quickly and say a quick thank-you prayer for Olympian hair dryers. My thick black mane goes from wet to dry in under five seconds. A little eyeliner and lip gloss, and my face is presentable again.

I throw on a little white dress, and can't help smiling. Davin bought it for me, last week, during an afternoon shopping excursion. He's so sweet. And his fashion sense is impeccable.

When I emerge from my changing room, Davin is sitting in the lounge, sipping a drink and looking gorgeous in black dress slacks and a green V-neck pullover that matches his eyes. He stands and smiles when he sees me. "You look lovely, Ari."

"I am so sorry I snapped at you earlier. Forgive me?"

"There is nothing to forgive."

I wrap my arms around his waist, pulling him close as I whisper, "No matter what happens, Davin, you are my Warrior. My angel."

His lips brush against mine, making me burn with desire. "I'm happy that you feel that way," he whispers back.

"Really?" I feel lightheaded.

"Really." His lips explore my neck, lighting little fires inside me. "You are my strength and my weakness," he says softly, as his lips dance across the sensitive skin behind my ear.

He lifts his head, and as his lips seek mine, all traces of self-restraint crumble into little pieces. I fall into his kiss, surrendering to my passion, and pull him close—so close that he gasps, as my fingers hungrily trace every muscle in his back. Then, taking his face in my hands, I stroke the perfect lines of his jaw, as I whisper, "I want to be your everything."

His expression melts into an angelic smile. "Do you have any idea what you do to me, Ari?"

"Of course," I say breathlessly, as I bury my head in his shirt. "I work very hard at it."

"Your efforts are quite effective," he says softly.

"I think we need to go because I'm about to totally lose control." But instead of letting him go, I tighten my grip.

"Mmm," he moans, as his hand strokes my back, hovering just north of naughty.

"Your left hand is not helping at all, Davin."

"I was hoping to keep you here to see what happens when you lose control."

"We *really* should go." I groan. "Prom is tomorrow, and I need my beauty rest. You haven't forgotten the prom, have you?"

"I haven't. But if I did, Tal would remind me.

Tal. And Ella. Complications. Davin has been my protector for the past two months. He drives me to school every morning, and picks me up each afternoon. If I go shopping, he tags along. Don't get me wrong. I really enjoy being with him. But…

If I go somewhere with Ella, Davin brings Tal along. And Tal is almost as gorgeous as Davin. And Ella is…

Well, Ella is crushing on him. And she invited him to the prom. I told Tal that if he breaks her heart, I'll break his face. He thinks I'm kidding. I'm not.

"Yeah, I'm sure Tal will remind you."

"I've talked to him about it, Ari. He will be careful with her."

"Yeah, well we'll see how that goes." There's nothing I can do about it. I can only hope that Ella doesn't get too attached.

"Are you still excited to go?"

"Yes, but only because I'm going with you. I'm dying to see you all dressed up." I smile, as I picture him in a sophisticated black tux. My oh-so-suave Warrior.

"I have something for you, Ari." He places a small box in my hand.

I open the box and gasp. "It's beautiful, Davin." It's the most unique pendant I've ever seen—a bas-relief infinity symbol, sculpted from smooth black stone. In the center is a round metallic setting, holding a smoky gray gemstone. The chain is choker-length and silver-colored. It looks like woven metal.

"You really didn't have to do this," I say.

"I had it made because I wanted to. The design symbolizes eternal beauty and the jewel, a black diamond, symbolizes strength." He smiles as he takes the pendant from the box and clasps the chain around my neck.

I shiver with pleasure as his hand brushes my skin. Then he steps back, admiring the pendant, like an artist would his greatest masterpiece.

"It complements your hair and your eyes perfectly."

"And you—you complement *me* perfectly." I wrap my arms around him and bury my head in his chest. "I will treasure it forever, Davin."

I will treasure *him* forever.

Chapter 16

When I get home, I change into yoga pants and a tee, and then plant myself on the family room sofa. As I switch on the TV, an episode of *Ancient Aliens* is playing. The narrator catches my attention:

> IS IT POSSIBLE THAT TALES RANGING FROM FALLEN ANGELS TO GREEK DEMIGODS, TO ALLEGED EXTRATERRESTRIAL ENCOUNTERS ARE ALL ONE IN THE SAME? AND IF SO, IS IT ALL PART OF A GREATER AGENDA? MIGHT EXAMINING THESE EXPERIENCES PROVIDE NOT ONLY EVIDENCE OF EXTRATERRESTRIAL EVOLUTIONARY INTERVENTION IN THE REMOTE PAST, BUT ALSO REVEAL THE TRUE NATURE OF MANKIND'S ORIGINS?

"Uh-huh," I mumble to myself, "If they only knew."

"Did you say something, honey?" Mom asks, as she comes through the front door.

"No. Just talking to myself. How was your day?" I ask, as I mute the TV.

"Busy," she says, as she plops her purse down. "Looks like you had a busy day, too. Is Thalia overworking you?"

I must look as tired as I feel.

"Just an ordinary day. Davin and I worked out at the gym. I'm just a little tired."

"I see. And why are you blushing?" she asks, with twinkling eyes. "On second thought, please don't answer that."

"Mom! You're getting as bad as Ella."

"Poker face, honey. Always remember your poker face," she says with a big grin. "So when were you going to tell me what's going on?"

That catches my attention. "Huh?"

"Ari, have you ever been able to hide anything from me?"

"You think I'm hiding something from you?"

Does she think that Davin and I are having sex? Does she suspect I've changed?

She sits down beside me and begins stroking my hair. She's trying to make it easier for me to come clean.

"Ari…"

"Mom?" I brace for the worst.

"There is nothing you can say that would shock me, honey."

Oh yes there is.

"What do you think is going on?" I ask, innocently.

"I'll make it easier for you, sweetheart." Her expression is serious. "As a physician, I am trained to be observant. As your mother, I've had the privilege of observing you for over eighteen years. I haven't missed much."

"What? What haven't you missed?" I ask, as panic begins to set in.

She drapes an arm around my shoulder. "Well, let's see. You never get sick—not even a cold—and you exhibit an extraordinary ability to heal. Am I correct?"

"Yes."

"And remember the time you tried to make French fries and splashed hot oil on your arm?"

"Boy, did that hurt. Yes, I remember."

"I dressed the burn and then drove you to the hospital. Dr. Ellison removed the dressing, laughed, and called me a doting mom. The second degree burn I'd witnessed in the kitchen was nearly healed. Not even a blister remained. Shall I go on?"

"Uh, no," I mumble. But I know her question is rhetorical and I brace for more.

"Then, of course, there was your encounter with Luke—"

I cut her off. "If you knew all this, why didn't you run tests on me?"

"I have, Ari. I've analyzed your blood, your urine, your DNA. Your body is unique. It's as if God got bored with ordinary humans and decided to get a little creative. I have no logical explanation. Much of what I've seen under the microscope simply cannot be explained. Some of the conversations I've had with Thalia—about her research—make me want to pick her brain. But I can't risk anyone finding out about you. The consequences could be dire."

"Yeah. I could get dissected, huh?"

"It's not a joke, sweetheart."

"Oh, I know. And neither is what I'm about to tell you..."

I tell her everything. The whole story. Mom gives me her full attention. When I explain the healing at the Falls, her eyes widen in shock, and she turns white as a sheet.

"It was a soft blue light? Are you sure?"

"I'm positive. Why?"

She rubs the bridge of her nose—a telltale sign that she's tense. "Several times, when your dad and I were intimate, I glimpsed soft light radiating from his hands. It was as if he was giving me a part of himself. The feeling was indescribable." A tear trickles down her cheek and she brushes it away.

"Oh, Mom," I whisper, as I wrap her in my arms. "Dad was..."

"Unique," she says. "Honey, look at me."

"Huh?" I'm confused.

"What do you see when you look at me?"

"I see a very beautiful woman."

She smiles. "Think, Ari. Be objective. Look past your familiarity. How old am I?"

She is gorgeous and youthful. Far too youthful for a woman her age. "Forty-three—"

"Exactly. Do I look forty-three?"

"Well, no. But there are celebrities and…"

"Yes. But they don't leave their homes until they've had a professional makeup job. And they tend to have lots of cosmetic surgeries. The bottom line is that if I really wanted to, I could easily pass for twenty-five."

"How long do you think it's been since you stopped aging?"

"I'm not exactly sure. A long time. At least ten years. At first, I thought I was just lucky. That I had good genes. But I don't get sick. Not even a cold. And, just like you, I heal very quickly." She sighs. "Do you believe me?"

"Of course I do."

"You have no idea what it's been like. Most women spend thousands on cosmetics and clothes—to make themselves look younger. I, on the other hand, do the complete opposite. It's really a pain in the butt. Sometimes I just want to throw on a little black dress and—"

"Mom!" I laugh out loud.

"Yes, well. It's been frustrating."

"I'm sorry, Mom. I think I understand."

"Are you sure you understand, Ari? Do you understand that we cannot stay here very much longer? People will realize. They'll start to ask difficult questions."

And there is the very real risk that we will pique the government's curiosity. "I know, Mom. I really do. Is your DNA the same as mine?"

"It's similar. But your body is able to manufacture very strange clusters of cells. I thought it might be a malignancy, but it is anything but that. The clusters are like an armada of little ships that patrol your body. They are also a little like capacitors because they are full of energy. I just don't have the equipment to do anything more than observe them."

"And you don't have these cell clusters?"

"It's a little different. You have two types of clusters. One type is bound to specific organs and structures. I have those, too. But I do not have the roving clusters—they are unique to you."

"So I really might be a new model, eh?"

"It would seem so," she says.

"Mom, how did Dad and you meet?"

"You've never asked me before. It's a good story," she says. "It was during my senior year of pre-med. I'd been accepted at the UVA School of Medicine and I was freaking out over the tuition. I was freaking out over a lot of things." She pauses. She's remembering the accident.

Her parents and kid brother were killed by a drunk driver during the summer after her freshman year. Fortunately, her parents did leave her a house that was almost paid for and enough insurance to fund her undergraduate degree. But she was just a teenager, and teenagers don't deserve that kind of burden.

"I had just turned twenty-one," she continues, "and I decided to go to a bar with some friends. I guess I drank a little too much. The next thing I knew, a couple of guys were hitting on me. I'm not sure how it happened, but they managed to drag me outside into the woods, behind the parking lot. I was terrified—and helpless. That's when Dad showed up. He moved lightning-fast. Before I could say a word, both of my attackers were on the ground—writhing in pain. He picked me up, as if I were a child, and placed me in his car. We spent the night in his house. *This house*. And he was a perfect gentleman."

"You were attacked by two strange guys, and you went home with another strange guy? I'm surprised at you, Mom." I chuckle.

"Yes, well, it was certainly impetuous of me. But I felt such a connection, and so totally comfortable. I was upset and he made me feel better. He even made me a cup of tea. I was in the guestroom, but I wouldn't let him leave me. I made him lay down beside me—on top of the covers, of course. He was a perfect angel."

"Of course," I say, as I roll my eyes.

"You're having fun with this, aren't you?"

"Yeah. I am, actually."

She sticks out her tongue, then purses her lips. "By the time I fell asleep, I was hopelessly in love with him. We were married three months later."

"Wow. That was fast. A whirlwind romance, huh?"

She nods slowly. "It was. But we were perfect for each other."

"Do you ever wonder if Dad somehow survived the crash. Do you think he might have been like us?"

She squeezes her lips into a thin smile. "I've wondered about Dad's heritage for a very long time. I do believe that he was more than human."

"He might be alive, Mom. Are you prepared for that eventuality?"

"He's been gone so long. If he does come back, he'll have a lot of explaining to do. But if he is the same man I knew..." She pauses and sighs. "I'll always love him, Ari. But all I have right now are memories..."

I don't know how to respond so I give her a hug. "I love you, Mom."

"I love you, too," she says. "I think I'll call Thalia tonight and see if we can get together. Alone. Are you okay with that?"

"Of course," I say. "But maybe I should call her first—to let her know you're in the loop."

"Good idea," she says, as she moves toward the stairs. She climbs halfway up, stops, and then turns. "Ari, there's a good chance that our only solution will be to leave our world behind. Are you prepared to make that decision?"

"Actually, I already have."

"That's my girl," she replies, looking relieved.

I grab my phone and call Thalia. As I wait to connect, I realize that AT&T has no idea how far its long distance can actually reach. The Olympians run a special network through the portal—effectively allowing intergalactic cell calls. As far as the phone company knows, the calls terminate at the Institute. No clue. No trace. Perfectly secure.

Thalia picks up on the second ring. "Hello, Ari," she says cheerfully."

"Something has come up," I say.

"What's wrong, dear?"

"My mom knows. She knows, Thalia. She suspected that I was different and she ran tests."

"She didn't use the hospital lab. Did she?"

"No. She has a mini-lab in the basement. She ran blood tests, urine tests, and she's analyzed my DNA."

Thalia does not seem very concerned. In fact, she is totally calm.

"There's more. She hasn't aged in over ten years. She doesn't get sick, and she heals fast. She's..."

"She's an angel," Thalia says, as if she's describing Mom's hair color.

"Um, you're not surprised."

"I'm not."

"You knew?"

"I had a strong suspicion."

"You ran tests. Didn't you?"

"Well, I'm sure you know that when your mom gets really engrossed in thought, she has this habit of running her fingers through her hair."

"Yeah. Oh. You snagged some hairs, huh?"

165

"I did."

"Why didn't you use a scanner?"

"The readouts are in Olympian."

"Oh. But why didn't you tell me?"

"She and I have spent a considerable amount of time together. Enough time for me to conclude that she did not know about Olympus. I decided to let her figure things out on her own. I did not want to alarm her. And I did not want to alarm you."

"You really should have told me."

"In retrospect, you may be right. I'm sorry."

"Do you have any idea how this happened? I'm pretty sure an angel couple did not leave her on my grandparent's doorstep. You know?"

"I have a few theories. I think that once everything is out in the open, your mom can help us figure things out."

"So what now? She wants to talk to you. She wants to meet with you tomorrow."

"Tomorrow will be perfect. She's an angel, Ari. And we have become friends. Everything will be fine."

"Are you sure?"

"Of course. She and I will sort everything out tomorrow. In fact, I think I'll treat her to lunch at Nagi's. Do you think she'll like torik?"

I sigh. "Yup. And if you want to seal your friendship, make sure you get her to try a slice or two of *Death by Chocolate*. With the farzberry coulis."

She laughs. "I will do that. And do not worry, we will be fine. She will be fine."

"Okay. Just try not to shock her."

"She will not be shocked, Ari. She'll be relieved."

"And make sure she gets home before I leave for my prom."

"I will, dear. Now, you have a relaxing evening and do not worry about a thing."

"I'll try."

We end the call and my head is buzzing. What an incredible roller coaster ride it's been. My mom is an angel. But...

How did she become an angel? It had to be Dad. He has to be the wild card.

Oh boy.

Mom and Thalia will be okay. Mom will be in good hands. I have to believe that. I have to. If not, I'll be a hot mess and I'll blow my last chance to be a carefree human girl.

Carefree. That's my mantra. I chant it to myself as my thoughts drift to the prom and I smile, wistfully. I'm ready to be a happy-go-lucky human girl for the last time. I'm ready to be swept off my feet by my handsome Warrior.

I park on the sofa, turn up the sound on the TV, and wait for Ella to arrive.

What could possibly go wrong?

Chapter 17

Ella arrives at seven, and we camp out in the family room with a huge bowl of our favorite homemade snack mix: popcorn, cheese puffs, and honey-roasted peanuts.

"You know, we shouldn't be eating this the night before we have to squeeze into prom dresses, sweetie."

"We'll be fine as long as we don't refill the bowl," I say, grinning.

We spend most of the evening talking about Davin and Tal. Ella knows nothing about Olympus, so I have to be very careful not to slip. As far as she's concerned, Tal and Davin are graduate students at the Institute. A couple of ordinary human college guys—who happen to be totally extraordinary in every way.

"You're in love with him, aren't you, sweetie?"

I don't hesitate. "Yes."

"Have you told him?" She tilts her head and looks at me expectantly.

"Not exactly." I sigh. "But I think he knows."

"Not exactly? What does that mean?"

I haven't the foggiest idea. "I don't know. I guess I act like I'm in love with him. I tell him things..."

"Things? He's a guy, sweetie. Males lack the intuition gene, ya know? They need things spelled out. If you're sure you love him, you need to tell him." She props her chin up on her fists and stares at me with pursed lips.

She is relentless.

"I've never loved a guy before. I'm not sure what to say."

"How about, 'I Love you, Davin'?"

"Hmm. I guess that would work."

"I think you're afraid he won't tell you he loves you. Are you afraid?"

"Of course not. Well, maybe a little."

"Sweetie, if he doesn't tell you, it doesn't necessarily mean he doesn't love you. It just means he's not ready—or willing—to admit it. I've seen the way he looks at you, the way he strokes your hair. That guy is in love with you. I'd stake my life on it."

"So you think I should tell him?"

"If you don't, I will," she says, grinning mischievously.

"You would?"

"Uh-huh. It would be a public service. You two belong together, like coffee and cream."

"You drink your coffee black," I say with a smirk.

She narrows her eyes and glares at me. "You know what I mean."

I want to tell him. I'm just waiting for the right time. The perfect moment. "Then I guess I'll have to tell him," I say with a contented smile.

"That's more like it," she says.

"So, how do you feel about Tal?" I ask, holding my breath.

Ella gazes up at the ceiling. "It's kind of evolving. There's a spark between us. A really hot spark. But he's a little weird about things sometimes. I mean, we'll have this passionate make-out session, and then he'll just stop and be a Boy Scout the rest of the night. It's a little infuriating. He's got enough hot to heat a small city—but something is a little off. Ya know?"

I hate lying to her, but I have no choice. "I'm sure he's just a little shy. Maybe a bit old-fashioned. I think everything will work out."

The fact is, Warriors are extremely honorable. Tal is simply being cautious. He's being a Warrior. He also knows that if Ella finds out he's immortal, things could get really, really complicated.

"Yeah," she says through a yawn, "I'm going to go with the flow and see where it takes me. He is a mighty unique guy."

"He is. Do you love him?"

"I think I could fall in love with him, but I'm not there yet. Maybe tomorrow will be our breakthrough. I'll let you know."

"You do that. So, I assume you broke things off with Tom?"

"I did. Interestingly, he understood. I think he felt as uncomfortable with me as I did with him. It's funny how things work out sometimes."

"Yeah. I'm glad Tom's okay. He wasn't a good fit for you, but he is a nice guy," I say, as we head into the kitchen to clean up.

Ella sighs and nods.

I wash out the snack bowl, dry it, then grab a couple of cold water bottles from the fridge. "Let's go upstairs and get some sleep. Maybe we'll have sweet dreams," I say.

"Sounds like a plan, sweetie."

Bright lights. Sunshine. Eyes hurting. I look at my phone. It's almost noon.

Across the room, there is a snoring lump on my sofa. Ella. I decide to let her sleep.

I grab my robe and tiptoe to the bathroom.

Stepping into the shower, I close my eyes and let the water gently massage me. My mind wanders. I'm an angel. Will I be strong enough to play the hand I was dealt? Am I really in love with Davin? Or am I using him to stay grounded?

I towel off and run a comb through my hair as I stare at the new and improved Ari in the mirror. Since my awakening, I've noticed subtle changes in my appearance. Smooth and unblemished skin. Softer, healthier, and blacker hair. Gray eyes that now sparkle like jewels. Arms, legs, and abs that are more defined. Breasts that seem fuller. I've always considered myself pretty, but the girl in the mirror is different. She's a woman—a very beautiful woman. And there's only one reason it matters. I want to be beautiful for Davin. Only for Davin. I'm still the same old Ari inside. My smile spreads to my eyes as I realize that I do love him, I love him with all my heart. There will never be anyone else. Only Davin.

And tonight I will tell him.

I walk back out into the bedroom. Ella is starting to stir. "Wake up, sleepy head," I urge, while nudging her gently. Ella could sleep through a hurricane. One eye pops open. Then the other. "Let's get some breakfast. Okay?"

She stretches and yawns. "You go ahead, sweetie. I'm going to clean up. Meet you in fifteen. Okay?"

"Don't go back to sleep," I nag, as I get dressed.

She stands on wobbly legs. "I won't."

"See you in the kitchen," I say on my way out.

The house is quiet. No sign of Mom.

Is she with Thalia?

I find a note in the center of the kitchen table. It's wedged between the salt and pepper shakers.

ARI,
SPENDING THE DAY WITH THALIA – AT THE INSTITUTE. IT'S ALL GOOD. SEE YOU TONIGHT IN TIME FOR PICTURES AND HUGS. LOVE YOU — MOM

I picture Mom and Thalia sitting in Nagi's restaurant, chatting casually, about angels, and space portals. And I smile, because what else can I do?

Davin, Tal, Mom, and Thalia arrive together at six-thirty. Mom runs to fetch her good camera, while Tal and Davin stare at Ella and me as if we're prey. Our dresses are, in a word—*hot*. Ella's white strapless gown has a form-fitting skirt with a thigh-high slit. Mine is black and features a scooped tunic bodice over a curve-hugging, floor-length, double-slit skirt.

"You are the two most beautiful creatures I've ever seen," observes Tal, looking as if he is about to drool all over his exquisite black tux. "Don't you agree?" he asks Davin.

Davin looks like he's trying really hard to say something, but his mouth seems a little stuck. "Davin, you look very handsome."

No response.

"Davin?"

He walks across the foyer, takes my hands in his, and finally finds his voice. "Ari, the dress is stunning. You are...you look like a goddess."

The poor fella looks awestricken, and I'm liking it, a lot. "Thank you, Davin," I say, as a camera flash makes me blink.

Mom and Thalia are snapping away. Then they get serious, making us pose for what seems like a hundred photos. They are really enjoying themselves—and I feel like royalty.

I don't get a chance to talk with Mom and Thalia about their meeting, but I do get an opportunity to give them each a questioning look—to which Mom responds with a wink, and Thalia a thumbs-up. So their meeting was good. I flash a big smile and give each of them a little nod. The details will have to wait, but I have a feeling it will be all good.

We finally manage to sneak out the door, while our personal paparazzi keep snapping pictures until the four of us are seated inside Tal's black Porsche SUV.

"Ella," Mom calls out from the doorway, "Say 'hi' to your mom and tell her I'll be posting a bunch of pictures on Facebook."

Ella's mom, a teacher at our high school, will be a prom chaperone tonight.

"Okay, Doc. Will do," Ella replies.

Tal pulls up to the main entrance of the Sandhaven Hotel. Built in the 1920s, the Sandhaven is the Valley's showpiece, having hosted Presidents, royalty, and captains of industry in grand style. It's a storybook setting for a prom.

The valet hands Tal a claim check and then opens the doors for us. Davin tracks the Cayenne as the valet drives it away.

"What are you looking at?" I ask.

"Our car. I want to see where he parks it—in case we need to find it."

I nod. The guys probably have spare keys in their pockets. I have a lot to learn about strategy and tactics.

"Hey, y'all," comes the grating voice of Jen Hilliard. She's Edgewood's head cheerleader and the shallowest person I've ever known.

Her ample assets are in danger of popping out of her gown, and I'm hoping it won't happen in front of me. She's a pretty girl, but it's obvious that's all she has going for her. Life after high school might easily prove to be a rude awakening. I feel sorry for her. Maybe she'll find herself at college.

"Where'd you get the pretty fellas?" Jen asks, as she checks out the guys. She certainly isn't shy about it, either.

Ella glares at her. "They were selling them down the road. Did you miss the kiosk? They came with a Porsche. All for one low price. We just need to get them back before midnight or they'll turn into garden gnomes," she says with narrowed eyes.

Jen's date walks up just in time to rescue her.

As we walk inside, Davin leans in close, and whispers, "She would make a great Warrior."

I smile in silent agreement. Indeed she would.

The grand ballroom is immense. A posh dining area rings a polished wood dance floor. The room has to be two hundred feet long, half as wide, and about forty feet high. The décor is early twentieth century and totally gorgeous. I love everything about it. It would make a great setting for an old movie—and it probably has.

The ballroom ends in a solid glass wall, which opens onto a large ornate balcony—perched high above the Valley.

We find our table and are quickly greeted by a server, who brings us water and takes our dinner orders.

After dinner, the DJ switches from mood to dance music, and Ella looks ready to party.

"Alright y'all. We have to dance the first dance. Follow me," she says. She stands and waits for Tal to take her arm.

I'm a little less forward and wait for Davin to ask me.

As we make our way onto the dance floor, my cheeks flush as I realize how many girls are ogling Davin. It's almost indecent the way some of them gawk. I lean close and whisper, "I think you have some fans here."

He looks around. "In case you haven't noticed, almost every guy in this room is staring at you. I guess we make a nice couple," he says, looking happy and relaxed.

Davin holds me close as we dance. Every nerve in my body is on high alert and I'm oblivious to anyone or anything, except him. The side of my face finds a cozy nest on the left side of his chest. It's a perfect fit.

"You're a very graceful dancer," I say.

"Thalia worked with me. We watched videos."

"How cute," I say, imagining them practicing. "Thank you for coming to the prom with me."

"I wouldn't have missed it for the world."

He's being sweet, because I'm pretty sure being surrounded by a bunch of human teenagers is not his idea of a fun evening. "Thank you. It does mean a lot to me."

I look up just as an adorable smile begins to form on his lips.

"I know that your human heritage is important to you. This dance is important to you. I want you to be happy."

"I'm happy whenever I'm with you, Davin," I say, as I softly knead the nape of his neck.

"Mmm, if I kissed you now would you get into trouble?"

"I don't care, because if you *don't* kiss me now I just might explode into little pieces all over your nice tuxedo."

So he kisses me. It's a wonderful kiss, a kiss that might never have ended had the music not come to a scratching, screeching halt.

Our blissful interlude shattered, we stare up at the stage. A large man is standing behind the DJ, holding a gun to his head.

This can't be happening.

The man grabs the mike and announces in a perfectly clear voice, "Boys and girls, may I have your attention please? Please give me your undivided attention."

He gets what he asked for, because everyone stops talking and looks at him. It's then that I realize how grotesque he looks.

"Davin, I can sense him. Is he—"

Davin doesn't answer. I hear a loud pop, and the front of the DJ's head explodes in a macabre spray of blood and tissue. It takes several seconds for reality to sink in—and then all hell breaks loose.

Kids are running around aimlessly, screaming and crying. I see one girl fall and get trampled by two other kids. She manages to get back on her feet and takes off running.

Tal appears beside us, holding Ella protectively, as more shots ring out. She's shaking.

"Ari, take Ella and go to the balcony," Davin commands, as he points to the glass doors at the back of the ballroom. "Get down to the Valley and go straight to the river. Tal and I will secure things here, and then we'll find you. Go!"

"I want to help you."

"Tal and I are in no danger, but Ella is. PLEASE!"

He's right. "Be careful, Davin."

"I will. Now GO!" he roars over the deafening din.

Ella is sobbing uncontrollably. "Did you see his head—?"

"Shh," I whisper in her ear. "I'm going to get us out of here. It'll be okay."

I kick off my shoes, pick her up in my arms, and rocket to the balcony at full speed. To any human observer, we probably appear as an unidentifiable blur. Taking one last, heart-rendering look inside the ballroom, I leap up and onto the balcony wall.

"Ari, you're not going to jump!" Ella screams. She's writhing like an eel, struggling to squirm out of my arms. "You'll kill us both!"

"Stay as still as you can. We'll be fine."

"Please let me down, sweetie. Please."

"Close your eyes and trust me. You know I'd never hurt you."

I don't want to prolong her agony, so I hold her tight against my chest and launch us off the balcony, toward the Valley, forty feet below. The soft ground cushions our landing and I look down to make sure she is okay. Her breathing is steady, but she's out cold.

I jog to the riverbank, set her down on the grass, and brush the hair away from her face. She's coming around. Now she's glaring at me. Her expression quickly progresses from confusion to anger. I brace for the tirade I know is coming.

She sits up slowly and leans against a tree, fixing me with a look of grim determination. And then she erupts. "You picked me up like I was a little kid. Then you took off running like a freaking express train. And…and that jump into the Valley should have killed us both. But it didn't. When did you become a superhero, huh? What the *hell* is going on?"

"I can't tell you right now. When Davin and Tal get here, we'll go somewhere and talk. It'll all make sense. I promise."

I lied. I have no idea whether the Warriors will want Ella to know what we are.

"Really? You can't tell me?" she asks, as I start walking upstream. "You get back here right now!"

"I'm just going to look for the guys. I'll be right back."

"Ari! You need to tell me. Right. Now."

Maybe I can give her a partial explanation. I turn and start to walk back toward Ella when a man's voice resonates through the darkness— startling me.

"My, such a pretty young lady." His tone is deep, rich, and evil.

I turn toward the voice just as its owner emerges from the shadows. Steely dark eyes and an aquiline nose dominate his face. His oily black hair is slicked back. I suddenly know what Davin meant by a Warrior's instinct. He reeks of evil, causing the Essence to surge through my skin, as my body generates a protective shield. "You are Zon," I hiss.

"Oh, my. A Warrior," he croons. "A most serendipitous encounter. How can this be?"

"It's your lucky day, I guess. Are you responsible for what happened in the hotel?"

"I am responsible for many things, my lovely." He bows at the waist and continues. "Allow me to introduce myself. I am Artemus Bodden."

"What do you want, Artie?" Energy is boiling inside me. I'm coiled and ready to spring.

"What do you think? I want to create chaos, provoke panic, and cause you to tingle with terror. And then I want to taste your fear, my dear."

He's got my attention. I place my hands on my hips and stare daggers at him. "Can't have any."

"Well, let's see." He pauses and stares at me—running his gaze the length of my body.

I'm totally creeped out.

"Hmm. First I'll make you moan with pleasure and then I'll make you scream in agony." His face contorts into a perverted, sickening smile.

"What the hell is going on?" Ella bellows. "Are y'all crazy?"

"Ella, stay back there. Everything will be okay. The guy is nuts."

He is trying to charm me. I can feel it. He's testing my power.

"I'm completely sane, ladies," Artemus says, with a lilt. "I just have a highly evolved sense of pleasure." He's leering at me now. God, I hate it when guys leer at me. Okay, this is going too far, and I'm about to pop.

"You've got less than ten flippin' seconds to live. I suggest you start praying for redemption."

Davin once asked me if I could look a snarling Zon in the eye and destroy him without hesitation. One look at Bodden and there's no doubt. I can do this. I can tear him to pieces.

"If you attack me, your human friend will die." His tone is smooth and ice cold.

I turn toward Ella. A man is crouched next to her. He smells like Artemus and looks even crazier—and he's wielding a wicked-looking knife. Crap!

Ella looks petrified, her face a mask of abject fear.

I'm not prepared for this at all. What would Davin do? If I charge, she will surely be stabbed before I reach her. I could project energy, but I don't have enough control yet. I could unintentionally hurt my best friend. Maybe even kill her. My only hope is that Davin and Tal will arrive in time to help. I have to buy us time.

"What to do, what to do," Artemus says, in a sing-song cadence. "Your fear is palpable. I haven't felt pleasure like this in centuries."

He's acting like a total perv.

"You're sick," I say. "Let my friend go and I will be merciful."

"You are not in a position to bargain, Warrior."

"If she is hurt, you will die. There will be no negotiating. Do you want to die?"

"Oh, please don't be angry. It's such a useless emotion. Fear is so much tastier. How can I terrify you?" He looks at me and then at Ella. "Ah, I think I know," he says with a maniacal cackle.

He turns to the beast beside Ella. "Lander, stick your knife into the pretty little human, but try not to kill her too quickly."

"No! Please don't hurt me," Ella pleads.

Lander smiles wickedly as he leans close to Ella. "Are you afraid, little girl?"

He runs his knife along the front of her neck, drawing a thin line of blood. He looks at the knife and moans. And then he licks Ella's blood off the tip of his blade. Ella is sobbing, and Lander is getting more excited.

"LEAVE HER ALONE!" I shout.

"Watch closely," Lander says. He sticks his knife into Ella's stomach, inserting it slowly. Then he twists it.

Ella screams in agony as my heart shatters into little pieces.

"NO-NO-NO-NO!" I scream, as blood gushes from Ella's abdomen, turning her beautiful gown red.

I leap toward Lander, screaming, or perhaps roaring. He pulls the knife out of Ella and lunges. But he's not quick enough. My foot connects with his midsection, and he flies into the river.

I kneel beside Ella, who is lying on the ground, moaning. "Hang on, honey, help is on the way," I tell her.

"Ari, you roared," she says in a weak voice.

Ella looks behind me and her eyes go wide with fear, causing me to turn, just as Bodden raises a handgun and aims. I move in front of him, shielding Ella, as he fires. The bullets are repelled by my shield. He curses and throws the gun onto the ground.

"You will not leave this forest alive," I say. The words come out as a guttural snarl.

"Such a spoil sport," he whines. "Regrettably, I will take your leave and live to fight another day. It was a *pleasure* to meet you. Now you'd better tend to your little friend. She does not look well at all."

I'm about to kick his evil face into pulp when a sudden movement in the shadows catches my attention. Gliding like a panther, Davin appears in front of us. His fist shoots out like lightning and the left side of Bodden's head explodes.

"Ari, behind you!" Davin shouts.

I turn to see Lander charging up the riverbank toward me. He's moving fast, too fast for me to plant for a killing strike. I slide to my left and strike the side of his face with a straight right hand. He staggers backwards, but recovers quickly and lunges. Davin steps in front of me, but this is my battle, and I won't be denied. I shove Davin out of the way and launch myself at Lander. I'm on him in an instant, pinning him to the ground. He sneers, trying to speak, but I cut him off. "You will never hurt anyone again." I snarl, grabbing two handfuls of his hair.

"Please…"

Is he begging for mercy? Because if he is, I have none to offer.

"NO!" I roar, as I slam his head into the ground.

He tries to spin free, but the Essence within me is far too strong. I drive his head into the hard, rock-strewn soil, over and over, and over again. I can hear the bones in his neck cracking. Blood pours from his nose, his ears, and his eyes. I want to rip the heart from his chest.

"THIS IS FOR ELLA, YOU BASTARD!"

A gentle hand grasps my shoulder. "Ari, he's dead. You can stop," Davin says, softly.

I can't look at him. I can't stop smashing Lander's head into the ground.

"HE'S NOT DEAD ENOUGH!" I bellow.

Davin lifts me off my feet and holds me against his chest, breaking the spell and bringing me back to what remain of my senses.

"Ari, are you hurt?"

I look down at my dress. It's covered in blood—Lander's blood.

"I—I'm fine. He tortured her, Davin. Is she…?"

We both turn toward Ella. Tal is kneeling beside her, pouring something into her wound.

"What is he doing?" I ask.

"He is administering a medicine that will help slow the bleeding. It is similar to what your mom would call a hemostatic agent—but more effective."

"Will it heal her?" I ask, hoping it would.

"It will buy her time." Davin doesn't look confident.

"Help her, Davin. Don't let her die. Please!" I begin to sob.

"She is human, Ari. I cannot share the Essence with her. But you might be able to. I think there is a chance…"

I can't move. I can't speak. I just stare at him, wide-eyed, unable to stop sobbing. He grasps my shoulders and gives me a firm shake.

"Ari, *you* need to help her. It's her only chance."

"BUT YOU HEALED *ME!*"

"Because you have angel DNA. Ari, please, there's not much time. Your powers are unique. I believe you can help her."

181

"This is my fault. I hesitated, Davin. I should have saved her. This is all my fault…"

"It is not your fault. Get hold of yourself and go to her. Now!"

I shake my head, trying to clear my mind.

I have to try.

I go to Ella's side and gently grasp Tal's shoulder. "I'm going to help her heal, Tal."

Tal gives me a curious look and nods. He looks devastated. Defeated.

I kneel down next to Ella and inspect her wound. Blood is everywhere. Lander didn't just stab her—the monster tore her open.

"What do I do, Davin?" I ask, as I lay my hand gently on her stomach. She flinches and moans—but doesn't wake up.

Davin kneels beside me and places a hand on my arm. "Ari, release your energy into her. See it in your mind. Think about how much you love her."

I nod, unsure whether I can do it, but I'll try. I'll try as hard as I can.

I focus—pulling energy inward. Whatever Tal poured into her wound is working, because the bleeding has slowed to a trickle.

Please God, give me a little help here. Maybe a miracle?

I push out hard, releasing energy into her torso. The air around me warms, and a faint glow appears over my hand. It's almost imperceptible. But then it grows brighter—until Ella's entire body is bathed in a soft blue halo. Her eyes open wide and she gasps, trying to speak. But all she can do is mouth my name.

Davin leans in closer and whispers, "It's going to hurt a lot, but you must stay connected. Do not let go."

Ella's eyes close again. I watch the slow rise and fall of her chest. "Don't give up, Ella," I beg, as tears stream down my face.

Ella convulses, and I feel hot, really hot, as if every muscle and organ in my body is on fire. I groan in agony, refusing to scream, fearing I'll lose my focus.

"Hold on, Ari," Davin says. "You're doing it. I'm here with you."

After several long, agonizing minutes, the pain begins to subside and I can breathe again. Ella's eyes open and she looks at me.

"Ari?"

"I'm here Ella."

"I know that. I can see you."

I smile at her through a steady stream of tears.

"You healed me, sweetie. It was as if you and I were…as if we were one person. How…?"

Her voice is weak and raspy. I look at the guys for help, not knowing what to tell her.

"I will explain everything when you are stronger," Tal says.

"No you won't," Ella says. Her voice may be weak, but her mind is strong as ever. "You will explain now. That creepy dude called me human. Why would he do that, huh? And Ari and Davin did some things that were clearly more than human. I'm nobody's fool, Tal."

"You need to rest, and then I will tell you everything," Tal says, as he rubs her forehead and temples with a very aromatic ointment.

"Stop it. That stuff is gross. You better tell me…" Her voice trails off and her eyes close.

She's sound asleep.

"What did you put on her head, Tal?"

"A sedative. She needs to rest."

"That was one hell of a sedative. Is it safe?"

"Yes. She will sleep for a couple of hours and then wake feeling refreshed."

"Will you stay with her?"

"I will not leave her side."

"Thanks. She cares for you a lot. If any human can handle our little secret, it's Ella. If we hide the truth from her, she'll know, and she'll be terribly hurt. She's a lot smarter than you think. You need to tell her what you are. What *we* are."

He looks at me with a wistful expression and sighs. "Sometimes I think she is smarter than most angels. I will talk with her tonight. You should get some rest, Ari."

"I think you're right. If her condition changes, come get me."

"I will," he says, and then he grasps my hand. "You were amazing tonight. I am very proud of you."

"Thank you, Tal. But I should have done more."

"You did all you possibly could. You displayed courage and good judgment. You are a true Warrior. Neither Davin nor I could have done more."

I smile and give Tal a pat on the shoulder. "Coming from you, it means a lot. Thanks."

He nods and smiles back at me.

"Take care of her, Tal."

"I will," he says.

I stand up on wobbly legs.

Davin wraps an arm around my waist for support. "How do you feel?" he asks.

"A little drained, and I have a really big headache. Oh, and every muscle in my body feels like mush," I say, wincing. "Other than that, I'm pretty good."

"I know the feeling," he says.

"Is that how you felt at Renegade Falls?" I ask, remembering how drained he looked after helping me to heal my leg.

"Yes."

"How did you know I could heal her? *Did* you know?"

He knew.

He takes a deep breath. "I didn't know for sure. But I suspected you could. Warriors cannot heal humans. But you are more than a Warrior, Ari. Much more."

"This is all so incredible, Davin. I felt as if I was inside her soul."

"There is something we need to consider."

"What do you mean?"

"Think of what you've learned about angel genetics. How do we heal?"

We heal from the Essence. In the event of a major injury, we can help another angel by sharing energy. But angels heal themselves because they are genetically equipped to do so. I gasp. "The Essence. She used the Essence."

Davin nods.

Is he implying that I changed her?

"Oh, Davin. You don't think…"

"There is a very real possibility that you have altered her DNA."

"How can we find out?"

"Let's go sit down and wait for Thalia," he says, pointing to a large SUV parked under a tree. "She will know."

"Oh God," I whisper.

Davin gives me an odd look, then smiles. "Precisely."

Chapter 18

Davin and I are sitting in the cargo area of a large black Range Rover, which turns out to be a lot more comfortable than the ground. In fact, it's quite luxurious.

"Who are they?" I ask, as I look out through the open tailgate.

Several people are scurrying about. Some are spraying a powdered substance on the ground, while others wield instruments that look like high-tech metal detectors.

"Thalia sent in a team to clean up the area and dispose of the Zon bodies," Davin replies, as he strokes my hair.

"You called her?"

"Tal called her just before we found you."

"Oh," I say, as I watch a Warrior walk up from the riverbank, carrying a large bag. From the shape of its contents, I assume it's a body. I shudder.

"What happened after I left the hotel?" I ask. "Were there more casualties?"

"Yes."

"How many?"

"I'm not sure. After we dealt with the shooters, we left to find you and Ella."

"How many bad guys?"

"Two."

"Are they dead?"

"We put them to sleep and carried them to the river with us."

Putting an adversary to sleep is a Warrior euphemism for knocking someone out—usually with a very hard punch or kick to the head.

"They are alive?"

"Yes. They're in custody and will be interrogated."

"Will they be killed?"

"We cannot allow them to live. Their executions will be painless."

I want them to die, I want them to pay for what they did.

"Was this my fault? Did the Zon come for me?"

"I doubt it. Did either of the Zon who attacked you say anything that would indicate you were targeted?"

"No. Bodden, the one who did most of the talking, seemed very surprised. He thought I was a Warrior."

"Ari, many seemingly random acts of violence are the work of the Zon. Given our proximity to Washington, it's not unusual. They are quite active in this region." He gently grasps my hands. "It had nothing to do with you. It was not your fault."

"I hope you're right."

I hear footsteps approaching from behind. It's Thalia.

"Are you two alright?"

Davin and I nod.

She hops up onto the tailgate and sits, facing us. "Ari, Tal told me what you did. Are you sure you're okay?"

"I'm fine. Did you examine Ella?"

"I did a quick scan. Her wounds are nearly healed. I gave her something to help replenish her fluids, and something for the pain."

Thalia looks uneasy. Apprehensive. Halting. "I love you like a big sister," I say, "but you are holding something back. I've been through a lot tonight, and I really don't want to be wondering what it is you aren't telling me." I fold my arms across my chest and we lock eyes. "Did I change her?"

She purses her lips and nods slowly. "She is an angel. We'll know more once I can do more extensive testing."

I lean into Davin and groan.

"She's going to be fine, Ari," Thalia says.

"Let me guess. In all of recorded Olympian history, this is totally unprecedented. Right?"

Thalia's lips slowly curve into an impish smile.

Davin hugs me tight and sighs. "I am humbled in your presence."

I punch him in the arm, and Thalia's smile widens.

"Why are you smiling, Thalia? Is this funny?" I ask.

"BFF," she says.

"Huh?"

"Best friends *forever*."

"I know what it means. I want to know why you think it's funny."

"You've given the acronym a more literal meaning. You will not have to watch Ella grow old, Ari. This is a gift. A wonderful, magical, priceless gift. For both of you."

She's right. Having to watch my best friend grow old and die, while I remain young, would really suck. She's my sister from a different mister; my partner in crime. "Is the change dangerous to her in any way?"

"The genetic changes will cause her body to evolve. She will undergo an awakening—just as you have. There is no danger."

"Can I talk to her?"

"I had Tal take her to my home in Portal City. You'll see her in the morning."

"Okay." I still can't get my head around the fact that I changed her. "How was I able to change her?"

"You seem to have the ability to alter DNA. This is not unheard of. The angels who altered the course of evolution on the mortal worlds were special angels, blessed with the ability to manipulate DNA through touch."

"The Prostáti?"

"Yes. And you seem to have that ability."

"Can the Prostáti turn mortals into angels?"

"Not that we are aware of."

"I'm worried that I'm some kind of freak. I really am."

"You are not a freak, Ari,"

"I'm different than the other angels, Thalia. There is no one else like me. And no one can tell me why."

"We will figure it out. I do have a theory."

"Anything you'd care to share?"

"Not until I work out a few details. Soon. I promise."

"Does your theory have anything to do with my mom?"

"It does."

"What did you—"

She raises her hand to stop me. "I know you're anxious. We're very close to a breakthrough, Ari. Can you give me a day or two?"

"I guess."

"Thank you."

"By the way, do you know where she is?"

"Your mom?"

"Yes."

"She is at the hotel helping to treat the wounded. She will meet us here as soon as possible and then return with me to my residence in Portal City. She knows you are safe."

"Does she know she's going to be staying on Olympus tonight?"

"Yes. She's excited."

I'll bet she is.

Davin gives us a curious look. He knows something is up.

Thalia nods to me. "Tell him," she says.

Davin looks at me, expectantly.

"Mom knows. She figured it out," I say.

"She knows you are an angel?" Davin asks. He doesn't look very surprised.

"She's suspected for years. She ran DNA tests—discreetly. I told her everything. That's why she and Thalia spent the day together."

Davin gives Thalia a sideways glance. "I wondered why she was at the Institute. I guess we'll have a lot to go over tomorrow."

"There is something else," I say tentatively.

Davin arches a brow.

"Mom hasn't aged in over ten years. She's not human."

He runs his fingers through his hair and sighs. "Whew."

"Are you upset with me?"

He steals a glance at Thalia, then turns back to face me. "We've known all along that your situation is complicated. I'm actually excited. This is significant."

"I guess it is." I sigh. "Maybe I won't be your little enigma anymore."

Davin sits up straight and glares at me. "You're not my little enigma."

"Then what am I, Davin?"

"You are my angel."

My heart flutters and nearly stops. "I am?"

"You *are*," he states emphatically.

Thalia is smiling so wide that I'm afraid her face might break.

"Ari! Are you there?" Mom emerges from the shadows at a jog.

"Over here, Mom," I call out, as I hop down out of the SUV.

She looks drained. Exhausted. I give her a big hug. She feels tense.

"How many people, Mom? How many casualties?" I ask.

She grasps my hand and grimly rattles off the names of three students who were killed. Six more students and four teachers were wounded—four critically.

"Oh, God," I mutter, as I lean forward, hiding my face in my hands. They weren't close friends, but I knew them. Edgewood is a small school. They were good kids. Amy Madison was a softball player and had a great sense of humor. Michael Turner was captain of the debate team and would have been class salutatorian. Beth Miller could sing like an angel. All gone. There will be no graduation. No college. No happy endings.

And I will not be able to rest until every Zon is destroyed.

"Ari…" She's rocking back and forth. Something is wrong.

"Mom? What is it?"

"Maggie Douglas…she was killed."

Oh no. I lean against the SUV and bury my face in my hands. "Dear God, no."

My heart hurts and I begin to sob.

"Ari," Davin says. "I'm sorry. Was she a good friend?"

"She…" I take a deep breath and swallow a sob. "She's Ella's mom."

Davin gathers me in his arms, and I collapse against his chest.

Ella will be devastated. "We should have searched for her. I should have tried to find her in the ballroom. We should have done more."

"We needed to get Ella out of harm's way. There was no time," Davin says.

"I can't believe this. I just can't believe it. Does she know? Did you tell her, Thalia?"

"I didn't know until now, dear."

"I should tell her. I'm her best friend."

"I'll tell her," Mom says. "You've had enough trauma to deal with tonight."

I know from her look that there will be no negotiating. Her decision is made, and it's final.

"But she might need me." I counter weakly.

"I agree with Andi. She knows you saved her life," Thalia says. "She will understand."

This battle is lost. Mom is not going to budge.

"Tell her I love her, Mom. Tell her she'll always be my best friend."

"I will, honey."

Mom wraps me in a hug.

"Won't the Sheriff's department be looking for her?" I ask.

"I already called Sheriff Johnson and told him Ella would be staying with me. If the good sheriff needs to talk, he has my number. According to Thalia, my cell phone will work in Portal City, hopefully without astronomical roaming charges," she says, rolling her eyes.

She hasn't lost her sense of humor, which makes me feel a little better.

"Should I go home?" I ask.

"No." Mom and Thalia answer simultaneously.

Thalia's eyes move from me to Davin, and then to Mom. "I've got a full house, Andi. Ari can stay in Davin's guest apartment. He lives nearby. She will be safe there."

Mom's eyebrows nearly pop off her face. "Davin? Will my daughter be *safe*?" Her tone conveys two distinct meanings.

Davin does not hesitate. "Of course, Dr. Worthington. She will be totally safe."

Mom walks up to Davin and hugs him. "Thank you," she says. Then she stands on her toes and whispers in his ear.

Davin nods, and Mom steps away. "Get a good night's sleep," she says to Davin and me.

"Goodnight, Mom."

What was that all about?

"Davin, your car is parked up on the road," Thalia says, as she tosses him a key fob.

"Thanks," Davin replies.

Thalia gives us a quick wave and a warm smile. Then she and Mom walk off toward the road.

I take Davin in my arms and hug him to me like a security blanket. "I think Mom likes you. What did she whisper in your ear?"

Davin sighs. "She said she trusts me. But if I hurt you, she will find me when I'm sleeping and torture me." He pauses and clears his throat. "She has an interesting sense of humor."

"I don't think she was kidding," I say grimly.

"Of course she was."

"She has access to powerful drugs and sharp surgical instruments," I say with a wink.

"Very funny. Let's go."

We walk up to the road and get into Davin's car.

As he starts the engine, I realize that my gown is ruined, almost to the point of indecent exposure. And I'm barefoot. To top things off, my phone and wallet are in Tal's car. I'll need to retrieve them tomorrow.

"Can we stop by my house so I can get a change of clothes and some essentials?"

"Of course."

Davin parks in my driveway. The house is dark. "How will we get in?" he asks.

"Well, we could use our angel strength to break down the door. Or we can use the key hidden out back," I say. "Come with me."

We walk behind the deck, where I retrieve a key from beneath a large flowerpot.

"You Worthingtons think of everything," he says, as I unlock the back door.

"That we do. Just a second," I say, as I grab a hose and spray my feet, which are encrusted with a thick layer of muck.

"That's better."

I turn off the water, wipe my feet on the welcome mat, and unlock the door.

"Have a seat," I say, pointing to the family room sofa. "I'll just be a minute."

Standing in my bathroom, I strip out of what's left of my dress, chuck it into the trash, and take the quickest shower ever. After detangling my hair, I tie it into a high ponytail, then change into yoga pants and a clean tee shirt. I throw a few changes of clothes and some toiletries into a backpack, and I'm ready to go.

"That was quick," Davin remarks, as I come bounding down the stairs.

"I just want to get out of Edgewood as quickly as possible."

I want to put some distance between me and the horrors I've witnessed. A thousand light-years seems about right.

Davin places his hand over the panel on his front door, which glows blue, before sliding open with a hiss.

I've visited his place several times, but never to spend the night. The house has two levels and is roughly the size of a typical suburban home on Earth. In terms of technology, though, it's purely Olympian. You enter into a large open space, which contains several intimate seating areas. Off to the right are the kitchen, a large study, a guest suite, and a powder room.

The walls are computer controlled and Davin can change the color, texture, and even the artwork, at the touch of a button.

The building is underground, but you'd never know it. Simulated skylights provide simulated sunshine or moonlight, while a large virtual picture window can display any type of scenery—in high definition, full-motion video.

The second floor is limited to one very large bedroom, a bathroom that looks like a tropical rainforest, and a closet bigger than my bedroom in Edgewood.

Davin leads me into the kitchen and we sit at the table.

"Hungry?" he asks, as he hovers over the food prep system.

"Yes," I reply. "Something light. An omelet. With cheese. And some torik sausage. The spicy kind."

Davin casts me a sideways glance and smiles.

"Can you schedule delivery in thirty minutes? I'd really like to take a shower before I eat."

"Of course."

"Do you mind if I use your shower?"

The shower in Davin's bedroom is equipped with the latest in Olympian bathing technology. Stepping inside is like stepping into an alternate reality.

"Not at all," he says, as he keys in our food choices. "I'll use the guest bath. Do you remember how to program the shower?"

"I think so." I give him a quick kiss, grab my suitcase, and head upstairs.

As I climb the steps, I think of Ella. Her life was torn apart tonight. How long will it be before she can smile again? Before she can move on with her life? I want to hold her in my arms. I want to comfort her.

I enter the bathroom and let my suitcase fall to the floor. Plants and flowers are arranged to appear as if they're a natural part of the room. The walls are covered with video screens that simulate a tropical rainforest. It's all so amazingly realistic.

I program the shower for a gentle tropical rain and crank the temperature up to the equivalent of one hundred and four degrees, Fahrenheit.

I strip off my clothes, fold them neatly, then place them on a counter. A blue light flashes on the shower door. I wave my hand across a panel, the door slides up and open, and I step inside.

The enclosure is large, easily twenty by twelve feet. The floor, walls, and ceiling are natural stone, and there's a small pool on one side, deep enough to sit in.

The computer-controlled effects transport me to a topical isle—in the midst of a gentle rain. The sounds, the smells, the lighting, and the gentle breeze that whispers over my skin, combine to alter my reality. I'm somewhere else, somewhere exotic.

I imagine how wonderful it would be to share this space with Davin. Someday. Once we have a more permanent solution in place.

I'm startled by Davin's voice. "Ari, are you alive or have you drowned in my shower?"

"Davin?" I ask, looking around for him. "Where are you?"

"In the kitchen, waiting for you. You've been up there forty minutes."

I instinctively wrap my arms around myself to cover my nakedness. "You can't see me, can you?"

"No," he laughs, "It's just an intercom. Audio only."

"Oh," I say in a small voice. "I'll be right down."

I turn off the shower and step outside, feeling foolish. He did that on purpose.

Stepping under the dryer, I watch as the droplets of water on my body quickly evaporate. In less than a minute, I'm dry.

I slip on a black silk sleep camisole, and matching shorts, then assess my look in the mirror. A mischievous grin spreads across my face. This will get him back for the intercom thing.

I stop in the doorway, between the great room and the kitchen, and strike a seductive pose. "Sorry I took so long," I say with a come-hither smile.

Davin looks up and stares at me for several seconds before speaking. "You look very relaxed."

He abruptly pushes back his chair and stands, but he isn't paying attention to what he's doing. He's focused on me, which is probably what causes him to slam his knee into the table, really hard. "Ahh!" he grunts.

"Are you okay, Davin?" I ask, as I fight to suppress a smile.

"I'm fine," he says through a pained expression. "Sit down and I'll get our food."

"You're limping," I say, suddenly feeling guilty.

He looks gorgeous in a clean tee shirt and a pair of very comfortable-looking shorts.

"I'll be fine in a minute," he says.

He will. But I still feel guilty.

We both attack our omelets with gusto, finishing them quickly.

"That was delicious," I say. And then I lean back, inadvertently pulling the thin fabric of my cami tight against my breasts.

Davin looks up at just the right moment. His gaze stops at my chest, and his lips form a cute little smile. "Did you have enough to eat?"

"Yes. That really hit the spot," I say with a shy smile.

Davin leans back in his chair, looking pensive.

"You're suppressing your emotions, Ari."

I stare back, pondering his assessment.

"No. I'm not," I state evenly. "I'm just trying to not let my emotions consume me. I watched my best friend get tortured tonight and I couldn't stop it. Then I healed her and, in the process, turned her into an immortal being. And I killed a man. So yes, I could easily let myself fall apart—but if I do, the Zon win, and I won't let that happen. I've seen evil, I've smelled it, I hate it, and all I want is to destroy it. It's an instinct. Right?" I let out a deep breath and reach for his hand, squeezing it tight.

"You're not going to go easy on yourself, are you?" he asks, with a glint of pride in his eyes.

"Would the Zon go easy on me?" I ask, rhetorically.

"No," he agrees. "But it's not really about hating the Zon."

"Then what's it all about?"

"We fight so that goodness and love can thrive. We fight to protect the innocent. And the *man* you killed tonight was a fallen angel."

I feel humbled. Ashamed. "I'm sorry, Davin. I'll try to keep things in perspective. And I'm sorry I pushed you. I didn't hurt you, did I?"

"No, you did not hurt me. But you are getting impossibly strong. I will need to be careful around you," he says, smiling. "We should get some sleep now. Tomorrow will be a busy day."

I don't want to be alone in the guest suite. It's not that I'm afraid. I just want Davin close to me. I need the comfort only he can provide.

"I'd rather not sleep alone tonight."

"Ari, your mother—I promised her."

"I don't intend for us to do anything that would cause that promise to be broken. Please?"

He moves to my side and places his hand on my shoulder. "Are you sure?"

I stand up and wrap my arms around his neck. "I'm very sure," I whisper, speaking directly to his heart. "I want you near me."

"I know you do. But…"

"No *buts*," I say softly. "I'm an angel. And I happen to be in love with you."

He looks startled. He looks as if he wants to speak, but he can't find his voice.

"Do you not want me to love you, Davin?"

He arches his brow and stares.

I'm getting worried. Did I just make a complete fool of myself?

"Davin?"

His poise seems to return and he smiles.

"It happened the night we slept on your sofa—"

"What? What happened?" Did I miss something? Something important?

His smile widens and lights up his eyes. They're sparkling like jewels.

"I fell in love with you."

My heart flutters and I feel warm all over. "You did?"

He nods slowly. "I did."

"You didn't tell me."

"I wasn't sure how you felt. Love between two angels is a very powerful force. It is…"

"Forever," I say, completing his thought. "Are you afraid I don't understand that? Do you think my human side makes me prone to frivolous fits of infatuation? Because if you do, please allow me to set you straight." I take a long breath and gaze into his eyes. "I am in love with you, there will never be anyone else, and that's all there is to it."

He shakes his head and chuckles.

"What?"

"This is why I love you."

"It is? What is?"

"I believe the term is moxie. You are bold and fearless. You are spunky."

"You love me because I'm spunky?"

"Well, that…and because you are kind, and selfless, and brilliant, and very beautiful?"

"You think I'm all that?"

He loses his voice again and just stares.

"Davin?"

"Come here, my Padawan."

Before I can respond, he laces his fingers through my hair and pulls me tight to his chest. "You are the most extraordinary angel ever born and I…I am the most fortunate."

He kisses the top of my head, as he whispers, "Forever and never ending."

His words and his touch make me shudder with ecstasy. "Kiss me, Davin. Kiss me like your life depends on it."

"It does," he says, as he captures my upper lip softly between his teeth.

Our kiss deepens and I smile inside, because I realize that each kiss we share seems to be better than the ones before, and we have eons of time and kisses to look forward to.

"We should get some sleep," he says, as he slowly pulls away. "It's been a long and difficult day and we have much to do tomorrow."

I nod and smile. "True. But I'm really liking how this day is ending. Shall we go to bed, Darling?"

"Yes, but remember…we need to be careful."

"We do?"

"No kisses like this, or we could go missing for a very long time."

I want to go missing. I would love nothing more than to go missing with Davin. But there are things to do. People to see. Responsibilities, obligations and…

"I will be strong," I say with a crooked smile. "But only because I don't want my mom to torture you."

"Go ahead and use the bathroom first. I have some data to review," Davin says, staring at the information screen embedded in his desktop.

"Okay. I won't be long."

I close the bathroom door, grab my toothbrush, and stand in front of the mirror.

"You look awful," I say to the haggard-looking creature staring back at me. She looks like she's had a very, very hard day. "Things can only get better," I tell her. She looks at me like I'm crazy. I sigh. "Go to bed," she tells me.

Davin is still sitting at his desk, reading. "The bathroom is all yours," I say.

"Thanks," he replies, as he shuts down the computer and walks into the bathroom, leaving me alone in his bedroom.

I pull back the cover and slide onto the luxurious silk-like sheet underneath. The bed is really comfortable, and it really belongs to my boyfriend. No, *boyfriend* is not the right word. He's my angel, my comfort, my strength. He's the most important person in my world.

"You are not sleeping, yet you appear to be dreaming."

His voice startles me. "I was. It was a good dream." I pat the space next to me. "Get in."

He lies down beside me. "What did you dream about?"

"Us. I dreamt about us and whether you sleep with your shirt on or not."

He just stares at me. Then he shakes his head slowly and smiles. "Maybe I should wear a long flannel nightie," he teases.

"I want you to be comfortable. Sit up," I say.

I rise to my knees, reach under the hem of his shirt, and gently lift it over his head, letting my fingers brush lightly over his bare skin. I reach down and tap his hip, allowing my hand to linger. "Do you normally sleep in your shorts?" I ask. "You needn't be shy."

"These are my sleeping shorts. There is nothing underneath them except me."

"Got it. In that case, we can leave them on. Are you comfortable now?"

"I'm never uncomfortable when I'm with you. But you look exhausted. Lie down and put your head on my incredibly soft pillow. I promise you'll get the best night's sleep you've ever had."

"That sounds delicious," I say, as I lay my head on the pillow. "I love this pillow."

Davin lays down beside me, and we turn to face each other. "You were remarkably brave tonight," he says.

"I really didn't have a choice."

"You are wrong. We always have a choice. And the choices we make define who we are."

"Who am I, then?" I ask, with a smirk.

"You don't know?"

"Hmm. I'm your angel. And since you chose me, I must help to define you."

"Good. And since you chose me, we must help to define each other. Descartes would cower in our presence."

"I would have found him boring," I remark.

"He was boring. Very boring. And he never bathed."

"Eww."

I lean over and gaze into Davin's eyes. "The cat's out of the bag, Warrior. We're stuck with each other now. You know that, don't you?"

"I do," he says.

"Forever and always," I say softly.

His eyes widen momentarily, and he gently tucks some loose hairs behind my ear. Our closeness seems so perfectly natural. This is where I belong. Beside him. Always.

As I begin to drift off, he whispers in my ear. "Never ending."

I purr contentedly as he wraps me in a tender embrace.

Chapter 19

I awake to the gentle rays of a virtual sunrise and the rhythmic beat of Davin's heart, as I lay with my head on his chest.

He loves me. He really loves me.

I run my fingers across his abdomen, trying to tickle him awake. He trembles, as a soft moan escapes his lips.

"Mmm, this is a wonderful way to wake up," he says.

"Almost perfect," I whisper.

"Almost?"

"The me-and-you part is perfect, more than perfect," I say, as I make little circles on his chest with my finger. "But I'm worried about Ella."

"Of course you are. I am, too. Thalia is expecting us at noon. We should eat something before we go."

Right on cue, my stomach rumbles, making Davin chuckle. "I want pancakes and bacon," I say, patting my belly.

"Your wish is my command. But I would like an appetizer."

"An appetizer?"

"Yes."

Slowly and softly, his lips glide down my neck, stopping only when they reach the lace top of my cami. Little sounds escape my throat. Sounds I never imagined I could make.

"Delicious," he whispers, into my chest.

Unfair. Totally unfair.

"Better than torik?" I ask.

"Much better. More delicate. So tender."

"Feel free to have a second helping," I say, breathlessly, as my heart threatens to leave my body.

"I would, but then we might not leave this room for a very long time," he teases.

"You're bad."

"The good bad or the 'bad' bad?"

"Both," I say, rolling my eyes.

We shower *separately*, eat, and are out the door by 11:45.

Davin's house opens into a small courtyard. On the left is an elevator that leads to the surface. On the right, a clear door, behind which is parked Davin's personal vehicle, which puts his Carrera to shame. Thalia's house is within walking distance, but Davin always rides to meetings—just in case something comes up that requires him to travel. He likes to be prepared.

We hop inside, and Davin punches in our destination—Thalia's house. The transport hums as it levitates several inches above the ground, suspended by a magnetic field.

We accelerate smoothly, under the control of Portal City's transportation network, and arrive at Thalia's in less than a minute. Davin's transport pulls off the main line and parks itself in a guest area.

I feel anxious as we walk toward the door. Ella is strong. But what she endured last night is beyond tragic. I steel myself and pray for the best.

Davin waves his hand across the door panel, and the scanner flashes blue. Several seconds pass, and then the door slides open.

Ella is standing there. I've never seen her look so lost.

"Ella," I say, as my eyes fill with tears. Reaching for each other at the same time, we meet in a fierce hug, and we sob.

"She's gone, Ari," she whispers in my ear.

"I know," I say.

She steps back and looks me in the eye. "She died a hero. She stepped in front of Cindy Greenwood. She shielded her."

I didn't know that, but I'm not surprised. Maggie always put others before herself. "Oh, Ella..."

"It hurts. I'm going to miss her so much."

"So am I, honey. So am I," I say, as the tears begin to flow again.

Davin steps beside me and puts his arm around Ella's shoulder. "If there is anything you need, anything at all," he says, as he gently leads her inside the house.

"Thank you, Davin," she replies, with a sniffle.

I'm no more than three feet into the house when Tal sweeps me up into a bear hug. "I thought I lost her. Thank you for saving her."

Tal releases me, and we stand, facing each other. "We both almost lost her," I say in a soft voice. "Have you two talked?" I ask, loud enough for everyone to hear.

Ella answers. "I know everything. I know I just spent the night on another planet. I know that you healed me. And I know that you changed me."

She doesn't look angry. She looks...resigned.

"How do you feel about that?" I ask.

She runs her fingers through her hair and gazes up at the virtual skylight. "I'm having a hard time focusing on things right now. I don't know. I need some time."

"Of course. Take all the time you need. I'll be here for you. Always."

"I know, sweetie. I just wish Mom were here to see all of this," she says with a tremble.

I don't know how to respond, so I hug her tightly. "I love you, Ella. I always will."

Thalia and Mom emerge from the kitchen and greet us. "Please come and sit with us in the kitchen," Thalia says.

Thalia's kitchen is much larger and more formal than Davin's. The table is huge, and being an Olympian kitchen, there are no appliances. It looks more like a conference room.

"Well," Thalia says. "We have a lot to discuss."

Ella comes up beside me and kisses my cheek. "I'm going out for a while. I'll see you soon."

"Where are you going, honey?" I ask.

"Tal and I need to talk. We'll be back before you leave."

I nod and stand, facing Ella. "I'll be here if you need me," I say, as I grasp her hand.

"I know, sweetie," she says as she takes Tal's arm.

"I'll see you later," I say, as Ella and Tal walk outside.

The door slides closed and Thalia sighs. "Ella is not happy with Tal, and the fact that he did not confide in her."

"She's probably not so happy with me, either," I say.

Mom reaches over and squeezes my hand. "She'll be alright. She'll understand. We're family now."

Ella's grandparents are gone. She has no close relatives left. And she's still seventeen.

"She'll be a minor until July," I say to Mom. "Won't social services…"

"Maggie designated me as Ella's guardian in her will. I called Mr. Jarvis this morning. He will file the necessary court papers on Monday, and I will be her legal guardian until she turns eighteen."

"How could I even doubt for a moment that you wouldn't be two steps ahead of any potential problem?"

"You doubted me?" Mom asks, smiling.

"Not really. What about the funeral?"

"Thalia and I will take care of the details tomorrow. I've made preliminary arrangements with a funeral home."

Thalia clears her throat. "We are all part of the same family now. I wish we could take Ella's pain away. But she is strong. She'll get through it."

Mom and I nod. Ella is one of the strongest people I know. She will get through this.

Thalia puts on her business face. "I've arranged for a team to take down Bodden's Zon organization. They will study the intelligence reports and decide on a schedule. It seems they run a rather large prostitution operation in Charlottesville—featuring high school girls." She grimaces. "Apparently they were recruiting in Edgewood and decided to have a little *fun*. The mission should be interesting because the brothel's patrons include a United States senator and two congressmen. I'll keep you posted."

"Thanks," I say, "but I have other priorities right now, such as how my mom and Ella were changed. It almost seems miraculous."

Thalia sits up straight. "Perhaps, in a way, they were miracles, Ari."

"I've learned much from you, Thalia. I've learned that all beings, including angels, are subject to natural law. Is there something you have failed to tell me?"

"The fact that life exists…" She reaches across the table and squeezes my hand. "The fact that *we* exist is pretty miraculous. Don't you think?"

I remember many evenings, sitting by the lake behind my house, gazing at the stars, and wondering where it all came from. How was the universe really formed? How could reality have become…real? How remarkable is it that I can even ponder such things? "Now that you put it that way…"

"There is no limit to what is genetically possible. There is still so much we don't know," Thalia says with pursed lips.

"We don't know how my mom and I came to be angels. Do you really have a theory?"

Thalia locks eyes with me. "I do."

I watch intently as Thalia taps her data panel. A holographic image of a man slowly forms over the table.

It's my dad, and somehow I am not surprised. Not in the least.

"That's my dad."

Mom doesn't look surprised, either. She and Thalia must have discussed this yesterday.

"Where did you get the image?" I ask Thalia.

"It is nearly one million years old. Your father is being honored. The occasion was a ceremony marking the defeat of the Zon and the formation of the Olympian Governing Council. He was known as Damas—which means father in the ancient dialects. His given name is actually Damian, a fact that is not widely known on Olympus today. He was the Elder leader."

"My dad was the leader of the Elders?"

"Yes, dear," Thalia says.

"Why? Why did he keep this from us?" I ask.

Thalia gives me a helpless look and shrugs.

"Never mind, I'm just thinking out loud."

"Ari...?"

"Yes, Mom?"

"He's alive."

I gasp and suddenly feel a little lightheaded. "My God," I whisper.

"There is something else," Thalia says. "This morning, I discovered an obscure reference indicating a daughter."

"In addition to me?" I ask.

"Yes."

"And you know who she is?" Mom asks.

"Her name is Solana. She is a brilliant scientist and a dear friend of Davin's and mine. Up until last night, it was assumed she was orphaned during the rebellion."

"So my husband was previously married?"

Thalia nods. "Unfortunately, Damian's Promise, Calana, was one of several Elders who rebelled against Paradise. She feared being stuck on Olympus—tending to the needs of mortals."

"What happened to her?" I ask.

"She..." Thalia pauses and looks me square in the eye. "She attacked Solana. Your father killed her in order to save his daughter."

Mom gasps.

"He had no choice, Andi."

"My God," Mom says. "I can't begin to imagine the anguish he must have felt. All those years..."

"Quite," Thalia remarks.

"How did you find out about Solana?" I ask.

"She is mentioned by name in a social missive between Damian and another Elder, written many years later. It was an informal communiqué, which are not normally catalogued. I was very fortunate to have discovered it. The other elder's name is Euclid, who is your sister's father of record. Her adoptive father."

"Wow," I mutter. "You're sure of this?"

"The evidence is compelling."

"We have to find her, Thalia. Do you know where she is?" I ask.

"She is on holiday for the next three weeks. I will arrange a meeting as soon as she returns to Portal City."

"I cannot wait to hear what she has to say about this," Davin comments, with a stern gaze.

"It should be interesting, "Thalia says. "But do keep in mind that Solana might not know the truth. She was, after all, an infant when her mother was killed."

"I suspect she knows who her father is," Davin says.

"You're probably right," Thalia replies. "But we need to give her the benefit of the doubt."

Deep in thought, Davin nods. I'm not sure if he actually heard what Thalia said.

Mom looks at me, somberly. "You always wanted a sister. I guess you got your wish."

"I envisioned a slightly different scenario."

"So did I," she says, reflectively.

"Back to my dad," I say. If he changed my mom and me, what were his motives?"

"The obvious answer," Thalia asserts, "is that he was motivated by his love for you."

"But he left us," I retort.

"He did. But we don't know why. Perhaps it was necessary," Thalia replies.

"Perhaps it has something to do with the prophecy Galen described," Davin says. "There has to be a logical explanation."

"And what do we do if the explanation defies logic?" I ask. "I mean, the whole notion of a prophecy, that I'm the most powerful angel ever born, is way out there…beyond logic. Thalia thinks I might be destined to save the human race from the Fallen. Right, Thalia?"

"Yes, I do think that is a possible explanation for your existence. But we each must keep an open mind. The pieces will fall into place," Thalia says.

"For what it's worth," Mom interjects, "Albert Einstein once said, 'Logic will get you from A to B. Imagination will take you everywhere.' I think we need to be prepared for the unexpected. Nothing is off the table, as far as I'm concerned."

Thalia grins. "Albert was such a remarkable man. And such an amazing sense of humor!"

"*Albert?*" I ask, rolling my eyes.

Thalia shrugs her shoulders. "We were very good friends."

Mom just shakes her head.

"Can we find my husband using the DNA sample I gave you, Thalia?" Mom asks.

"Yes…" Thalia says.

"Wait. You had a sample of Dad's DNA?"

"I kept a few locks of his hair, honey."

I wonder what other interesting things she's been squirrelling away.

Davin looks at Thalia. "Have you done a long-range DNA scan?"

"Yes," Thalia replies.

Mom looks at Davin. "We can track him from his DNA?"

"Yes, Dr. Worthington. It would still require a significant investment in time—but armed with a DNA scanner, the mission becomes quite viable. Unless, of course, he is not on Olympus. Our scanners do not reach Paradise."

"Thank you, Davin," Mom says. "And please, call me Andi."

She really does like him.

"He is here," Thalia states. "I've already done a planet-wide scan. He is somewhere in the Northern Outlands. That's where we will begin the search."

"So you know where he is?" I ask.

Davin answers me. "A planet-wide search does not yield precise coordinates. We can detect his trace, but it is more like picking up a scent as it blows with the wind. We need to get closer in order to find him."

I nod. "That makes sense."

"Who will go on this mission?" Mom asks.

212

"The logical team would be Davin and Ari," Thalia says.

Mom looks annoyed. "I should go. He's my husband."

Thalia's expression is sympathetic and understanding. "While I'm sure that the mission will be perfectly safe, there is always a risk that something might go wrong. Ari has undergone rigorous training and would be better able to defend herself if the need arose. She and Davin make a formidable team. There is also the Governing Council, and certain protocols that even I must follow. I'm afraid I could not justify sending you on a mission until you have been trained."

"I see," Mom says. But she looks disappointed.

"Ari will be safe," Davin says, looking and sounding totally confident.

"It really will be a safe mission, Andi," Thalia adds.

"So when do we go?" I ask. I'm excited. A mission to find Dad. A mission with Davin. And we'll get to fly all over Olympus.

"In several weeks," Thalia says.

I'm a little deflated. "Why so long?" I ask.

"You need to take exams and graduate. If you don't, the human authorities will want to know why."

"I'm really not happy about going back to school. It seems so anticlimactic."

Thalia smiles. "I've taken care of that. I had the president of the Institute contact your principal in Edgewood. He has agreed to allow Ella and you to take your finals at the Institute. You will still need to attend graduation, though."

"Thanks." I guess that won't be too bad.

"We also need to put you through a little more training. And there is the matter of your celebration," Thalia adds.

"Celebration?"

"Everyone wants to meet you. It'll be like an old-fashioned formal ball on Earth. You'll love it," Davin says.

"A party for me?" I ask, in a small voice. "Who will be there? How many—"

"Don't worry, dear," Thalia says. "There will be no more than two thousand people attending." She is grinning from ear to ear. "And it will be beamed to every entertainment device on Olympus!"

"Holy shit," I mutter.

Mom glares at me. She has a thing about cussing.

I glare back as several more highly colorful words try really hard to escape my lips.

Davin and Thalia are seriously laughing, which must be contagious, because Mom stops scowling and joins the party.

"I'm glad everyone finds this so amusing. Maybe you'd like to hear some more cuss words, because I know some really good ones. Two thousand people? Really?"

"Ari, it will be grand," Thalia says, wiping tears from her eyes. "And a great honor. We will have fun designing a gown for you and picking out flowers. And I will even give you dance lessons." She is beaming.

"It does sound like fun," Mom says.

"It sounds pretentious. Like I'm God's gift to the world. Ya know?"

"But you are God's gift to us," Thalia says, with a sly grin.

Mom chuckles and gives me a *gotcha* look.

I shoot her a we'll-discuss-this-later look.

Thalia puts on a serious expression. "Davin and I can't keep you from the Council forever. They need to meet you."

"Why have you kept me away from them? Will they be hostile?"

"No. They will, however, be extremely curious. We wanted to make sure that you were fully trained before you met them. They will be captivated by you. There is nothing to fear."

"Alright. If you say so."

"There is nothing to worry about. Now, would you like to know about your father's DNA?"

"Yes. Of course."

"He seems to be an amalgam of Serafeím, Warrior, and something else—perhaps Prostáti; perhaps something entirely new."

"Am I like my dad?"

"The best way I can describe it, at least for now, is that you are an improved version of your dad. A significant improvement. You do share one very unique ability, though."

"And what is that?"

"You both changed a mortal into an angel."

"You think he changed my mom?"

"Yes. And I believe he changed her before you were conceived. And that implies—"

"It implies that Ari was born an angel," Mom says.

"It also means you stopped aging before I was conceived," I say, "which implies…"

Mom gasps. "I stopped aging nearly twenty years ago."

"Exactly," I say with a big smile. "So we need to get you a more youthful wardrobe."

Mom looks a bit shocked. "I need a little time to digest this. My wardrobe is the least of my concerns right now. Though I did have my eye on a cute little black dress…"

Thalia and I both chuckle, while Davin looks totally confused.

"So, my dad and I share an ability to turn mortals into angels. I assume this is without precedent?"

"It is," Thalia says."

"Geez. What about Solana?" I ask. "How is she classified?"

"She is classified as Serafeím. But now I am not so sure."

215

"What do you mean?" I ask.

"Your sister is in charge of our central DNA laboratory."

"She could be hiding what she is?"

Thalia purses her lips and nods. "Perhaps when we are able to question your father, we will be able to determine exactly what you are. What you all are. For now, all I know for sure is that you are a first edition."

"A collector's item, eh? You wanna have me stuffed and mounted? I'd look great hanging on your wall."

Thalia frowns. "That is disturbing. I care for you very much, Ari. It is true that we don't know what you are. But we do know *who* you are—a wonderful person who is loved and admired by everyone sitting around this table."

"I'm sorry. I overreacted. I know you're all trying to help me. It's just that it gets a little overwhelming sometimes."

"Apology accepted," Thalia replies. "Now, do you remember our discussions about amplification clusters?"

"Yes. They are like armies of little cellular robots. They store the Essence. They help us to heal, and they are responsible for our strength and powers."

Thalia nods. "What's going on inside you is extraordinary. For example, projecting energy is very difficult and usually takes many decades of study. What you did on Friday is unprecedented, given the circumstances."

"I almost barbecued Davin." I wince at the memory, which is still fresh in my mind. "So how was I able to do it without decades of training?"

"I'm not sure. But it's got something to do with the special clusters your mom discovered. Essentially, they are organic capacitors—able to store large amounts of energy—much more than an amplification cluster can. You are like a perpetually-armed particle beam weapon."

That sounds really dangerous and unstable. "Can I blow up?"

Thalia smiles. "You cannot blow yourself up. Davin will teach you to control it."

216

"When do we start?"

"Monday. And there is something else."

Oh great. "What?"

"Since we do not understand the extent of your abilities, additional training will be difficult...unless we can find someone who understands what you are capable of."

"I guess an ad on Craigslist won't do it, huh?"

Thalia smiles. "Your father, Ari. We need to find him."

Ella and Tal arrive back at Thalia's in time for dinner, looking much happier than they did before they left. Thalia briefs them, and then we discuss our plans for the immediate future.

Mom, Ella, and I are official Olympian citizens now. As Sages, Mom and Ella will be personally tutored by Thalia and her staff—and will live in Thalia's house while they train.

I'll continue to live at Davin's.

Mom will be resigning her position at Edgewood Memorial. They'll be sorry to see her leave—but will surely understand that a research fellowship at Bryce Institute is an offer she simply cannot refuse.

In the fall, Ella and I will attend classes at the Warrior College, as we slowly disappear from the human grid. We'll never achieve the career goals we've dreamt about, but it doesn't really matter. We'll be able to achieve so much more.

The Olympian Governing Council will assign someone to manage our properties in Edgewood. Ella's house will be sold as soon as she turns eighteen. Mom doesn't want to dispose of our house until she speaks to Dad. They fell in love in that house, and she has every right to be sentimental about it.

As angels, we'll have access to as much money as we need. We'll be fixed for life. A very long and happy one. I hope.

It all seems like a dream. But it's real. And Davin is real. And Mom, and Ella, and I are together. And Dad is alive. And when it comes right down to it, things are not looking too bad at all.

Chapter 20

"It's good to be home," I say as Davin and I enter his house.

My words surprise me. Is this really my home? Yeah, it is. It really is. Just to prove I'm home, I kick off my shoes.

Davin casts me a sideways glance. "You will domesticate me yet."

I wrap my arms around his neck and bury my head in his chest. "Never. I love your wild side."

"You haven't really seen my wild side yet. I can be quite feral."

He has mischief in his eyes, and he's flexing his fingers. I'm in trouble. "What are you going to do?"

"I'm not entirely sure," he says, with a sinister chuckle.

The anticipation of being tickled is worse than being tickled. I know this to be true. And Davin does, too. He's going to tickle me, and so I pray that my dinner remains in my stomach until it is properly and completely digested.

The problem is simple. I am utterly defenseless against these attacks. It has nothing to do with strength, agility, or balance. You cannot fight when you are giggling. You can't.

"You're so easy," he says as he gently lowers me to the floor and captures my foot. "I am merely looking at your toes, and you are already convulsing."

"Not fair!" I shout.

"Your Achilles heel," he says, as he slowly draws his finger along the bottom of my foot, from my toes to my heel.

"If you don't stop, I might have an accident. And you can clean it up."

"We need to conquer your weakness. If our enemies should discover that you are so ticklish, you will be in great danger."

"You know I'm not ticklish when I'm fighting. Stop it or I'll…"

"You would hurt me, Ari?" he asks, as he begins to kiss the parts of my foot he just tortured."

A moan escapes my lips. "That feels…"

Heavenly.

I spin out of his grip and roll on top of him. "I'm going to kiss you until your toes curl." I stare at him, my lips millimeters from his.

"But then I won't be able to walk."

"And then you cannot escape. You don't want to escape, do you Davin?"

"There is no escape for me. There can never be…"

He surrenders to my kiss and, for a few blissful moments, we are symbiotic organisms, joined at the lips.

"That was intense," I say, breathlessly, as I roll off to the side. "One of these days, I'm not going to be able to stop."

He smiles at me. "I know."

We both know. But he respects my decision to wait. Being in love is new to me. I need time to adjust, to become comfortable with my feelings.

"Would you like a glass of wine?"

"Sure. Something sweet?"

"Certainly," Davin replies.

Davin selects a tawny port and we sit on the sofa, sipping and talking.

"You're really not happy about your celebration?" he asks.

"Oh, it was just a shock. I'll get used to the idea. And I can't disappoint Mom, Ella, and Thalia."

"No. That would be bad."

"I think it would be very bad."

"And you wouldn't want to disappoint *me*, would you?" he asks.

"How would I do that? I didn't think you were the partying type."

"The celebration is not just a party. It is a political function. You will get to meet each of the Governing Councilors. It's important that they get to know you."

"I hate politics, Davin."

"It's not all about politics. You will meet some very nice angels."

"Yes. But I'll be a curiosity. I'll feel like I'm being studied."

"You're wrong. You will be a magnet. Everyone will want to meet you, and everyone will love you, in a manner of speaking, of course."

"Of course. I hope you're right."

He smiles reassuringly. "By the way, as an Olympian citizen, you now have your own personal account. And you will be given a transport, as well as your own residence."

My own residence? The thought makes me shudder.

"But I'm comfortable here. I don't have to move out, do I?"

Davin smiles warmly. "No. I want you to stay with me, Ari. It would make me very happy if your residence remained vacant."

"So you're officially asking me to live with you?"

"I want you to stay with me because I need to know you are safe." He rubs his temples briskly. I'm afraid he might rub his hair off. "I have also grown very fond of our living arrangement."

"And I want to stay with you because we love each other. I'm not leaving unless you kick me out. Are you going to kick me out, Davin?"

"Of course not—"

"Then it's official. We are living together. As a couple."

He chuckles. "If you were human, I would urge you to go to law school. You are incredibly good at making a point."

"Thank you. I was the star of my school's debate team."

He stares at me for a moment. "You must have been a frightening opponent."

"Terrifying," I answer, with a crooked smile.

Davin's expression suddenly changes, as if a switch was flipped. He looks distracted. Something is on his mind.

"Is there anything wrong, Davin?"

"I was thinking about your sister…"

"Go on," I urge, because he seems to be stuck.

He's rubbing his temples again. Not a good sign. "She is very close to Reyna—"

"Your almost-fiancé?" I have no idea why, but I feel a pang of jealousy. Just a small one.

"Yes. They are best friends."

"Why is this an issue?"

"Reyna has been behaving strangely of late."

"I thought the two of you agreed to break up. Why would…" I pause. "Does this have something to do with you and me?"

He averts his eyes. "I'm not sure, but the timing would seem to indicate a connection."

"Is she jealous? Does she want you back?"

"I'm not sure."

"Did you break off the relationship, or did she?"

"I did."

"And she was not happy with that. Right?"

"She took it badly. She was mortified. She wanted everyone to think our breakup was mutually agreed upon. I played along."

"How long has it been since the breakup?"

"A long time. A few hundred years."

"Well, that's a pretty long time, even by angel standards. She has to be over you by now."

"I thought she was. Up until a few months ago, our relationship was civil."

"When you say she acts strangely, what exactly do you mean?"

"I really don't think you want to know."

"Davin…" I'm not going to give in.

"Ari, I really—"

I narrow my eyes and scowl at him. "Spill it, Davin."

He studies me for a moment. "She throws herself at me."

I'm not getting a very good visual. "She throws herself at you? What does that mean?"

"Well, it means that if you were there when she did it, you would probably want to hurt her."

Oh geez, this is not good. "And how does Solana feel about all this?"

"She is neutral. She cares for Reyna, but she also understands that her behavior is not acceptable."

"By *unacceptable*, do you mean that she is delusional, unstable, and possibly dangerous?"

Davin looks queasy. "I think that covers it."

"She sounds lovely. I just don't understand why she would go weird after all these years. I'm not the only girlfriend you've had since Reyna and you broke up. Right?"

"No. Of course not. Ari, I just wanted you to be prepared. Reyna and Lana are inseparable."

"*Lana?*"

"Solana's friends call her Lana."

My eyes widen. It can't be. "Can I see a picture of her?"

"Sure," he says, as he taps an info panel.

An image of a woman appears on the screen.

"Oh, my God…"

"What is it?" Davin asks, looking concerned.

"The hair is different. But her face…" I pause, unable to process what I see.

"What about her face?" Davin asks.

"I know her. She was my nanny!"

"Your nanny?"

"Yes. When Mom was doing her residency, Dad hired a nanny to take care of me. She lived with us from the time I was born until Dad left."

"The plot thickens."

"It sure as hell does. Is she a good person, Davin?"

"She is a wonderful person and a good friend. Was she a good nanny?"

"Yes. I loved her dearly."

"I'm sure there is a logical…"

"I'm sure, too. I just wish this were a book so I could skip ahead a few chapters. You know?"

"That would be convenient. But I'm afraid we will have to wait until we can talk with her. And we will do that."

"Can we conference with her tonight?"

"She is on holiday for the next few weeks. I think we should wait until she returns to Portal City."

"Okay," I say with a hint of disappointment. "Do you think I should tell my mom?"

"I don't see what harm it would do at this point. But I would not mention what I told you about Reyna. That would probably worry her."

"Agreed."

"Ari...?"

"Yes?"

"I'm sorry I didn't tell you everything about Reyna before."

"There is nothing for you to be sorry about," I reply.

"I'm glad you're not angry with me."

"If you ever make me angry, you will totally know it. Now let's forget about Reyna and go to bed. Okay?"

Sleep eludes me. I'm unable to stop thinking about Lana and Reyna. When I finally expel Lana from my thoughts, Reyna creeps in. Why is she acting strangely?

I lean over to face Davin and loop a leg across his thighs. "Hey. You awake?"

"Hmm, I think so. What's up?" he asks, groggily.

"I was thinking."

He looks down at my leg and smiles. "About me? I really like it when you do that with your leg."

I laugh. "You are an incorrigible smart-ass, Davin."

He sighs. "I think it comes naturally. Now tell me what you were thinking about."

"I was thinking about Reyna."

"In what context?"

"Is she on a mission to sabotage our relationship? And if so, why?"

"I'm really not sure what her motives are. But I am sure that nothing could ever come between us. Reyna's behavior defies logic. She is not a bad person. I've asked both Lana and Seto for their opinions, but they are at a loss."

"Seto?"

"Yes. He and Reyna have been in a relationship for quite some time."

I'm a little surprised. Seto is my agility instructor. And a really sweet guy.

"Something is going on, Davin. I'm not sure what it is, but it can't be good."

"I don't doubt that. Do you have a theory?"

"It's not really a theory. It's more like intuition."

Although I haven't really thought things through, it feels as if I'm on the right track.

"Ari?"

"Sorry," I say. "I was thinking that my dad was the only Elder to have more than one child. Was I really a gift? Or did he break a few rules? Do you see where I'm going with this?"

He nods. "Tell me more."

"Okay. If I'm a gift, there might be fallen angels somewhere who might want me out of the way. They could perceive me as a threat, a weapon. And there could be others, like Galen, who want to control me. But if I am the result of a forbidden union, then I could be perceived as a weapon for evil, a disruptive force. I could threaten the balance of things. Make sense?"

Davin stares at me for several moments. Clearly, he's digesting and processing what I've said.

"Fascinating. You have suggested two plausible scenarios. I was considering Reyna's actions from a behavioral perspective only. I had not considered it in conspiratorial terms."

"So what do we do?"

"We continue to protect you, and we wait for the answer to come to us. And it will come to us—one way or another."

"Shouldn't we question her?"

"No. We are blind. We could stir things up that we are unprepared to deal with. Knowing that Reyna could be part of a conspiracy gives us an advantage. We have to wait. Of course, that does not mean we cannot have her monitored," he says, with a smile. "And Lana might be able to help us," he adds.

"Do you think I could be evil?"

"Of course not. This is why we must proceed with your celebration. Once everyone meets you, they will know you are not evil."

"How will they know?"

"Because you smell so nice."

I laugh out loud. "That's very scientific."

"Well, there is your charming personality, too."

"That's better. Anything else?"

"Your amazing beauty."

"Is that all?"

He leans closer to me, and I can feel the warmth of his breath. "Because I'm in love with you, and I'm known for my impeccable taste in women."

"Shut up," I say, as my fingers walk slowly from his navel to his chest.

He opens his mouth to respond. "Shh," I whisper, as my lips find his.

I kiss him as if I'm dying of thirst and he's a cool mountain stream. The problem is, I want to dive into the stream and swim around for a few hours.

"Thank you, Davin," I say, as I lean back onto the pillow.

He casts me a questioning look. "Hmm?"

"Thank you for being my strength. For being my inspiration. For believing in me. For respecting me. For loving me."

He smiles. "You make it very easy."

"I'm glad I do," I say, through a big yawn.

"You look very tired. We should get some sleep."

"Good idea. I love you," I whisper.

"And I love you," he says, as he plants a sweet kiss on my lips.

Davin rolls over, and I wiggle my body into his. We fit together like a living, breathing puzzle. I smile contentedly as sleep wraps me in a warm and happy embrace.

I'm home.

Chapter 21

"Something is happening, Davin!"

Davin is trying to teach me how to project energy. We've been at it for ten days, and it hasn't gone very well. But today I feel close to a breakthrough. I'm not sure why, but I just feel it. In my bones.

"Can you feel the Essence pooling?" Davin asks.

"Yeah."

It's as if a bubble has formed in my chest. I concentrate on it, trying to move it out of the way, so I can breathe. It moves toward my shoulder, but now it's stuck. It's pulsing, and beginning to hurt. I focus harder.

Still stuck. No, it's inflating, getting larger. And it's moving down my arm.

"It's moving. I'm moving it!"

"It feels like flexing a muscle, right?" Davin asks.

"Yes!"

Stepping clear of Davin, I point my hand, fingers outstretched, toward the first target—a stone obelisk, fifty meters away.

Snap, crackle, **BAM**! The obelisk explodes, disintegrating in a mist of fine powder.

"Holy crap! The target is gone," I say, hardly believing my eyes.

Davin comes up behind me, wraps his arms around my waist, and whispers in my ear, "That was extremely sexy. If you do it again, I will need a cold shower. Can you do it again?"

"I think so."

I hope so.

"Do it," he says softly, stepping away from me. "But this time, release the energy gradually. We want a steady stream, rather than a projectile."

"Okay. I'll try."

The remaining target is a solid metal cube made of an Olympian alloy similar to titanium. I point my hand at the target and concentrate on moving the bubble down my arm. But this time I flex gradually. A steady stream of white energy shoots from my fingers hitting the target dead-center. Counting the seconds, I watch, transfixed, as the cube begins to change shape. It's melting.

"Try to hold it, Ari," Davin calls out.

Beads of sweat drip down my head and into my eyes as I hold the beam. I'm still counting. Thirty seconds.

I am almost spent.

Five seconds more.

I'm out of juice.

Davin stares at the spot where the cube was and lets out a whoop, because all that remains is a puddle of molten metal. I let out a breath and crouch. My legs are feeling a bit wobbly.

"How'd I do?"

"You are a weapon of mass destruction," Davin says.

He pulls me into his arms, smiling like a proud coach. "I knew you could do it."

"Really?" I ask with a raised brow.

"Really," he says as he kisses my forehead, my eyes, my nose, and my lips.

"Can we take tomorrow off?" I ask.

His lips are pursed. He's thinking. "I think we should practice more. We want this to be second nature."

"Yeah, I guess that makes sense. Practice makes perfect. Especially with finals next week. I'd hate to melt the classroom. Or the proctor."

Davin chuckles. "On second thought, let's take tomorrow off. We can make a day trip to Genobli. A little sightseeing?"

"Your hometown! I would like that, Davin. Maybe Ella and Tal could join us?"

"Sure. Let's call them tonight."

I nod and try to shake the knots out of my arms.

"Are you tired?" Davin asks.

"A little. I was beginning to think I wasn't going to be able to do this. I'm kind of proud of myself."

"You should be. What you've accomplished is truly amazing. I hope you realize that."

"I do now," I say with a big grin. "I couldn't have done it without you."

"I have a feeling that someday soon there will be things you will be teaching me."

I smile. "You're already a great Warrior and a fabulous kisser. What could I ever teach you?"

"You never know."

The following week is considerably less taxing. Ella and I complete our high school graduation requirements, breezing through finals. The last test is in the books by Friday, which means we have a ten-day holiday before training resumes.

We say goodbye to Mr. Elliot, the proctor from Edgewood, and rocket out of the classroom. Davin and Tal are waiting for us outside the building.

"Well, you think you passed?" Davin asks.

"Are you kidding me?" I tease. "It was child's play. So where are we going?"

"You'll see," Tal says, grinning slyly.

"Well, let's hit the road," Ella says. "We're not getting any younger, ya know?"

"We're not getting any older either," I say, unable to suppress a giggle.

"That's a technicality, sweetie. Actually we are getting older, we just..."

"When you two are done philosophizing, we can go," Davin says, shaking his head.

"Sorry," Ella says, smiling innocently. "So where did you say we were going?"

"Shopping," Tal says. "Ari and you need to buy swimsuits."

"We're going swimming?" I ask.

"I would like us to go to Carina—a lovely island in the South Promethean. It's been in my family for a very long time," Davin says. "I thought we could go tomorrow, stay through Thursday night, and have you back in time for graduation next Friday."

Six nights on an island with Davin. Wow. "I would love to." I give him a quizzical look. "Your own island? Really?"

"It's a very small island," he says, smiling.

There are no malls in Portal City, but there are several very nice clothing stores in the shopping district. Our first stop features an amazing swimsuit selection. Ella buys two really cute bikinis. Practical me settles on a bikini and a sleek one-piece. The suits come with coordinating sarong cover ups.

Our next stop is a chic dress boutique, where the guys help us pick out a couple of new dresses, just in case we go out dining and dancing. When it comes to selecting my clothes, Davin is almost as good as Ella, though he's definitely biased toward *sexy*.

We make one last stop and pick up jeans, shorts, footwear, and some really cool accessories.

We're ready for a much-needed vacation.

"Where to now?" Ella asks.

"Let's go to Thalia's so we can tell Mom about our plans," I say.

Thalia's house is empty.

"Where do you think they are?" I ask.

"There is a message on her data screen," Tal says. "They are at Thalia's office."

"Let's call her and see if she'd like to go out for dinner," Ella suggests.

"Good idea," I say. "Where do you think we should go?"

"Does she like Italian food?" Davin asks.

"Ooh, yes. She'll love Umberto's," I say.

Davin took me there once and I was blown away. Eating in a restaurant on another planet is fascinating enough. Eating in an *Italian* restaurant on another planet is downright amazing.

"You'd better call her before she and Thalia decide to go out to a nightclub," Davin says with a little chuckle.

"I'd love to see that, actually," I say, as I take out my communicator.

Mom is excited to spend some time alone with us. A girl's night out. We agree to meet at the restaurant, which is halfway between Thalia's house and Davin's.

"This is the best veal I've ever had," Mom says. "And the fact that a cute little baby cow didn't pay the ultimate price makes it taste even better."

"It is amazing, no doubt. But wait until you try the cannoli. They're to die for. Save room for dessert."

"Mmm. I love cannoli," Ella says.

Mom laughs. "Look at us, girls. Eating Italian food on an alien planet!"

"Look at you," Ella says with a big smile.

"What? Is my makeup smeared?"

"You look so beautiful, Doc. You look so young."

Mom is wearing a little black dress and she looks stunning. We could pass for sisters.

"You really do look gorgeous, Mom," I say.

"I told you I used to work hard at looking older," she says with a big smile that makes her eyes sparkle. "I'm so happy to not have to worry anymore. I'm so happy to be here with you. Both of you. Do you ever feel like we're in a fairytale?"

"We kind of are," I say, smiling. "And I'm beginning to think it'll have a happy ending."

"I hope so," she says with a sigh.

I'm sure Mom's idea of a happy ending is contingent on finding Dad. And Davin and I *will* find him—even if we have to search every square inch of this world.

I squeeze her hand. "Everything will work out. I know it will."

"I have a feeling it will," Mom says. "Thalia is confident that we'll locate Dad. I just can't get him out of my mind."

This is my opening. Mom and Ella need to know about Lana. I've put off telling them long enough. "Davin and I were talking about my sister."

"Solana?" Mom asks.

"Yes. It seems her friends call her Lana." I pause, allowing Mom and Ella an opportunity to make the connection.

Mom looks puzzled for a moment and then her nose wrinkles. Her mind is in overdrive. "*Lana?* You don't think she could be...?"

"Davin showed me a picture. It's her, Mom."

"Our Lana?" Ella gasps. "From Edgewood? Your nanny?"

"One and the same."

"Oh. My. God," Mom mutters. "It makes perfect sense. Who better to watch over you?"

"Yeah. So, the orphaned angel-angle is out of play. She knows who her real daddy is. And that means she will..."

"She will know where he is," Ella finishes.

"Precisely," Mom adds, with a cautious smile. "This is very good news."

"It is," I agree. "Davin says that Lana is very trustworthy. Just promise me you won't get too anxious. I didn't want to keep this from you, but I also don't want you to be consumed with worry. Okay?"

"I'll be fine, sweetheart. I've waited a long time for answers. I can handle it."

I smile at her. If anyone can handle it, Mom can.

She smiles back and gives me a thumbs up. "Have you been training hard, honey?"

"Oh yeah. But it's paying off. I've gained a lot of control with my energy projection."

"Thalia thinks that Ella and I can project energy. Once we complete Sage basics, she wants to merge our training with yours."

"That's wonderful, Mom!"

"It is. So do you have plans for this week, now that finals are over?"

"In fact, we do. But I wanted to run it by you first."

"I'm all ears," she says.

"Davin wants to take Ella, Tal, and me to his island for the week. He'll have us back in plenty of time for graduation. What do you think?"

She stares at me for a moment with pursed lips. "*His* island?"

"Yeah, it's a small island."

She shakes her head slowly and smiles. "Do you want to go?"

Ella and I nod.

"And if I told you that you should not go, would you *not go*?"

"I don't think you would do that, Mom. I think you would lay out reasons for us to reflect on, and then we would consider the whole picture."

"Well, that sounds like an excellent idea. Can you think of any reasons why you should not go?"

"No. I really want to go."

"And you want my approval?"

Oh, she is good.

"It's not that I'm seeking your approval, though that would be nice. Basically, I don't want you to think we're being impulsive."

She looks at Ella and me with a knowing smile. "The men you care about have invited you on an island vacation, and you think the fact that you want to go might be impulsive?"

Unconsciously, I begin to rub my temples, really hard, just like Davin does when I confuse or confound him. It makes me smile. "No, I don't think it's impulsive. Well, maybe a little."

"Ari, you and Ella are not human teenagers. Even when you were, you were so much smarter and more mature than your classmates. But now you are angels." She chuckles. "And, of course, I'm not a normal mom anymore."

"I'm not sure if any of us were ever really normal. But now we have an excuse," I say, smiling.

Mom laughs heartily. "I trust my girls to make good choices." She pauses for a moment. "Ella, would you happen to know why Ari is blushing. She looks as if she might burst into flames any second."

I make a quick mental note to ask Thalia if it's possible to control blood flow to my cheeks.

"She always blushes. You know that," Ella says, with a dismissive wave of her hand. Then her expression turns serious. She sits up straight and continues, "It hasn't always been easy, Doc, but we've been making good choices. I know you trust us, and we would never do anything to violate that trust. You have my word."

"I know, Ella. Now, I understand the cannoli here are quite good."

"Indeed they are," I say.

As I walk along the path back to Davin's, I turn and watch as Ella and Mom walk toward Thalia's. We are together and somehow I know everything is going to work out.

Chapter 22

When I get home, Davin is sitting in the study, watching a movie. "What are you watching?" I ask.

"*The Questor Tapes.*" He removes his VR glasses and looks up at me.

"Never heard of it."

"It was made long before you were born and has become somewhat of a cult classic here."

"It was made on Earth?"

"Yes. In the 1970s."

"What's it about?"

"In a nutshell, Questor is the last in a line of super-powerful androids, designed by an advanced extraterrestrial race to serve and protect mankind. Each android lives several hundred years, builds a replacement, and then dies. But Questor has a problem. His programming is damaged. He knows he is special, but he doesn't know why. The plot focuses on his adventures as he travels the world in search of his purpose."

"Sounds corny. So, do I remind you of Questor?"

"No. Well, perhaps a little. But you are much prettier, far stronger, considerably faster, and significantly funnier. More importantly, you are the appropriate gender, and you have a more natural body—no wires, gears, or little motors that make whirring sounds. And when you sleep, you—"

"Stop!" I'm laughing so hard I think I might hurl.

He grabs my hand and pulls me onto his lap. "I love it when you laugh." He draws little circles around my mouth with his finger. "Do you know how perfectly beautiful you are?"

"Davin, you are extremely prejudiced, and I am far from perfect. I have pouty lips and small hips. My eyes are too large, and my hair is too thick—"

"Those are all things I happen to love about you—especially the two parts that rhyme."

"Um, lips and hips?"

"Yes, those. I'm glad they rhyme because as far as body parts go, they are remarkably poetic." His eyes are sparkling, and *his* lips are curved into a *very* sensuous smile. "But you also must consider what's in here." He pats my chest. "When you combine your outer shell with what's inside, you are the most beautiful woman I've ever known—on two worlds."

I gaze into his eyes. I want to ravish him.

"Ari, are you alright?" He looks concerned.

I guess it's my un-blinking stare. I must look catatonic.

I shake my head rapidly. "I'm fine. Tell me about Carina. There's a house there, right?"

"There are three structures, actually. A residence for the caretakers, a sanctuary, and a beach house that we will use."

"A *sanctuary*?" I ask.

"It's a kind of shelter. A bunker. A refuge. My parents wanted to make sure the family always had a safe haven in the event of an attack."

"Ah. Kind of like an alien version of *Doomsday Preppers*," I say.

"Yes, In a manner of speaking. So, your mom is okay with our trip?"

"She trusts us."

He wrinkles his brow. "Sages have remarkable powers of perception and intuition. Especially where it concerns those whom they love." He sighs. "I'm glad she trusts us because I really like having you close to me."

His smile is seductive. His eyes are scintillating, smoldering, sparkling, and they seem to be calling to me. Oh boy.

"Davin, you're looking at me as if you're starving and I'm a big, juicy steak."

"I..."

"Shh, it's okay, sweetheart, because right now you look like a big chocolate truffle," I say.

"Chocolate is your favorite."

"I can't get enough of it, if you really want to know."

"Do you want to drive me crazy?"

"I want to make you happy, Davin."

"Ari..."

"I'm not finished," I say, cutting him off. "I'm a fully-evolved angel and I'm in love with you. That's never going to change."

"Ari..."

I hold up my hand, cutting him off again. "There is no reason to wait any longer."

I look into his eyes, hoping he understands how much I love him and how ready I am to show him. Please understand, Davin. Please.

"May I speak now?" he asks, with a playful smirk.

I nod.

"Thank you. I need to get up," he says.

I slide off his lap and stand. "Where are you going?"

"I'll be right back."

He walks to his desk, retrieves something from a drawer, and places it in his pocket.

"What did you get?" I ask, as he stands in front of me.

"I can't show you yet."

"When can you show me?"

"In a moment. I have an important question that you must answer first."

"You do?"

"Yes," he says, as his lips curl into a delicious, dimpled smile.

"How important is it?" I return his smile, not knowing what he's talking about.

"Extremely important." His smile gets wider and he grasps both my hands. What could possibly be so important? Unless...

"Will you commit to be my Promise?"

The words are so uncomplicated; the implications so profound, so life-altering. I gaze into his eyes, as the only possible answer forms on my lips.

"Yes," I say, as my eyes fill with tears. Happy tears.

"These are tears of joy?" he asks, as he brushes his thumb along my cheek.

I smile and nod.

"Davin, I love you so much... so *very* much."

He speaks slowly, clearly, and so very tenderly. "Ariel of Edgewood, Serafeím, Daughter of Damian and Andrea, I commit to be your Promise. Will you be mine?"

There's nothing to think about, nothing to consider, and no misgivings. I know the protocols, and I know exactly how to respond.

"Davin of Genobli, Warrior Master, Son of Lecco and Annia, I commit myself to you. I am yours, you are mine, and so it shall be for all time."

"And now it is done," he says.

"And now we are one," I finish.

His lips curl into a joyful smile. "You knew exactly what to say."

"Thalia has taught me many things about angel culture," I whisper.

"So, you know what comes next?"

"I do."

241

To complete our commitment, we will brand ourselves with an infinity symbol placed just above each of our hearts. It's a beautiful tradition. A magical tradition.

Davin removes the brand from his pocket and hands it to me. It's smooth, black, and roughly the size and shape of a domino. One side is blank and the other glows with a pulsing white light, which makes me smile, because it means that Paradise approves of our commitment.

"You place it, glowing side up, over my heart. When it is straight, the light will stop pulsing. Hold it still until the light turns blue."

Davin removes his shirt. My hand is shaking a little as I place the brand over his heart, turning it slightly. The light stops pulsing, and then it turns blue. A small puff of vapor rises from his chest, along with a slight odor of burning flesh. He doesn't flinch.

I lift my hand away. The mark is small, less than an inch tall, and perfectly formed—a crisp, black infinity symbol.

Davin takes the brand from me and holds it between his fingers. The light begins to pulse white. He gently pulls down the left side of my top to expose the area above my heart. The brand feels warm as he presses it against my skin. I brace for the pain, but there is none. None at all.

I look down at my chest.

"It's beautiful," I say, as the magnitude of our commitment sinks in.

We are bound. Married. We will finalize our commitment within a year at a public binding ceremony. But that's merely a formality. He is my Promise and I am his. Forever.

"Are you happy?" he asks.

"I am the happiest women, the happiest angel, in the entire universe." I wrap my arms around his neck. "I love you, Davin. With all my heart and soul," I whisper, as I brush my lips gently across his.

"Forever and never ending," he says.

And we kiss. It's the kind of kiss that's possible only when you love someone completely. The kind of kiss you feel in your soul.

"I should call Mom," I say, as I pull away from him, reluctantly. "She needs to know before anyone else."

Davin smiles. "I agree."

"What if she doesn't approve?"

"She will approve." Davin's smile gets wider.

I narrow my eyes. "Davin?"

He chuckles. "Your mom and I have talked. She will respect your decision."

"She knows you were going to commit to me?"

"Yes. But she thinks it will happen the evening before your celebration."

"Okay. I'm really happy you spoke to her. That was really very considerate of you."

"Thank you."

I step back and we lock eyes.

"Davin, would you do me a favor?"

"Anything."

"I'm going to run into the guest bathroom and brush my teeth. And then I'm going to call Mom and Ella. Would you mind programming the shower upstairs for a really hot and steamy monsoon?"

"A monsoon?" His eyes widen.

"Uh-huh," I say, as I brush a finger along his bare chest.

"How hot?"

"Scorching." I bite my bottom lip and gaze into his eyes. "Oh, and if I'm not there when it's ready, just get in and wait for me. Okay?"

"Ari, you have no idea what you do to me."

"Perhaps. But I know exactly what I'm going to do to you tonight." I flash him a sexy smile as I head for the guest suite. "Think about that while you're waiting."

His eyes are wide as saucers, and a smile lights up his face. I hope he can make it up the stairs without melting. I hope I can, too.

Chapter 23

"Mmm, that feels so good," I moan. Am I still sleeping?

It's as if the softest feather is being brushed across my shoulders. It feels exhilarating, stimulating, intoxicating. I open my eyes and look down. The *feather* is Davin's lips, and he's using them to shower every inch of my bare skin with soft kisses. Electric kisses. It awakens a hunger inside me—a deep, primal hunger. A hunger I thought was sated just a few hours ago.

"Good morning," Davin says." His voice is thick with sleep and something else. Joy? Pleasure? Contentment? All of the above? I've never seen this side of him. I like it.

"I won't be able to go on vacation with you if I die of a heart attack in your bed," I whisper.

"After last night, I would say your heart is very strong. And this is *our* bed."

Our bed. A purring sound escapes my throat. I'm so happy.

"It was amazing, Davin. We were amazing."

"There are no words to describe how I feel. It's as if a part of me was missing and now I'm whole."

"That's exactly how I feel. It must be genetic, huh?"

"It's love, Ari."

"I was just thinking."

"You were? Really?" he asks, with a playful smile.

"Smart-ass. I was *thinking* that Mom and Dad were married three months after they met. Do you know how long we've known each other?"

"Is this a trick question?"

245

"Davin..."

"Three months."

"To the day."

"I'm glad we didn't wait as long as *my* parents," he says.

"And how long was that?"

"A thousand years. More or less."

"I'm glad, too," I say, unable to stifle a giggle.

Davin sighs. "You know, Ella and Tal will be here any moment. I think we need to get dressed."

"You sure know how to ruin a mood," I complain. "But I guess they would wonder what was going on if we kept them waiting outside for several hours. Or a day. Or maybe even a week."

"I'll see you in a little while," he says, as he gets out of bed and grabs a pair of shorts off the floor. "I'll shower downstairs."

I nod. Good decision. If he showered up here, I'd probably follow him inside—and we'd go missing for a very long time.

Ella and Tal arrive, as expected, promptly at eight. Mom and Thalia arrive two minutes later. Somehow, we're not surprised.

We have an impromptu commitment celebration over breakfast, complete with hugs and tears. Thalia even insists on toasting us with Kristovi—an Olympian beverage similar to champagne. It's nice to see us all so happy.

After breakfast, we hug and cry a little more, pack the transport, and prepare to hightail it out of Portal City.

Ella looks a little tentative.

"Sweetie, are you sure Davin and you are okay with us tagging along? I feel like we're intruding on your honeymoon."

"We're fine, Ella. An Olympian honeymoon is traditionally taken right after the binding ceremony. You are not intruding at all…" I pause and smile. "And besides, Davin told me the bedrooms on the island are soundproof."

"Ooh. Okay. That's really good," Ella says, beaming like a high-voltage light.

"Let's get this show on the road," I say, as we take our seats inside the transport.

Ten minutes into our journey, the transport slows to a stop and moves sideways off the main network.

"Why did we stop?" Ella asks.

"We are exiting the transport level. The rest of our journey will be by air," Tal answers.

"Oh," she says, as the transport slowly rises toward the surface.

"Did you and Davin fly to Genobli?" Ella asks me.

"We did."

"Wow. Had I known, I would have changed my plans so Tal and I could have gone with you. This is so freaking awesome!"

The transport rises through a shaft and hovers in the sunlit Olympian sky. Then we shoot forward—accelerating and climbing steadily through wispy white clouds.

"How is this thing flying?" Ella asks. "There are no wings, no rotors, and I don't hear an engine."

"Plasma field," Tal says. "A fusion reactor turns the surrounding Essence into plasma. Groups of cells, which cover the craft's surface, selectively respond to pilot input—becoming positively charged and emitting a beam, which pushes against the plasma, generating thrust."

Ella looks intrigued. "Fascinating," she says. "Will I be able to study about this at Warrior College, sweetie?"

"Absolutely." Tal answers.

"Epic." She pauses, deep in thought. "Since the propulsion system uses the Essence, rather than air, can we fly above the atmosphere?"

"We have transports specifically designed for that purpose," Tal says. "This model, however, is not outfitted for space travel. Maximum safe altitude is approximately eighty-thousand feet."

"How fast are we going?"

Tal glances at the control cluster. "Mach 3.5, which would be..." He pauses for a moment, and then continues, "a little over twenty-five hundred miles per hour."

"Amazing," Ella says, with a hint of awe in her voice.

We're in the air for perhaps an hour when I feel the transport begin to descend. An island, tucked inside a ribbon of white sand, and surrounded by vivid blue water, looms below.

As we get closer, a stately white house comes into view. It's nestled in a small clearing, several hundred yards from the beach. A second building, U-shaped, with a large central courtyard, sits right on the beach. The walls are light beige, and the roof blue. The surf is no more than a hundred yards away.

The transport slows to a hover and Davin eases us down, landing behind the beach house. "Welcome to Carina," he says.

I look at Ella, who's grinning from ear to ear. "I think we just landed on Paradise, sweetie," she says.

The transport's doors open and we get out. Snow white sand comes right up to the house, which is landscaped to look like an oasis. Breathtakingly beautiful flowers and tropical-looking trees are perfectly placed amidst masterfully built stone paths and walls.

"This is so beautiful, Davin." I reach up and give him a quick kiss.

Carina seems like the kind of place human billionaires might go to for some rest and relaxation—for an obscene price, of course.

"Is the weather always like this?" I ask.

It's very warm, but not stifling, and it's just humid enough to let us know we're near the sea. It feels perfect.

"We are near the equator, so the temperature is consistently warm throughout the year. Let's go inside and get settled," he says, as he and Tal gather up our luggage.

"Are the caretakers here?" I ask.

"No," Davin replies. "I gave them several days off."

"Good thinking," Ella says with a big smile.

We follow the guys inside the house.

The décor and layout are typically Olympian. But unlike urban homes, the beach house is above ground, which gives it a different dynamic—especially when you consider the glass wall along the back that looks out onto the sea.

Davin gives us a quick tour. In addition to the main room, the house has a large kitchen—with automated food and beverage systems—and a study, equipped with all manner of infotainment equipment.

Two large bedrooms, with full baths and private beach access, flank the main room. The showers are large and programmable, like the one in Davin's Portal City house—but the outer walls are completely transparent, making it feel as if you're on the beach.

Ella looks perplexed as she eyes the clear walls. "Um, can you see in from the outside?"

Tal chuckles. "No one can see inside."

"That's good to know, sweetie," she says, obviously relieved.

I notice a staircase in the corner of the main room. "What's downstairs?"

"Six guest bedrooms," Davin answers.

"Do you have a lot of guests?" I ask.

Tal snickers, and Davin shoots him a warning glance. "Not really."

"I see. So this is not your little angel den of iniquity?"

"Angels are never iniquitous, at least by human standards," Davin states with a crooked grin.

"Hmm," I tease. "Not a single wild party?"

Tal sputters, unable to keep a straight face. "I can honestly say that there has not been a *single* wild party here."

Ella rolls her eyes. "Dude, we need to work on that sense of humor. Timing is everything and you're really not supposed to laugh. Ya know?"

Tal pouts.

By nature, Angels are not licentious. Our brains are simply not wired that way. We have an enlightened sense of decency, as Thalia likes to say.

"I'm not concerned with your past, Davin. All that matters is our future."

Davin looks relieved. "Thank you."

"Well," Ella says, "is anyone up for a swim?"

"I'm in," Tal says.

Davin looks at me and I nod.

"We'll change clothes and meet you in the courtyard," Tal says, as he and Ella walk out of the room.

"Sounds like a plan," I say.

I stand in front of the bathroom mirror, appraising my new bikini. It's definitely skimpier than any swimsuit I've ever worn, but not to the point of being indecent. I make a few adjustments and confirm that my vital parts are securely covered, before wrapping my bottom half in a matching sarong.

I like the look. Of course I do. Ella picked it out.

"Wow," Davin says, as I walk out into the bedroom. "You look amazing."

"Thanks. You look pretty good, yourself."

He's wearing black board shorts that hug his hips like they were made just for him.

"The house is spectacular, Davin, especially considering how old it is. How often do you have to fix it up?"

"Every forty years or so," he says. "Materials keep getting more durable, so the remodels are getting less frequent."

"Still, it's one of the inconveniences of immortality, eh?"

"Yes," he replies with a grin.

"I wonder what Rome would look like today if Romans were immortal?" I muse.

"I love the way you think."

"When it doesn't give you a headache?"

"You never give me headaches. Well, I wouldn't actually call them headaches. They are more like twinges. Yes, *twinges*. Little ones."

I smile, as I punch his arm, playfully.

We meet up with Tal and Ella in the courtyard garden. Ella is wearing a crimson sarong over a black bikini. She looks like a movie star. She is stunning.

"Tal and I need to conference with Thalia. We won't be long," Davin says to me.

"Perfect," Ella says. "We need to catch up on a few things anyway."

The courtyard garden is full of lovely flowers, neatly trimmed shrubs, a large dining table, and several seating areas.

"Am I dreaming? This is really happening, isn't it?" I ask.

Ella laughs out loud. "Either this is real, or I'm in your dream." She gives me an appraising glance. "You're positively glowing, sweetie. I've never seen you so happy."

"I am beyond happy, Ella."

"Did you expect him to commit to you?"

I shake my head. "It was a complete surprise."

"You know, he asked your mom if she would approve. It was kind of like in the old days when a gentleman asked for a lady's hand."

"So Mom is really okay with this?"

"Absolutely. After she told me about her talk with Davin, we cried. It was so sweet, Ari. Your mom has come to terms with the fact that what you are—*what we are*—changes everything. We're not girls."

"I know. When I began to fall in love with Davin I was terrified by our age difference, so I asked Thalia for guidance. She told me that when an angel awakened, age became irrelevant."

"Right," Ella says. "Thalia told me that by the time we awaken we're emotionally and intellectually the same as any other angel, which is really good since there is a definite shortage of male angels our age."

I chuckle because all of the male angels I know are nearly one million years old.

"It's all so remarkable, and I really need to spend more time shooting the breeze with Thalia, because there are several thousand questions remaining on my list of things to ask her."

"Do you know if she's ever been bound?" Ella asks.

"She was. Her Promise renounced Paradise. According to Davin, it was just before the rebels escaped through the portal. She was devastated."

"That's so sad."

"It is. But Davin says she's had a very active social life. She's just too busy to commit."

"I guess when you have all the time in the universe, you can afford to take things slowly."

"Very true," I say. "So, do your new abilities scare you at all?"

She looks up at the clear sky, pondering my question. "No. They thrill me, actually. I've always had a thirst for knowledge—and this reformatted brain of mine is like a sponge. I'm not scared. I'm positively elated. How about you?"

"It's a little bit complicated sometimes."

"Complicated?"

"Thalia said you can sense what people are thinking. You can't read my mind. Can you?"

She snickers. "Of course not. But I can sense feelings. Depending on the situation, I can tell if someone is hurting, happy, scared, or sincere. I can tell that you feel a little uneasy about something. But I don't know what it is."

I hem and haw for a moment, unsure of how to put my fear into words. "I'm afraid of what I can do. Killing Lander was too easy." I shudder as a vision of Lander's lifeless face enters my mind.

"He was evil, Ari. You were my avenging angel." She puts a hand on my shoulder. "What's happened to your mom, you, and me—there is no precedent. We're enigmas—but we are what we are for a reason. And I have a feeling we're close to discovering the reason. How exciting is that?"

"It's exciting, but it's also a little frustrating. Sometimes I feel like I'm a science project for Thalia. And when I healed you—"

"I know. They can do all the tests they want. I understand that our powers are genetically-based. But what you did to me was a miracle."

I nod slowly. "I'm inclined to agree."

"It's going to be an adventure, sweetie."

"That it will," I mutter.

Ella's expression grows somber. "My only regret is that my mom won't be able to share it with me."

"I know, Ella. I know."

She sits up straight and smiles. "Enough serious talk. Have you set a date for the binding celebration?"

"Not yet. It's traditional to wait a year, so we have a little wiggle room to get used to each other."

"Wiggle room, my buns. You two are destined to be together, sweetie. We may as well start ordering the flowers as soon as we get back to Portal City."

"I know," I say, smiling. "So, what can you sense about your relationship with Tal?"

"Do you think I would be willing to share a bed with him, on this island, if I wasn't sure he loved me?"

"Well, he's really hot, Ella," I say, trying to suppress a grin.

"I have my principles," she says in mock indignation.

"I know you do. And so does Tal."

"I was thinking of testing his resolve, but I have a feeling he would never waiver. He's so noble and honorable," she says with a little sigh.

"Do you love him?"

"I do. Sometimes I can't believe how much. It's as if he's imprinted on my brain, on my heart, and on my soul."

"And he knows this?"

"No. But he will tonight."

"Good girl."

"So, was it worth the wait?" she asks.

"What?"

"Your commitment night, silly."

I feel a flush of heat, as I remember last night. Ella notices my reaction and smiles.

"You know I'd never kiss and tell."

"Well, we're talking about more than kisses. Right?"

"My lips are sealed."

"You're expression says it all, sweetie. Really, I am so happy for you."

"Thanks, Ella. Maybe you and Tal will be next."

Ella seems to ponder my statement. "Perhaps."

We hear footsteps approaching and turn to see the guys standing with their arms folded.

"We didn't want to interrupt your conversation, but I thought you wanted to swim," Tal says.

"Sorry," Ella replies. "Ari and I were just doing a little catching up, sweetie. Girl stuff. Let's go."

We remove our sarongs, and the four of us jog toward the sea. The sand is warm and feels wonderful between my toes.

"Are there any dangerous creatures lurking under the water that we should be concerned about?" I ask.

"There are predators. But they will not bother us. The energy we emit repels them," Davin replies.

"Does that go for Sages, too?" Ella asks.

"Yes," Tal answers. "But you might have to worry about *me*."

He lunges at her, but she's too fast.

"You have to catch me first, sweetie," Ella squeals, as she bolts into the water like a hellfire missile.

She must be training hard.

"I've never seen Tal so relaxed," Davin comments. "Ella has made some improvements."

He smiles and I can tell he's happy for his friend.

We frolic in the water like children until the need for food beckons us to shore.

After lunch, we linger outside and talk, sipping coffee laced with a delicious Olympian liqueur. I look out across the sea. It's so beautiful. The sun is behind us now, and I can make out a land mass in the distance.

"Is that the mainland, Davin?" I ask, as I point toward the horizon.

"Yes. Do you see the peninsula in the center?"

"Uh-huh. Is it a city?"

"It's a resort called Corbal. Nice restaurants. Very fancy. Would you like to have dinner there?"

"Yes!" Ella and I answer simultaneously.

"What do you think, Tal?" Davin asks.

Tal shrugs. "If the girls really want to…"

"Then it's agreed," I proclaim. "Dinner tonight in Corbal. Do we need reservations?"

"No, that won't be necessary," Davin says.

"I'm so glad Ella and I bought new dresses."

"And I'm glad you picked the sexier one," Davin adds with a grin.

"Davin, what am I going to do with you?" I ask.

His brow arches, and he gives me a devilish glare. "Do you need suggestions?"

"Ooh," Ella says. "That is *so* totally hot."

"ELLA!"

"Sorry."

Chapter 24

It's getting dark as we near the lights of Corbal. We could be approaching any small airport on Earth. But as we get closer to the ground there's no doubt we're on Olympus. No buildings are visible, but there are several large patios dotted with tables—near the beach. On one of the patios, several couples are dancing. Torches shoot flickering flames into the sky.

It looks exotic. Mysterious. Inviting.

"Wow. This is different," Ella says. "Where's the restaurant? And isn't there supposed to be a hotel?"

"The buildings are below the surface. In nice weather, people eat on the terraces," Tal answers.

"Oh." Ella gazes down at the ground. "Cool. I see people dancing. They're doing the Rumba. Right?"

"I think so," I say.

"Do you think Thalia can teach us to dance in time for your celebration?"

"I'm sure she can."

"Davin and I can help," Tal says.

"You know the Rumba?" Ella asks him.

He nods. "And also the Foxtrot, the Tango, and the Waltz."

"Dancing is a social convention," Davin says. "At most celebrations, dancing is usually restricted to the Waltz. It's not difficult to learn."

"Private dance lessons could be very romantic," Ella says, as she leans over and gives Tal a kiss.

As Davin approaches the ground, I can make out a large, well-lit clearing. A dozen or so vehicles are parked there. The transport touches down smoothly, and Davin powers it down.

We get out and the guys lead us along a torch-lit path toward the shore. They look like GQ models. Davin is in white linen slacks and a black button-down shirt. Tal's slacks are black and his shirt is a lovely shade of blue. Ella and I wear cocktail dresses—hers coral and mine black. We are a chic-looking foursome.

Davin takes my hand. "You look radiant. Happy. Content."

"I am all those things tonight, *and more*," I purr. "But it's all because of you, and you know what?"

"Hmm?"

"I think we're rubbing off on Tal and Ella. Do you sense that they are falling in love?"

"Something is definitely making Tal very happy. He keeps telling me how beautiful and brilliant she is. How she makes his heart flutter. I think there is a high probability that love may be involved."

"It sure looks like it. I'm really happy for Ella. For them both."

"Me, too." He squeezes my hand as we follow Tal and Ella up several steps to the terrace, and our table.

"Davin!" a male voice calls from behind us. "And Tal!"

Davin and Tal greet the man and then Davin turns to Ella and me.

"Ladies, this is Moras. He is Corbal's director."

Ella and I greet Moras, who looks middle-aged. Obviously, he's a mortal Olympian.

"Please, sit down and I will have someone attend to you immediately," Moras says, as he makes sure we are comfortably seated. Then he turns on his heels and rushes off—presumably to find an attendant to attend to our every need.

"He's a bit intense," I whisper. Davin nods slowly, and Tal chuckles.

"He needs to chill out, " Ella quips. "But that's not my problem. I'm starving!"

Right on cue, an attendant appears. Davin selects a wine and several appetizers.

"Excellent choice," Ella says, as she takes a sip of wine. "Mom would have loved it." She takes another sip and lets the wine swish around in her mouth. "I was a little surprised when you ordered a Bordeaux, but it actually tastes like a Rothschild. Decent vintage, too. May I see the label?"

Davin turns the bottle and hands it to Ella.

"The label is not authentic. Neither is the bottle. This was fabricated here?" Ella asks.

Davin arches his brow and smiles. "You know a lot about wine."

"It was Mom's hobby," she says with a wistful expression. "I was tasting wine when I was ten years old. I guess Mom thought that if I appreciated wine as an art, I would not abuse it. And she was right."

Ella begins to tremble.

I steel a glance at Tal, who gives me a subtle nod, as he wraps an arm around Ella.

"I'm fine, sweetie," she says to Tal.

"It's okay to be sad," I counter.

"Ari is right," Tal adds.

Ella smiles softly and sighs, then rests her head on Tal's chest.

"I know. Sometimes it's hard to deal with her being gone. I'll be alright in a minute."

Tal turns slightly and wraps both arms around Ella. I can't see her face, but I can hear the sobs. I know she has to grieve, that grieving is part of healing, but my heart aches for her.

"I'm so sorry," Ella mumbles.

"There is nothing to be sorry for," Tal says, while rubbing her back.

"Yeah, there is. I ruined your pretty shirt. It's streaked with mascara."

Tal smiles. "I have many shirts, but only one Ella."

Ella leans back and smiles at Tal.

"That's the sweetest thing you've ever said to me."

She wraps her arms around his neck and kisses him, sweetly.

"Hey, come with me so I can fix your makeup," I say, with a wink.

"You can come with me, but I'll fix my own face. I'd rather not frighten anyone, ya know?"

"I'm not that bad with makeup."

"Yeah you are. Give me a minute while I try to clean up my mess," she says, as she scrubs Tal's shirt with a dampened napkin.

"You make cute faces when you put on makeup. I tend to look terrified," I say as I watch Ella in the restroom's mirror.

"As well you should," Ella answers with a smirk, making us both chuckle. "I'm sorry you had to put up with my little meltdown."

"Honey, It's okay to miss her. It's okay to grieve. So please don't be sorry."

"Oh, Ari…" Her lower lip begins to tremble, her eyes fill with tears, and then she laughs softly. "I'm going to run out of makeup, sweetie."

"We'll just stay in this restroom until you dry out. I'm in this for the long haul."

"I love you, Ariel Worthington."

"I Love you more," I say.

"Let's go before the guys start to worry."

"You still hungry?" I ask.

"Starving."

"That's my girl."

The four of us take an after-dinner stroll down a meandering stone path that follows the contour of the shoreline. On one side is the beach. On the other, a seemingly endless progression of bars and cafés. We decide to stop for an after-dinner drink and choose a small, deserted patio café with a nice view of the sea.

We find a table and are immediately approached by a young server, named Melina, who can't seem to keep her eyes off of Davin and Tal.

When Davin orders, she pretends to have difficulty hearing him. So she leans in close, giving him a nice view down her ample cleavage.

"I think she likes you," I tease, after she leaves.

"The poor girl seems to have a hearing impairment," Davin says, with a straight face.

Ella snorts. "I think that girl is perfectly healthy, sweetie."

Davin stares at Ella and shakes his head slowly.

"What? You don't believe it?" she asks, in mock amazement. "It's one of my new talents. Y'all better be careful what you say or think around me." She tilts her head and grins, mischievously.

Davin looks at me. "You think she can…"

"Oh, I do. I really do," I say.

Davin appears to be deep in thought. "Fascinating. That's a very useful ability to have."

"We play guessing games all the time," Tal says. "I've had to master the art of hiding my thoughts from her."

Ella smiles at Davin. "Tal is being silly. I can't read thoughts. It's more like I can detect general feelings and attitudes. I didn't know the server's actual thoughts. But I do know that she was very attracted to both of you…and she wanted to touch you."

"What is Tal thinking right now?" Davin asks.

"I'm not sure. But he's very happy."

Tal looks into Ella's eyes and smiles, timidly.

"Aw, how sweet," I say.

Whatever Ella is, whatever she can do—it's because of me. I'm responsible and I hope she'll always use her ability for good.

I'm jarred back to reality by the sound of a woman's voice behind me. She must have walked up from the beach.

"Hello Davin. Mind if we join you?"

I spin around in my chair. She's pretty, with longish auburn hair, high cheekbones, and a nice figure, which is carefully poured into a very sexy black dress. And she's petite, with delicate hands that I notice only because they happen to be rubbing Davin's shoulders. It's more than a friendly little rub. It's foreplay. She has to be Reyna.

Davin must sense the surge of energy going through me because he plants his hand on my thigh and pushes down hard—like he thinks I might want to get up and rip her head off.

She looks me in the eye. "Hello, Ari. I am so pleased to finally meet you. I am Reyna."

No surprise there.

Her eyes seem to challenge me. She wants me to lash out, to lose my composure.

She isn't alone. A man and another woman stand beside her. The other woman is smiling, her amber eyes sparkling. Lana. As my nanny, she dressed down. Tonight, she's positively striking in a chic and sexy white dress that hugs curves I never knew she had. We make eye contact and her lips curl into a smile, but she fights it. I give her a subtle nod and a half-smile. It's amazing what you can say without words.

The man accompanying them looks like he just ate something very sour.

Davin handles the introductions.

Sourpuss's name is Cylar. He's a Sage.

I pry Davin's hand off my leg and stand to face Reyna, who is standing next to him.

Channeling my inner Gandhi, I bow to her. "I am honored to meet you, Reyna." She gives me a plastic smile that makes me want to deck her.

I bow to Lana and Cylar. "It is a pleasure to meet you all."

I smile politely at Lana, then turn away, stealing a quick glance at Ella, whose brow is arched. She gives me a wink.

I turn back to Lana, studying her more intently. She looks like a fairy princess. A crown of silky black hair, cut in a pageboy style, frames her oval face, which is dominated by large amber eyes, an upturned nose, and very full lips. She's the polar opposite of nanny Lana, who had long straight hair, who wore little or no makeup, and whose favorite outfit was an oversized tee shirt over faded jeans. I like the new look. I like it a lot.

Cylar doesn't look pleasant at all. He seems arrogant and aloof. His brown hair is cut short—not a single strand out of place. His features are pedestrian, dominated by a large mouth that seems remarkably adept at frowning, scowling, and smirking. And he looks a little dangerous—as if he's calculating killing scenarios.

Everyone takes a seat and that's when things begin to get a little weird.

Chapter 25

It has to be a test. The Fates want to test the limits of my patience. That's why Reyna is here. And that's why she's doing everything she can to annoy, anger, and antagonize me. Her primary weapons are her hands—one of which is in constant contact with some part of Davin's body. I manage to maintain a civil bearing, resisting the impulse to stab her with my spoon.

"Ari, dear, have you been to Davin's island?"

"Mm-hmm," I say, gripping my spoon tightly.

"Carina is so lovely. You know, he and I shared so many…" Reyna pauses and licks her lips, as she gazes up at Davin. "Well, let's just say that if Davin's bed could talk, I would be very embarrassed. Have you slept in Davin's bed, dear?"

She's trying to sound innocent and shy. It's not working.

"I am still getting acclimated to Olympian culture, Reyna. On Earth, such a question would be considered rude—even if the couple were committed. I'm really sorry, but I have no interest in Davin's past dalliances," I say, smiling demurely, as I lower my eyes and tap the commitment brand over my heart.

Davin's face is hiding inside cupped hands. I squeeze his thigh, hoping to reassure him that I'm not concerned about his past.

Reyna stands up and glares at my chest. She sees my brand.

Her lips slowly curl into a scowl. Her fists clench tightly. She turns bright red. "Davin and you are committed?" The words come out dripping with venom.

I shoot to my feet and send my chair flying backwards. "Yes. We are *very* committed."

265

Reyna wheels toward Davin, who is now standing between us. "You committed to this...this mutated human? What were you thinking?"

Ooh, she is seething.

"Reyna..." Lana reaches out and grabs Reyna's arm. "Stop this right now and apologize. Ari has done nothing wrong."

Reyna smacks Lana's hand away and starts in on me again. "You will only cause him pain. You do not deserve him." Her head is twitching. She looks like a demented, redheaded Barbie doll. And I've had enough.

I step in front of Davin and grab her arm, causing her to gasp. She looks afraid of me, which is a pretty reasonable response since I'm one heartbeat away from snapping her arm. "Put a cork in it or I'll..."

"Or what? Do you think you can intimidate me?" She tries to wriggle free of my grip but there's no way I'm letting go. Instead, I squeeze harder. "Let go of me!" she shrieks.

"Ari," Davin says, "let her go."

I release her with a little shove, just for good measure. Davin is right, though. Violence will only make things worse. I take a deep breath. Facing Reyna, I ask, in an even tone, "Why are you doing this?"

"Because you have ruined his life," she answers, glowering at me.

I watch with interest as Davin's face morphs through several shades of red. He's so good at controlling his emotions. I keep silent, waiting to see what he'll do next.

"Reyna, I am truly sorry that you feel this way," Davin says. "But I think you know me well enough to understand that you cannot change my mind."

"But you cannot be with her, Davin. She is poison. She is evil."

"She is anything but evil," Davin replies, calmly.

"Reyna has a point," Cylar says. "The girl is not like us. She was born on Earth, of humans. Doesn't this concern you, Davin?"

"She was born on Earth, of angels," Davin replies. "But she is not your concern."

Cylar looks unimpressed. He doesn't believe Davin.

"But she does concern me. And it should concern us all. Reyna simply wants to protect you. She is your friend and she can sense you are in danger, as can I."

Reyna is transfixed on Cylar's every word, nodding mindlessly, like a Stepford wife. Something is off.

Is he influencing her in some way?

I can almost hear Davin shift into a higher gear, as he locks eyes with Cylar.

"The only one in danger right now is you," Davin says in a dangerously calm tone. "I would strongly urge you to stay out of this discussion."

"Very well. But your emotions have blinded you…"

Davin slams his fist down on the stone table top. A crack appears down the middle. "Did you not hear me? Did I not make myself clear?"

Davin is about to pop. I can sense it. Cylar is seconds away from an exceptionally painful experience when Ella's voice startles us all…

"Wait. Something is very wrong."

Everyone, including Reyna, turns toward Ella, who continues, "I don't think she can control what she's saying."

"What do you mean?" Davin asks.

"I'm not sure yet." Ella gets up and walks around the table. "Reyna, did you mean to insult Ari?"

Reyna blinks rapidly. "Insult…?"

Ella places her hand on Reyna's arm. "Do you want to hurt her?"

Reyna looks like she's in pain. She turns to look at Cylar, but Ella shifts to block her view of him.

"Please, can you answer the question, Reyna?" Ella's tone is like that of a teacher talking to a first-grader.

Reyna's head twitches. She looks like she's trying to form words—but they won't come out. She just stares straight ahead.

Ella grasps Reyna's hand, startling her. "I don't," Reyna says, in a small voice.

"You don't want to hurt Ari?" Ella asks.

"No. I don't."

Ella places her hands on Reyna's shoulders. "It's okay. You're in control, Reyna. You don't have to say anything you don't mean."

"Reyna is only trying to help," Cylar says. "Obviously she still cares for Davin and wants to protect him. I will counsel her on the futility of trying to help friends who don't want to be helped."

"Really?" Lana asks, "When did you become her counselor?"

"I care about Reyna very much. I want to help her get over this," Cylar replies, trying, but failing miserably, to sound sincere.

"That's very thoughtful of you, Cylar," Ella says.

"Right. Well, we have been friends for many years," he replies.

"How sweet. So you are fond of her?" Ella looks at Cylar expectantly.

"Naturally," Cylar answers.

Ella steers Reyna to Lana's waiting arms and then turns to face Cylar. "You're lying. You are influencing what she says."

Cylar sneers. "Are you insane? This is utterly preposterous—and quite impossible." He gives Ella a dismissive wave, and I'm afraid Tal might rip his head off. As a matter of fact, **I** want to rip his head off.

Ella is undeterred and continues her interrogation. "So, is it an implanted device?"

"You cannot be serious, dear girl."

"I see." Ella says. "Then it must be a drug, right?"

Cylar flinches, but does not answer.

"Interesting," Ella says. "I have read of drugs that some counselors use when dealing with people who are under extreme duress. The patient receives one drug, and the counselor takes a second drug, which acts as a catalyst. The counselor is then able to influence the patient's behavior. Thalia says these drugs are used only as a last resort in extreme cases. Did you drug her?"

Ella is conducting a flawless cross examination, and Cylar doesn't stand a chance.

"Of course not!" Cylar exclaims. Contempt flavors his words. "The drugs you speak of are very carefully regulated."

"Only counselors can acquire them?"

"Yes," he hisses.

"Are you a counselor?"

"I've had quite enough of this!" Cylar bellows. "Your behavior is tactless and offensive."

Game, set, and freaking match.

Ella narrows her eyes and glares at him. "Excuse me? Were you saying something?"

Cylar looks flabbergasted. He is outclassed, outmatched, and overwhelmed.

Lana reaches out and takes Reyna's hands in hers. A soft glow radiates from Lana's fingers and snakes its way into Reyna's hands. She sighs and shudders, looking like a heavy weight has been lifted from her shoulders.

"Thank you," Reyna says, as tears run down her cheeks. "I am so ashamed."

"It's okay now, Reyna," Lana says. "It is done."

What is done? Does Lana know what's happening between Cylar and Reyna? I give Lana a questioning gaze, but she averts her eyes. Something is going on.

Cylar glares at Reyna and lets out a growl. "Fool! You are useless to me!"

Tal reaches out and grabs Cylar's arm in a vise-like grip. "You will tell the truth now—or I will rip your arm off." He looks and sounds deadly serious.

I've never seen Tal angry. He's scary.

Cylar gasps. "There is no need for violence, Tal."

"There is a need for the truth," Tal says, as he twists Cylar's arm. Cylar grunts, and Tal twists again, harder. "Speak!"

"Very well. I was sent to find *her*," Cylar says, through clenched teeth, as he points to me.

"By whom?" Davin asks.

Cylar fixes Davin with a scornful expression. "An Elder," he says.

Ella looks at Davin and nods. "He is telling the truth."

"What does this Elder want with her?" Davin asks.

This can't be true. Dad is an Elder. He's the *head* Elder. "Me? What would an Elder want with me?" I ask.

"He wants you to die," Cylar says. His tone is icy and I shiver.

"What are you talking about? Why would he want me to die?"

"Because you are an abomination."

"You are an imbecile," Davin says, looking more angry than I've ever seen him. "Where is this Elder for whom you work?"

"He does not…" Cylar pauses, looking perplexed. "I do not know where he is at the moment."

"Does Damas know of this?" Lana asks. "Does he believe this angel should die?"

Cylar's forehead glistens as beads of perspiration quickly form. "We do not know what he believes. Apparently, he has been gone for quite some time."

"Ari is Damas's daughter," Ella says.

"What you are saying is impossible." Cylar sounds confident and calm. Too calm. Too confident. He doesn't know.

Lana puts her hand up. "It is true."

"How do you know this?" Cylar asks.

"Your Elder seems to have withheld some rather important information from you, Cylar. I am Ari's sister. I held her in my arms when she was a baby. I changed her diapers. I rocked her to sleep. No Elder can make a decision of this magnitude without my father's approval, and I can assure you that he does not wish to see his daughter harmed. I suggest you return to whomever sent you and advise him that we will take this matter up with my father, when he returns to Olympus."

Lana looks at me and smiles.

I nod, returning her smile.

"It's so good to see you," Ella says, barely able to contain her excitement.

"I am happy…and pleasantly surprised to see *you*, Ella," Lana says, looking a little bemused.

"Well, I couldn't very well let my best friend go gallivanting across the universe without me. Now, could I?"

"Evidently not," Lana says. "You were always an overachiever."

Cylar rolls his eyes. "This is absurd. I have something that might help to explain my mission. May I show you?"

"Move very slowly," Tal says, releasing his grip on Cylar's arm.

Cylar reaches inside his pockets, then draws his hands out, slowly.

"Let me see." Tal commands.

Cylar turns his hands, palms up. Inside each hand is a silvery, golf-ball sized orb.

"What are those?" Tal asks.

"No!" Ella and Lana scream as one.

"Stop him!" Reyna shouts.

Before anyone can react, Cylar flicks his wrists, and the orbs fly from his hands.

One of the orbs strikes my energy shield and falls harmlessly to the ground. Next to me, I hear a grunt. I turn, just in time to see Davin stagger and fall. He's slumped over the table. Blood is everywhere. Oh no…

The other orb. It must have penetrated his energy shield. He looks at me with mournful eyes.

"It will heal." His voice is hoarse. He's gasping for air.

As I move toward Davin, a blood-curdling scream pierces the night air. It's Cylar. He's glowing like a light bulb, as a pulsing beam of angry white light pours out of Lana's outstretched hand and into his chest. The smells of ozone and seared flesh permeate the air. I watch in horror as clothing and skin melt together. His mouth is agape, as if trying to form a scream, but his voice is gone, and then he's gone—transformed into a small pile of fine gray ash.

"No," I whisper, as I turn toward Davin. "Oh, God, no."

I grasp his shoulders and gently lower him into a chair. "What do I do?" I ask him.

His clothes are saturated with blood. His breathing is ragged.

"I'm sorry," he manages to say before his head sags and he passes out.

"Davin, please don't give up. Don't leave me."

My sobs come in violent spasms. I kneel beside him and cradle his head to my bosom. He can't die. I won't let him die.

"Ari, let's slow his bleeding." Reyna is standing beside me, holding a small vile with a white, powdery substance inside.

She waves her arm across the table, flinging cups, plates, and flatware to the ground.

"Help me get him on his back, Ari."

I carefully scoop him into my arms and gently lay him on the table. Reyna pours the contents of her vial into Davin's wound. The hole in his belly is jagged and horrible.

I lean down and pick up the orb that struck me. It's covered with razor-sharp serrations. God, it must have hurt him so much. But the bleeding has slowed. The clotting agent Reyna administered is working.

"Thank you, Reyna," I say.

She nods and averts her eyes. She probably feels ashamed. But I have more important things to worry about. Her feelings can wait. Davin can't.

Tal and Ella are engaged in an animated conversation with Moras—no doubt briefing him on what happened. Moras finally turns and walks away. The poor man looks stricken.

Tal and Ella approach me slowly. Ella is openly weeping.

"It will be okay," Tal says, softly.

"I know," I say. "I'm going to heal him."

I place my hand over Davin's wound and push energy into him. My hand begins to glow, but it doesn't feel right. There's no pain—only a slight buzzing.

"Ari," Lana says, "The projectile is toxic. The wound will not heal until we remove it."

"How can we remove it?" I'm on the verge of panic. "Lana…?"

"He'll be fine, Ari. I'm a surgeon. We won't lose him. I promise."

Ella places an arm on my shoulder and finally speaks. "I'm so sorry," she says, choking back a sob, "I should have warned you sooner."

"You did what you could, Ella," I say.

"We must leave now," Lana says. "We must get Davin to Carina. There is a surgical theater there."

"I'll carry Davin to the transport," Tal says.

I shake my head. "I'll carry him, Tal. Take the others and get to the transport as quickly as you can. Have it ready to go. Okay?"

Tal nods. Then he, Ella, and Reyna take off sprinting toward the landing area.

Lana walks up to me and places her hands on my shoulders. "You are in no condition to carry him, Ari."

"I can do it. I have to do it."

"You are trembling. Please, we need to go. Let me carry him."

She's right. I'm a mess, and the last thing I want to do is risk hurting him more. "Okay," I say, choking back a sob. "Let's go."

I help Lana lift Davin into her arms, making sure he's as comfortable as possible. Then we set off down the path.

"You knew we are sisters?" she asks.

"I can be smart. Sometimes."

"You're far too modest," she says.

"It's a family trait."

A soft glow appears around Lana.

"What are you doing?" I ask.

"I'm sharing my energy with him. It will slow the effects of the toxin. It will help to sustain him until I can operate."

"What is this toxin?"

"The weapon Cylar used is called a core disruptor. It releases a deadly poison, while disrupting the absorption of energy. The victim cannot heal."

"But we can heal him after the orb is removed. Right?"

"Yes. I will remove the projectile, and then you will heal him."

"I wish I felt as confident as you sound. Are you a good surgeon?"

"I am very experienced."

"Can I really heal him, Lana?"

She gives me a warm smile. "You can."

I wonder if she knows the extent of my abilities…if she knows what Thalia, Davin, and I have been agonizing about for the past several months. "How are you so sure?"

"You really don't know?"

"Should I?

She smiles sweetly. "You are special."

That's really profound. *Profoundly cryptic.* "Meaning…?"

"Have you not been wondering how Dad was able to turn your mom into an angel?"

"Of course. And you know how?"

"I do. It was love, Ari."

"That tells me a whole lot." I look up at her and frown. "Can you take a more direct path to the point, please?"

"Love is the fuel of miracles. It helps to strengthen our abilities. There was enough love in Dad to change your mom. And there's more than enough love in you to heal Davin."

"Dad didn't change me. Did he?"

"He didn't have to. You were born an angel."

"He really did change my mom before I was conceived?"

"Yes."

I shake my head. *I was born an angel.* "Thalia was right."

"She figured it out, huh?"

"Yes."

"She is brilliant."

"I know."

"When did you and Davin commit?"

"Last night," I answer.

"Congratulations," she says.

I give her a tight smile. "Thank you."

"You do realize that every unattached female angel on Olympus will be utterly crushed?"

275

"As long as we are together, nothing else matters." I'm really not in the mood for humor, although I'm pretty sure she is right. Davin is *that* desirable.

"I can sense your love for each other. It is very powerful."

"I can't lose him, Lana. I just can't. And please, must you be so flippant about this. My heart is breaking," I say, choking back a sob.

"I'm sorry, Ari. You won't lose him. I promise."

"Last night I was dreaming about spending eternity with him. Now…"

"He is going to be fine. You are going to be fine. I'm sorry if I was crass, but it's only because I know he'll be fine. Davin and I have been friends for a very long time. And now we're family. I love him. I love you both."

"I just can't lose him."

"You won't. I…"

The words seem to catch in her throat.

"What's wrong?" I ask.

"It hurts me to see you like this. I didn't mean to sound flippant. I just…"

"You were trying to help. I understand."

"Are you sure?"

I nod. Lana's perspective is different. She knows more about what I am…about what I'm capable of.

She lets out a deep breath. "I assume you changed Ella. Am I right?"

"She was badly wounded and I healed her. I guess I did a pretty good job."

"You did. She was positively brilliant tonight."

"She was."

"Do you know how powerful you are?"

"Not really. I can only go by what Thalia and Davin say."

"Don't be frightened by it, Tink. It's a blessing. A really, really big one."

Tink. I smile at the memory. Mom had just started her residency, and Dad traveled all the time. So they hired Lana to care for me. I adored her. She was amazing. So full of love and laughter. She called me Tink because I reminded her of Tinker Bell. After Dad's funeral, Mom said that Lana decided to go back to college. I was heartbroken.

"I've missed you, Lana."

"I've missed you, too. I so wanted to be a part of your childhood. When Dad was called home, I was devastated. Then I had to return to Olympus. I didn't want to leave you. But I had no choice. I hope you understand."

Her eyes fill with tears.

"At the time, I was angry. I thought you didn't care about me. I was so young, and I loved you so much, and you left me. I didn't understand."

"I'll make it up to you. I promise."

"You did what you had to do. Let's just concentrate on moving forward, on being good sisters."

"That's a very worthy goal, Tink."

"Yeah. It is. Thank you Lana."

"For...?"

"For making my grief a little more tolerable."

"You have nothing to grieve over. This incredibly handsome angel in my arms will be fine," she says, as we approach our waiting transport.

Lana, Davin, and I are in the back row of the transport. I cradle his head to my chest, stroking his cheek, as I speak to him in a soothing drawl.

"We couldn't have come this far only to have it end. There are so many things we have to look forward to, so many adventures to share, so many things… "

Did his lips move? Is he trying to answer me? "Davin?" I lean down, placing my ear near his lips.

His voice is barely audible. "Monsoon. Remember."

Lana gives me a confused look. "Did he just say 'monsoon?'"

"He did."

"What could that mean, Ari?"

"It means his mind is working. It means *everything*."

My finger traces the strong line of his jaw. "I love you, Davin. I won't let you leave me. I promise."

Chapter 26

The ride back to Carina takes less than fifteen minutes, but it seems like an eternity. I'm curious when we pass the beach house and turn inland, toward an isolated area on the far side of the island.

"Where are we going, Tal?" I ask.

"If Cylar's associates have tracked us, we need to be in a secure position. There is a sanctuary here. It is impenetrable. And it has a fully-equipped infirmary."

As the transport nears the ground, a strobe light flashes. Then the ground slides away, and we land inside a lighted shaft, approximately twenty feet deep. Tal powers down the transport and opens the doors.

"I can carry him now," I say to Lana.

I need to hold him close to me. I need to touch him.

She nods.

As we disembark, the top of the shaft slides closed, and the lights inside come on.

We enter a large hallway, with several doors on either side. "The infirmary is in here," Lana says, as we approach a white door.

As she opens the door, my heart begins to beat wildly. I can't lose him. I can't live in a world without him. I can't.

It looks like a very high-tech emergency room. Banks of electronic instruments and monitors line one wall. Six gurneys are parked along another. A single bed stands alone in the center of the room, surrounded by computers and scanners. Lana walks toward it.

"Lay him down on the bed, Ari."

I carefully set him down. Overhead lights illuminate him, and the full impact of just how close to death he is hits me like a sledgehammer. The color has drained from his face, his clothes are red with his blood, he seems to be gasping for air, and my heart is breaking. I need Thalia. I need her reassurance.

"Should we call Thalia for input?" I ask.

"We can't," Tal says. "I activated an emergency lockdown. Communications in and out are blocked to prevent detection. Lana is a talented healer. Davin is in good hands."

Lana turns to the others. "I need you to wait outside while Ari and I tend to Davin."

"Of course," Tal says. "If you need us, we will be in the living quarters."

Ella and Tal hug me and then leave the infirmary, along with a sad-looking Reyna.

"We'll need to clean up and change into jumpsuits," Lana says. "Stay with Davin. I'll be right back."

She returns with two jumpsuits, a surgical drape for Davin, and a cleaning wand. Lana and I step out of our dresses, wave ourselves clean, and don the jumpsuits.

I carefully remove Davin's clothes and cover him with the drape, while Lana prepares the surgical equipment and tools she will need.

"Please be careful with him, Lana." My voice is cracking, and the tears begin to flow again.

"I need you to stay calm. Okay?"

I'm a long way from calm. "I can't stay calm. He's dying!"

"Ari, listen to me. He is going to be fine. We will not allow him to die."

I put on a brave face and nod.

"Good. Let's begin," she says, as she aims an injector gun at Davin's upper arm.

I stroke his face, trying to soothe him. I know he probably can't feel it, but it's all I can do.

Lana is now sporting a strange-looking glass monocle. "Ari, this is an imaging scanner," she says, as she positions a device next to the hole in Davin's belly. "The picture will appear on my eyepiece and on the wall screen."

I look up at the screen and gasp. It's not like an x-ray or an ultrasound. It's like watching a high-definition video. A video of Davin's insides.

"I see the orb, Lana."

"Yes. Thank God it is not embedded inside an organ."

"Now what?" I ask.

"I will remove the orb, and then you will heal him."

I watch in awe as Lana directs a thin robotic arm through Davin's entry wound, guiding it around organs and arteries until it reaches the orb. The robot wraps flexible tentacles around the orb, and then Lana pulls it back out through the wound.

Clearly, she's done this many times before.

"It is done," she says.

"That was amazing," I reply, as she passes a wand slowly across the gaping hole in Davin's belly. When she's finished, a thin membrane covers the wound. Its edges seem to feather into the surrounding skin.

I reach down and touch his face. It's warm. I place a finger above his lips—lips that can melt my soul—and feel the warmth of his breath. I have to save him.

But what if I screw up? What if I can't focus? The love of my life will be gone. Panic squeezes my chest in a vice. The room begins to spin, and I stagger.

Lana catches me and gently turns me to face her, as she cups my face in her hands. "You must have faith in your power, Ari. You have to believe."

"I'm trying, Lana. I'm really trying."

"You need him, Tink. He completes you. He is your destiny." She pauses and stares into my eyes. "I believe in you."

Gosh, she is one hell of a motivator.

"I'm ready," I say, steeling myself.

"Good. There is a bedroom through that door," she says, pointing across the room. "Let's move Davin inside. You will be more comfortable."

The room is spacious. A large bed centered on the far wall is flanked by two tables, topped with pretty lamps. Cheerful virtual paintings are embedded into the walls. There are three doors, not counting the one we entered through.

I lay Davin down on the large bed and inspect him. His breathing is ragged, he's covered in sweat, and my heart is about to shatter into little shards. I have to do this. I have to help him.

Lana tosses me a gown. "I'm going to turn off the equipment outside. Why don't you clean him up and dress him. There should be cleaning wands in the closet behind you."

"Okay," I say.

I clean Davin as best I can and carefully dress him in the Olympian version of a hospital gown.

Lana returns and sits down in a chair across the room. "Are you ready, Ari?"

"Yes."

"Place one hand over his wound and the other on his forehead. Focus on your love and then push your energy into him…all of it. Empty yourself, Tink. Become one with him."

I get up onto the bed and kneel beside him. "Hey, Warrior. I know you're strong, so you have to help me, okay?"

His breathing is shallow. Too shallow.

"Okay, here we go."

I focus on pushing all of my energy out through my hands. And it hurts. The pain is unrelenting. It's as if I'm being bruised, battered, beaten, burned, and bludgeoned—all at the same time. I know I'm screaming, but I can't hear anything because there are freight trains and stampeding cattle racing through my head.

A soft blue halo gives way to a raging red glow. We're like two halves of an angry setting sun. I'm either going to heal him or blow us both to kingdom come. The entire room seems to be fading in and out of view. I begin to tremble uncontrollably. It's not my emotions. The entire room is shaking. I brace for an explosion, and I pray it won't kill us all. But then the shaking stops. The noise in my head stops. The pain stops. And my world goes black.

I'm pretty sure I'm alive because every muscle, every joint, every tendon in my body is sore. Am I dreaming? Or am I trying to wake up?

My mind spins out of control as non-sequential thoughts fly every which way. Words and colors and shapes. One word rushes out of the maelstrom and hovers in front of my mind's eye.

Davin.

Davin?

"DAVIN!"

I bolt upright, eyes wide, as a warm arm wraps around my waist. Davin. He's looking at me—concern etched in his gaze. His hair is damp and falling into his eyes. His gown is matted to his body. It's the most beautiful sight I've ever seen. His eyes lock onto mine.

"I am here," he whispers in my ear.

"I–I thought I lost you," I stammer.

"I *was* lost, but now I am found."

"Just hold me," I say softly.

He pulls me to him. I'm sobbing.

"I was so afraid of losing you. I–I don't know what I would have done if…"

My voice fails me.

He laces his fingers through my hair and softly brushes my lips with his. Then he pulls away, abruptly. But he's smiling.

"What's wrong?" I ask.

"Nothing could be more right, Love. But I'm afraid we are not alone."

"It smells like a locker room in here, you know? I think both of you could use a nice long shower. Perhaps a monsoon, yes?"

I turn and look across the room. Lana is curled up in a chair, an enormous grin plastered across her face. "You guys can really sleep," she says through a deep yawn.

"How long have we…"

"Twelve hours and forty-two minutes."

"Is he healed?"

"Oh, yeah, he is very healed. You did good, Tink," Lana says.

"Tink?" Davin asks.

"Not important," I say, brushing him off, as I turn back to Lana.

"Lana, what do you mean by *very* healed."

What did I do now?

She grabs a scanner and walks over to the bed. "I'll show you."

She waves the scanner across Davin's body, then holds it out to me so I can see the readouts.

"Davin's energy reading should be close to 180, but it's over 400—and so is yours."

"I did this to him when I healed him? I made him stronger?"

"Yes. And somehow you made yourself stronger, too."

Davin scratches his chin. "How is this possible? Lana?"

"It's totally *impossible*, Davin. That's what makes it so wonderful."

Lana is positively beaming.

"You are definitely sisters," he says with a crooked smile and a tilt of his head.

"We have lots to talk about," Lana says. "But right now you two really need to get cleaned up. Ella brought fresh clothes for you this morning. They are in the bathroom."

"Alright," Davin says. "Is everything secure on the island?"

"Yes. No one followed us here. Tal insisted that we maintain lockdown until he knew your condition."

Davin reaches over to the bedside table and activates an info panel.

"Tal…"

Tal's voice comes over the speaker. "It's good to hear your voice, my friend."

"Thank you, Tal."

"And how is Ari?" Tal asks.

Davin gazes at me, lovingly. "She is perfect."

"Have you been monitoring the closed-circuit scanners?" Davin asks.

"Yes. We are clear."

"Good. Contact Thalia and give her a report."

"I will," Tal says. "Given the circumstances, we are safer here than we would be if we left the island. We should remain here until we are absolutely sure there is no risk. Agreed?"

"Yes. Make sure that Andi knows Ari is fine. Tell them we will conference later."

"I will."

"We're going to get cleaned up. I'll see you in about an hour."

"Take your time. And Davin…?"

"Yes?"

"Welcome back," Tal says, as the info panel winks off.

Davin turns to Lana. "We will meet you in the kitchen in an hour."

Lana smiles. "Take your time. I will be drinking coffee and talking with Ella."

Chapter 27

Davin and I stand motionless, lost in a tender embrace. A brisk tropical shower falls from above, as a warm breeze whispers over our skin. My hand moves lovingly across his stomach. I can't help but smile at how completely he's healed. All that remains is a slightly raised border where Lana patched him.

"Does it hurt?"

"Not a bit."

"He nearly killed you, Davin. I thought you were going to die," I say, choking back a sob. "I just want to hold you."

"It must have been hard for you," he replies. "I underestimated him. I was not prepared."

"I couldn't bear to lose you, Davin. It was terrifying. It was…"

"It is over. We are together."

"I know, but you have no idea…my heart was breaking. If you didn't come back to me I think I would have died, too."

"Don't say that, Love. You are stronger than that. I know you are."

"Everyone seems to have so much faith in me. But when you were wounded, I froze. I began to shatter into little pieces. If we were alone, Cylar would have escaped, because I was useless."

"What happened to Cylar?"

"Lana happened. She incinerated him. It should have been me, Davin. I should have avenged you. But I was helpless."

"Ari…"

I shake my head and gaze into his eyes, gently stroking his cheek. "Heal me, Davin. Make the pain melt away," I whisper, as my lips hungrily seek his.

Our kiss deepens and my healing begins, as Davin and I drift away to our own personal paradise.

I am home again. But for how long?

"Davin, it's been nearly three hours. They're going to wonder what happened to us," I say, as I dress.

"I don't think so." He's grinning from ear to ear. "I don't think they will wonder at all."

"Davin!"

"What?"

"Let's go," I say, with a huff, taking his hand and dragging him through the doorway. I look to the left and then to the right, and then it strikes me—I have no idea where we are going. I stop short and turn to face him, embarrassed. "Um, which way do we go?"

"I was wondering when you'd ask," he says with a chuckle. "Third door on the right."

"Thank you."

"Wait."

"What?" I ask.

"Lana called you Tink. What does that mean?"

I sigh. "Oh, it's just a nickname she gave me. When I was little, I reminded her of Tinker Bell."

"The little fairy?" he asks.

"Yes."

"That's cute."

"Yeah. It is."

As we enter the kitchen, Ella pops up and darts over to us. "Thank goodness Davin and you are okay." She pulls me into a hug. "I was so worried about you."

"We're fine, Ella."

She pushes me back and looks me in the eye. Then she looks at Davin. "Don't ever scare me like that again. You both mean so much to me," she says with tears streaming down her cheeks. "I love you guys."

"We love you, too, Ella," I say with a warm smile.

"Um, now that I know you're okay, I do have a question?"

"Hmm?"

"According to Lana, you and Davin have been showering and dressing for the past three hours. Which took longer? I think it was the shower. Am I right?"

"Ella!"

"Oh, you're so easy to rile."

"No, you're just very good at it."

"You love it."

"Says you."

But she's right. It's just Ella being Ella and I wouldn't ever want her to change.

"Uh, where's Reyna?" I ask, wanting to thank her for helping me.

"She's patrolling the island," Tal says.

"She is alone?"

"Thalia sent a recon team. Reyna wanted to help," Tal says.

"Seto is with her," Lana says.

"Oh. That's good."

"He will comfort her. She feels very ashamed."

"It's not her fault," I say.

"She knows that, but she is still ashamed," Lana replies.

"Is it safe outside?"

"Yes. And they are wearing armor, just in case."

"So what else has been going on?" I ask.

"Well," Lana says, "Ella and I have been talking about old times in Edgewood."

"That's nice."

Ella chuckles. "When she came out of the infirmary, she was a mess. Wild hair, no makeup, and totally worn out. She looked just like she did when we were kids."

Lana huffs. "Yes, well, it just goes to show you how hard I had to work at looking plain. And the only reason I looked tired all the time was because of my little sister and you."

"Lana," Davin says, "you always had that earthy, natural look. It becomes you."

Lana picks up a pastry and throws it. She gets him right in the nose.

"I don't like this kind. Try one of those," Davin says, pointing to a tray of chocolate squares, as he wipes his nose with a napkin.

"Okay, children," I say, "get us up to speed. What's the word from Portal City?"

Tal clears his throat and takes the floor. "A lot has happened. At dawn, your father conferenced Thalia."

I gasp. "Dad made contact? What about Mom. Did he talk to her?"

Tal nods. "Apparently, your parents had a very emotional reunion. Andi told me to tell you that it's all good."

Lana looks at me with a big smile. "He adores her, Tink. He always will."

Davin reaches up and catches a tear as it rolls down my cheek. "This is a happy tear," he says.

I nod as several more glide down my face.

"What else, Tal?"

"Graduation is off. Thalia said it would be too dangerous for Ella and you to be on Earth right now. The Zon have been extremely active."

"What's going on?" Davin asks.

"They are stirring the pot. Creating political tension. The plan is for Ari and you to remain on Carina, with Lana. She will help both of you learn to use your new abilities."

"New abilities?" I ask.

"Thalia did not elaborate. I'm sorry," Tal says.

I look at Lana, who nods. "Carina is perfect. We need privacy. And the water and sand will allow for soft landings."

Davin and I exchange glances. He looks as startled as I do.

"The rest of us will return to Portal City tomorrow," Tal says. "Thalia will brief us on the entirety of what Damian disclosed to her."

"When do Davin and I get briefed?" I ask.

"I'll take care of that," Lana says. "But there is one thing I must tell you all." She purses her lips. "Reyna allowed herself to be controlled by Cylar so that we could gather more information. She is a very brave Warrior. Thalia will explain the rest to you back in Portal City."

"When will we go back to Portal City?" Davin asks.

"You will return in time for Ari's celebration," Tal replies.

"Good grief," I say. "With all that's happening, they still want to have a party for me? That's ridiculous."

"Your father will be attending," Tal says.

"Oh, and what happens after the party?"

"We will have a brief holiday and then we go to Earth."

Davin gives him a questioning look.

"Paradise has declared war on the Fallen," Tal says.

"Rules of engagement?" Davin asks.

"The gloves are off, Davin."

"We can reveal ourselves?" I ask.

"Once the battle begins, our presence will be hard to conceal," Tal says.

"Oh, my God. The Fallen want to do what they did to Olympus. They want to start wars, and then, when the dust clears, they will enslave what's left of humanity. Do they actually think they can pull it off?"

Lana looks me in the eye. "They are prepared this time. They will not underestimate our power." Her lips slowly curve into a smile. "But they will be completely unprepared for you, Davin, and…Ella.

"Ella?"

"I told Dad that you changed her. He seems pretty sure that if you changed her, she is *special*. And after what I observed last night, I would tend to agree. Now that Thalia knows what to look for, we'll have answers in a few days."

I look at Ella. "What did I do to you, honey?"

"Don't get your knickers in a twist, sweetie. What's done is done, and if it means I can help save people, then I'm all in."

"You really think three people can save an entire world, Lana?"

"You'll have an army of angels with you. Including some secret weapons. They won't know what hit them."

"You like to push me, don't you?"

"That's what good coaches do, baby sister."

"Argh."

"Was that a growl I just heard?"

"You're pushing it."

"I know. It's one of my cuter talents."

Thalia's recon team is recalled to Portal City. Seto, however, opts to stay behind, refusing to leave Reyna. As they enter the sanctuary, I greet Seto and then pull Reyna off to the side. She looks a little frightened.

"Reyna, I know what you did. It was very brave. Thank you—"

"You don't have to thank me, Ari. It was my duty. But I do want you to know that I am happy for Davin and you. I loved him very much, but that was a long time ago. I would never do anything to hurt him." She takes a deep breath, and we lock eyes. "Do you believe me?"

"I do." I place my hand on her shoulder. "I really do. I understand that you and Seto are together. He is a good Warrior. A good person."

A blush paints her cheeks.

"You really care for him?"

"Yes. I…" She falters, averting her eyes from me.

We aren't friends, so I don't want to press. "Are you hungry?"

She looks down at the floor. "I was going to prepare dinner for Seto and me. I wasn't sure I was welcome to dine with you."

"Don't be silly," I say. "I insist that you join us."

Her eyes brighten. "Thank you, Ari."

Hmm. Maybe we *can* become friends. "Go get Seto and meet us in the kitchen."

"Okay."

Not surprisingly, Davin and I eat like two angels who haven't eaten all day. That is to say, like a pair of ravenous bears, newly emerged from a long winter's hibernation. Seto and Reyna smile as they watch us.

After dinner, we meet up with the rest of the group in the conference room. Lana is regaling everyone with legendary tales of Baby Ari and Baby Ella. It seems she has an excellent memory for detail.

"Ella, do you remember your chocolate art exhibition?"

"Um, not really. How old was I?"

"You were four, and your mom had dropped you off at Ari's for the day. I left both of you in the family room, watching a movie, while I cleaned up the kitchen. When I returned to the family room..." Lana pauses, looking wistful. "One entire wall was covered with stick-figures. Brown stick-figures. You'd used melted chocolate bars for your paint. It was a mess and I didn't know what to do, so I sat in a chair and stared silently at the wall, until Ari and you started poking me. I guess you wanted to see if I could still speak."

"I did that?" Ella asks. "I must have gotten into a lot of trouble, huh?"

"As much trouble as a four-year-old could. But you were so cute, and it was so hard to stay angry with you."

"Do you still paint with chocolate?" Tal asks.

"Yes. But I only do body painting now. Wanna be my canvas, sweetie?"

"Ah, no. I don't think so."

"Coward," Ella says.

"What did Ari do for fun?" Davin asks.

"Well, I wouldn't call it fun, because she was really serious about it, but one day—when she was about five—she decided to play doctor with the family puppy. I heard a pathetic whimpering sound coming from Ari's room, so I opened the door, and the poor little puppy was running around in circles—frantically snapping at her rear end. It seemed that Ari had tried to take the creature's temperature, with a rather plump electronic thermometer. I removed the device and looked at Ari. I was about to scold her, but before I could speak, Ari looked at me with doleful eyes and said, 'Princess doesn't like her temperature taken.' I laughed so hard that I began to cough. Ari looked at me with concern in her eyes and said, 'You sound sick, Lana. We should take your temperature, too.'"

Lana rolls her head back and laughs out loud. "From that moment on, whenever I was around Ari, I tried really hard to never turn my back on her!"

We all laugh until we cry. There isn't a dry eye in the room.

Tal stands up. "I think a round of brandy is in order."

"Excellent idea," Davin says.

As the brandy flows, the conversation turns serious. Davin, Tal, and Seto theorize about the tactics they think the Zon will employ. Lana and Ella seem to agree that the Zon will fail because their position on Earth is built on treachery and deception. But it's Reyna who startles me with her clarity.

"The Zon have one advantage that will prove difficult to deal with," she says.

"What is that?" Tal asks.

"They will have several billion innocent hostages."

The air suddenly feels thick, as I ponder the enormity of the task we face. It's not as simple as finding and destroying the Fallen. That's a very achievable goal. Keeping humans out of harm's way is another matter entirely.

Tal stands and stretches. "We are being picked up at first light. I think we should get some rest. And please, do not worry. We will devise a good strategy. We will not fail."

"I'm sorry," Reyna says. "I didn't mean to be negative. Casualties will be inevitable. But we *will* prevail. I know we will."

"She's right," Ella says. "If there's one thing I know about humans, it's that they don't go down without a fight. We just need to make them see who the enemy really is and then we turn several billion hostages into several billion angry allies."

"I hope you're right," I say.

"I know I'm right," Ella replies, as she and Tal head toward the bedroom wing.

I think each of us is a little apprehensive. Trouble is brewing and, except for Dad and Lana, no one really knows the whole story. No one.

Chapter 28

Davin and I stand on the beach, as the transport carrying our friends accelerates away with a whoosh.

"How do you feel?" he asks.

"After two nights in the sanctuary, it feels good to be in the open air."

"When my parents designed it, aesthetics were not a consideration."

"Clearly. But it did serve its purpose. We should thank your parents. Do you think they know we are committed?"

"I'm not sure."

"There is no way to communicate with them?"

Davin shakes his head.

"That's too bad. I'm sure if they knew…" I pause, unsure of what to say. I don't want to make him sad or uncomfortable.

"Their last visit was forty-five years ago."

"Oh."

Before I can say more, Lana emerges from the house with a tray of beverages and pastries.

One of the things I love about Davin is that when there is something on his mind, he usually doesn't mess around. The instant Lana takes a seat at the table, he gets straight to the point.

"Tell me about Cylar."

It's not a question.

"There is a bit of a backstory to this. May I…?"

"By all means," Davin says.

Lana shifts in her seat, sitting upright and facing Davin. "As you know, the fallen Warriors who survived the rebellion went into hiding—with their children."

Davin nods.

"In the confusion, one child became separated from his parents—"

"Let me guess," Davin says. "Cylar?"

Lana nods. "His mother was killed in the rebellion, but his father—Seth—survived. Before Seth escaped to Earth, he found Cylar and they established a relationship."

Davin winces. "Cylar then became a conduit between Olympus and the Fallen?"

"Yes. As a Sage, Cylar was able to travel freely between Olympus and Earth. He was a spy."

"But he wasn't actually Fallen." Davin says.

Lana nods. "Seth was able to manipulate Cylar into doing his bidding. He was a fool, but he never truly renounced Paradise."

"How do you know all this?" I ask.

"Dad is very resourceful. Not much gets past him. He discovered the connection while visiting Earth."

"How did he manage to travel to Earth without the Olympians knowing it? You can't just walk through a portal anonymously."

"Dad did not use the portal. He traveled from Paradise," she says.

"Silly me," I reply. "How does one travel from Paradise?"

"Typically, you go when you are summoned. A portal appears, a messenger beckons, and you enter. Dad has special privileges, though. He can come and go as he pleases."

"Interesting," I say. "So, are there more spies on Olympus?"

"Not that we know of."

"So, you were monitoring Cylar's actions?" Davin asks.

"I was stalking him."

"And he was stalking Ari and me?"

"Yes."

"And everyone came together on Corbal." Davin takes a deep breath. "Why do the rebels want us dead, Lana?"

"Because they are afraid of you."

"Why? Why are they afraid of us?"

"Because of who you are and what you represent."

"Can you just spit it out?" I ask.

"Ari, Dad is not like other angels. We are not like other angels. And we can add Davin to the list, now that you're committed."

"Excuse me?"

"We are…" She pauses, as if searching for the right words. "Royalty. We are the Royal family."

"What does that mean?" I ask.

"Our grandparents rule Paradise."

"They are gods?"

I steal a glance at Davin. He's taking it all in, but he looks a little incredulous.

"Yes. But it's complicated Ari. And it's best if we let them explain it to you."

"And when will I be meeting them?"

"Soon."

"Peachy," I say. "So are we all related? Davin and I aren't cousins. Are we?"

Lana chuckles. "No, Tink. Our grandparents had two children. Our mothers were not related to Dad."

"So who was the other child?"

"Dad had a sister. Her name was Chari."

"Was?"

"Before the mortal worlds were created, there was a coup. Our family was attacked. Chari was killed."

"She wasn't invincible?"

"She was young and not very experienced. She was not able to defend herself. After she died, Grandmother decided to keep her soul hidden."

"Where is her soul now?"

"I don't know."

"This is really weird, Lana," Davin says.

"Tell me about it," Lana says with an eye roll.

"If our grandparents only had two children, where did the other angels come from?"

"Paradise is a planetary system. The outer planets were seeded with life, much as Olympus and Earth were. The other angels evolved."

"Do our grandparents have names?"

"Calypso and Rafaíl."

"So Davin and I are like you and Dad?"

Lana smiles, wryly. "Dad and I are the same. You and Davin are something entirely different."

"Meaning...?"

"You are more like our grandparents."

"We are like gods?"

She clears her throat. "Yes."

"Um, uppercase or lowercase 'G'?"

"It's a matter of opinion, I guess."

"A matter of opinion? Really? Lana, there is more to this. Isn't there?"

"Yes, but I really can't tell you. Actually, there's a lot I don't even know. Our grandparents will tell you. Soon."

"Um, are Davin and I taking a trip to Paradise?"

"That is the plan. Yes."

"Have you been there?"

"I have. Once. And please don't ask me to describe it because the words do not exist. It is perfection, and it's simply indescribable. That's all I can say."

Oh boy. How does one even prepare for something like that? I turn toward Davin. He shrugs.

"So you altered your DNA records to hide what you are?"

Lana purses her lips. She is considering an answer.

"I did."

"That was pretty sneaky. I'm surprised at you."

She gives me an innocent smile, causing me to roll my eyes.

Davin sits up straight. "Tell us what you know about the rebellion, Lana. Are there things you can add to the official record? Things the Elders did not disclose to us?"

"There are. The rebellion would have been suppressed had the Serafeím helped. Had they not fallen. My father tried really hard to control them, but he couldn't."

"What do you mean?" I ask.

"Dad stood alone in challenging the rebel Warriors. The Serafeím disobeyed Dad, they refused to help, which caused more Warriors to rebel. Things got out of hand."

"Your mother was a rebel," I say softly, stating what I already know to be true.

"Yes. When she couldn't convince Dad to join her cause, she became furious. She tried to kill me. Dad—"

"He killed her. To save you. I'm so sorry, Lana."

301

"Thank you. But I was a baby. I never really knew her. As I grew older, I hurt only for Dad. Never for myself."

She has tears in her eyes. I feel bad for her. "Why did she rebel?"

"She did not want me. According to Dad, she felt that I was forced upon her, that she should have been given a choice. She just couldn't deal with it."

"Why did you allow everyone to believe you were orphaned?" I ask.

"Dad thought I would be safer if no one knew I was his daughter. If the Fallen knew who I really was, they could have used me as bait."

"Even though you're more powerful than other angels?"

"There are ways to suppress our strength. It's not easy, but it can be done."

"How?" Davin asks.

"Argolinos."

"What's that, Lana?" I ask.

"A very rare Olympian mineral."

"Explain," Davin says.

"If you place us in a space sealed with ground argolinos, we cannot absorb the Essence. We are rendered powerless."

"Kryptonite," I mutter.

"Precisely," Lana says. "The Fallen have been stockpiling the mineral on Earth for centuries."

"Cylar?" Davin asks.

"Yes, over the years, he managed to smuggle a large quantity of argolinos to Earth," Lana says. "The Fallen have several containment units scattered around the Earth."

"Angel prisons?" I ask.

"Yes."

"The angels we've lost over the ages. They are in these prisons?" Davin asks.

"I'm afraid not. Captured angels are held until they become weak enough to be killed."

"How many angels have been lost?" I ask.

"Twenty-eight," Davin replies without hesitation. He is angry. He didn't know about this.

"So, if we are put inside one of these units…" I pause.

"There is no escape, unless you are rescued from the outside," Lana finishes.

A shiver runs down my spine.

"Okay," Davin says, "let's change the subject. We can get back to this later. Why did the Serafeím fall?"

"After my mother died, the remaining Warrior rebels escaped. My father tried to stop them, but there were too many. He gathered the Serafeím and ordered them to go after the rebels. They refused."

"Why?"

"My mother was Serafeím. When my father killed her, the others accused him of treachery."

"That's horrible," I say. "Dad had no choice."

"True," Lana agrees. "And the others paid for disobeying him. They paid dearly."

"What happened?" Davin asks.

"A messenger was sent from Paradise to meet with the Serafeím. She informed them that their behavior had been offensive. They were given a choice…repent or be punished."

"And they did not repent?" I ask.

"No. They were banned from Paradise and bound to the mortal world for one million years. And then, right in front of everyone, the messenger announced that Dad would be rewarded for his valor, his loyalty, and his sacrifice."

"Ooh. That must have been really awkward. What was the reward?" I ask.

"He was promised a true love…and you, Tink."

"Um, can you elaborate, please?" I ask.

"Of course. The messenger said that Dad would find a true love, a soul mate. Their union would produce an extraordinary daughter who would grow into a powerful angel, the most powerful angel of all. And when she came of age, she would find a soul mate of her own, bind with him, and change him. With honor and grace, they would shine as brightly as a star, vanquishing evil, and presiding over all angels."

"So, Davin and I are parts of the promise?"

"Yes," she says. "The most important parts."

I'm not sure how I feel about this.

"So we had no choice in the matter? We were destined to fall in love?"

"Tink, that's not the way things work. You chose to fall in love with Davin. And once you did, you were destined to transform him. Do you understand?"

I sigh. I'm still getting used to what I am, and sometimes things feel a little out of control. "I guess so. Did the messenger say anything else?"

"No. She left."

"How did the Serafeím react?" I ask.

"They accused Dad of treachery, and then they left."

I sigh and blow out a deep breath.

"Where did the Serafeím go?" Davin asks. "When they stormed the portal, we were completely unprepared."

"They built an enclave on an island called Melori. As time passed, their bitterness grew. They sought out and organized the fallen Warriors and the Zon. When the first Earth portal was opened, the Serafeím orchestrated an assault. A fierce battle ensued, and many escaped."

"I know," Davin says. "I was there."

"You were there?" I ask, with a gasp.

"Yes."

"But the Elders were already gone. Right?"

"Correct."

"Let me get this straight. There are aspects of the rebellion that you never knew about. Why weren't you told everything?"

Lana clears her throat and answers. "The Elders were under orders, from Paradise, to be as discreet as possible. The children were to know only enough to be able to defend Olympus."

"That's crazy," I say. "If there was full disclosure, the children could have hunted the rebels before the portal was built. And we wouldn't be in this mess."

"Calm down, Tink," Lana says. "We can't change the past, and getting angry will not change anything."

I shake my head and sigh. "You really didn't know, Davin? You didn't know where the Fallen were hiding?"

"No. During that era, Olympian technology was not very advanced. Think of Earth during the early twentieth century. We did not have scanners, nor did we have transports. Searching was tedious and slow."

"The battle must have been terrifying," I say. "Were there many casualties on our side?"

"No. It was a rout. The problem was timing. Before we could mount a counterattack, many had already escaped."

A chill makes me shudder as I try to imagine how horrible it must have been.

"The million years should be up," I say. "I assume the Serafeím have not repented?"

"It was up twenty-two years ago. Dad went to Earth and met with Janus, the rebel leader. Janus was unrepentant. He mocked Dad, calling him a fool, and telling him that Paradise had abandoned him."

"Sounds like a nice fella. How did Dad react?"

"Dad told Janus that he would never lose faith and that the reward he was promised would come to pass. That very night, he met your mother. Four years later, you were born, Tink."

"Does Janus know about me?"

"Yes, and apparently it's driving him crazy. He harbors much ill will toward our family."

"Why?"

"Dad and Janus were once close friends. Janus was in love with Chari. When she was killed, Janus needed someone to blame. So he blamed Dad."

"What kind of angel is Janus?" Davin asks.

"Prostáti."

"What about my mom and Ella?" I ask. "What kind of angels are they?"

"I'm not entirely sure. I suspect they are very powerful. Dad will be able to provide an explanation."

"So, Davin and I are more powerful than you and Dad, and that's why Cylar tried to kill us?"

"Cylar tried to kill you before you changed Davin, because, together, your power is…well, it's immeasurable. And it changes *everything*."

"If Davin and I are so powerful, why don't the Fallen give up?" I ask.

"The hubris that caused them to rebel will not die easily," Lana says. "Reyna was correct. The Fallen believe that we will not want to put humans in harm's way."

"But we can't do that, Lana! Millions could be killed."

"Some will die, but there is no other way. The Fallen cannot be allowed to enslave the Earth. We will do everything we can to minimize casualties."

"Lana, why can't Paradise simply end this? Why can't our godly grandparents end this?" I ask in exasperation.

She leans on the table and locks eyes with me. "Paradise places a great deal of importance on free will. We all have choices to make. We always do."

Davin gazes intently at Lana. "And that's why you allowed your best friend to be used by Cylar. You made a choice. But why not just kill him? Why did you use Reyna?"

"Cylar had to be eliminated, but I couldn't just murder him. And I did want to see if he would reveal more information."

"Hmm," Davin says. "What was your plan?"

"As soon as Ari arrived on Olympus, Reyna began to act strangely. It did not take me long to realize that Cylar was drugging her. He wanted you dead…"

"Both of us?" Davin asks.

"Ideally, yes. But he did not want to be implicated. Instead, he would induce Reyna to murder you—in a fit of jealous rage. I told Reyna what was happening, and she agreed to play along."

"She was really under his control?" I ask.

"Yes, but not to the extent that Cylar believed. Reyna allowed me to give her a second drug, which minimized the effect of the drug Cylar gave her. And, as a precaution, we disabled the two core disruptors Cylar had given her. When Reyna failed to kill you, we knew Cylar would tip his hand, giving me a legitimate reason to kill him."

"But you almost got Davin killed," I say with a hint of annoyance in my voice.

"We had no idea Cylar was armed. The weapons are ancient—and very hard to acquire. No one was supposed to get hurt—except Cylar, of course."

"I see. But in order to change Davin, didn't I have to heal him? Was he destined to get hurt?"

"No," Lana says. "Once you were bound, the transformation became inevitable. It would have occurred gradually, triggered by your closeness."

"Healing me caused the change to happen instantly?" Davin asks.

"Yes," Lana answers.

"Can she change anyone?"

"We're not sure. We think it requires a strong emotional bond. And now that she's changed you, it is highly probable that you have the same ability."

Davin suddenly tenses. "If the Fallen think that we can transform others…"

"I know, Davin. Believe me, I know. But you still do not understand how powerful you both are. They do not have the strength to force either of you to do anything against your will."

"But they might be able to compel us to bend to their will. Coercion can be a powerful weapon."

Leave it to Davin to leave no stone unturned. The Fallen are prideful, but not stupid. If they realize that they can't outmuscle us, their only recourse will be to outsmart us. Or trick us. Or blackmail us.

"We will discuss this with my father, Davin. We will design a good strategy. We will consider all contingencies."

Davin clears his throat and flashes a tight smile. "There is much to prepare for."

"It begins with our training here," Lana says. "We are counting on their pride. We are counting on goading them into battle. And then we will annihilate them."

"You are the most confident person I've ever met," I say.

"We've had this discussion before. Trust me. Once you've been coached, you will be invincible."

"Something is still bothering me," Davin says. "When your father and you left Ari, who protected her?"

"When my father was called back to Paradise, he decided that Ari and Andi needed more protection than I could provide. So four Prostáti were assigned."

"I never knew." I say.

"They are stealthy. They also are quite powerful. You could not have been safer."

"They let me approach her. Why?" Davin asks.

"They probably sensed you were not a threat," Lana replies, smiling.

"They should have at least questioned me," Davin says, with a hint of sarcasm.

"They are extremely intuitive," Lana says.

Davin moans and rubs his temples briskly.

In a little over three months, I've gone from a high school senior to an angel—an angel who can shine as brightly as a star. Literally? Metaphorically? I am afraid to ask.

"So, what are you going to teach us, big sister?"

"Many things."

"For instance?"

"You will learn to fly."

"You'll teach us to fly?" I ask, unable to hide my excitement.

"Mm-hmm."

"I didn't know you could fly," Davin says.

"Would you like a demonstration?"

Davin grins. "That would be nice."

Lana moves several yards away and stands with her arms at her sides, her head slightly bowed, and her eyes focused on the horizon. A small smile spreads across her lips and she shoots straight up, like a Saturn rocket.

She has to be traveling hundreds of miles per hour. I crane my neck as I track her, squinting into the sun. She rotates her arms in a small arc, and suddenly she's flying parallel to the sea, looking less like my sister and more like a sleek fighter jet. The loops, rolls, and dives that she performs are absurdly cool.

I gasp. "She can really fly."

Davin's eyes are glued to her. "I'm going to enjoy training."

"Me, too. How fast do you think she's going?"

"Impossibly fast, Ari. It's astonishing."

"Davin?"

He doesn't answer. He looks like a little boy dreaming of a new toy.

"Davin, you're awestruck, and it's so terribly cute."

"I've always wanted to fly," he says, as he wraps an arm around my waist.

"Me, too."

"She's magnificent…"

"Shh. She's landing. Let's watch," I say.

I can do some pretty amazing things. I can run like a jaguar, jump like a kangaroo on steroids, sprint up vertical walls, and project lethal bursts of energy. But seeing my sister soar through the air, like a peregrine falcon, is the single most humbling experience I've ever had.

Epilogue

After our *briefing*, Lana goes inside to shower, leaving Davin and me alone in the courtyard. "I'm not very tired. How about a walk along the beach?" I ask.

"That's a wonderful idea."

Moonlight strolls are always romantic, but a stroll under two moons borders on the mystical. Together, they cast a soft amber glow over the beach. The effect is otherworldly, relatively speaking.

"You look very handsome in the moonlight, Davin."

He places his hand on my arm, and I turn to face him. "And with each passing day your beauty grows, as befits the goddess who will preside over all angels."

"Um, it is *we* who will preside. We're in this together, pal. And if I'm a goddess, then you are a god."

"I don't feel like a god. I'm not really sure I would want to."

"I guess we'll find out when we meet my grandparents. Do you feel like Lana was holding something back?"

"At first, I did. But I have a funny feeling there are some things she may not fully understand."

"I guess we'll find out. Eventually. In the meantime, let's just try to be ordinary angels."

"There is nothing ordinary about you."

"You're biased."

Davin laughs softly. Leaning close to me, his lips tease mine, and a tingling warmth spreads through my body. I melt into his arms.

"Mm," I say breathlessly, as my lips meet his. *My* lips do not tease. No, *my* lips are very serious.

Alone among the stars, the moons, and the sea, no words can describe the depth of our love or the connection we share. I can feel his soul as it sings to mine. If I could have only one kiss, one kiss to last until the end of time, this is the one I'd choose.

I rest my head on his chest, and his fingers lace through my hair, sending shivers down my spine.

Davin suddenly tenses. "Remain still and do not panic. Someone is approaching us."

"Friend or foe?" I whisper.

"I don't know."

Davin gently turns me so that I'm standing behind him.

A woman walks toward us. She's wearing a flowing white dress that touches the tops of her bare feet. Long golden hair blows in the breeze. Her movements are graceful, her bearing confident.

She stops several feet in front of us and smiles.

"I am Chloe," she announces in a clear and strong voice. "I bring you news from Paradise."

I'm speechless. Her eyes are deep violet and shine brightly in the moonlight. I've never seen eyes that color before. She is stunning. And she's a messenger. From Paradise.

Davin locks eyes with her. "How do we know you were not sent by the Fallen?"

"Do you think I am evil, Davin of Genobli?"

"If you are, I will know soon enough. What news do you bring?" Davin calmly asks.

Her expression is stoic and her voice even. "The Fallen have built a web of treachery and evil that will prove difficult to unravel. You will witness suffering and destruction on a scale never before seen, and your quest for victory will bring with it pain, sorrow, and despair. If you are to prevail, you must never lose sight that love is your standard and grace your sword."

"Your words trouble me, Chloe. Is this a prophecy? Is someone warning us that tragedy is inescapable?" I ask.

"I am sorry if my news disturbs you."

Davin's eyes meet mine. "It's not a prophecy. We do not even know if she was sent from Paradise. But be that as it may, we will make choices, and those choices will determine the outcome. Do you understand, my love?"

"I do. But it doesn't make me feel much better," I say.

Chloe smiles, reassuringly. "The Fallen and the humans will also have choices to make. I wish to help. I would be honored to fight by your side. Will you permit me to serve you?"

"You want to serve *me*?"

"I am an angel. And you are…"

"I am the *promise*," I say. It sounds silly.

"You and Davin are *manifestations* of the promise made to your father. You are the nemeses of the Fallen and the protectors of mankind. If you allow me to help, I will be a most valuable asset. I am Prostáti."

"Are you sure you want to serve us?"

"Yes. Serving you will help me to serve the Light."

"The Light? God?"

"They dislike that title."

"My grandparents?"

"Yes."

"Oh, well. Excuse me," I say, raising my eyes to the heavens like an idiot.

Chloe laughs.

"Four Prostáti protected my mother and me on Earth. Do you know them?"

"Yes. Lycos, Calliope, Nyx, and…me."

"Why should we trust you, Chloe?" Davin asks.

"That is a fair question," she replies. "I watched your Promise grow up. I protected her. When the Stratori called Galen tried to seduce her, I was ready to intervene. I allowed you to approach her. I was there when you healed her at the waterfall. I…" She hesitates and looks at me with an odd expression. "I care about you both."

"Where are Lycos, Calliope, and Nyx?" Davin asks.

He seems to be mellowing out. He believes her.

"Lycos and Calliope are in Paradise. Nyx, my Promise, is with Damian."

"You allowed me to help Ari when she was attacked by the human boy Luke?"

"I did. But I would have stepped in if necessary. Your reputation extends a lot farther than you know, Davin. We knew you would never harm her."

Davin blushes and I smile.

"And you were with us when she injured her leg?"

"Yes. If you were not so smitten, you might have been able to prevent her from falling into the water. I was angry."

Davin looks flummoxed. "I…" he sputters.

"Wait," I say. "You were smitten with me?"

Davin rolls his eyes.

"You did a wonderful job healing her," Chloe says. "But then when she kissed you, and you embarrassed her, I came very close to throttling you."

"Yeah, so did I," I mutter.

Davin cringes. "I needed to protect her, Chloe. If I allowed myself to be distracted…"

"Your souls had already connected. You had already chosen to accept the connection…to care for her. To love her. You could have been kinder, Davin." Chloe's face softens and she continues, "But you have more than made up for that transgression."

Davin gazes at her for a moment with a look of bewilderment, which slowly turns into a warm smile. "True. I will be forever in your debt for all you've done to keep Ari safe."

That's my Warrior.

"Chloe, come with us to the house. You must be hungry," I say.

"You will have me join you, then?"

I look at Davin and he nods.

"Welcome to the team," I say.

"Thank you," Chloe replies, giving me a slight bow.

As we walk to the house, I pray for strength, wisdom, and a miracle or two.

Lana is sitting in the kitchen. Any doubts about Chloe are dispelled as Lana stands and pulls her into a hug. Apparently, they are acquainted.

"I assume you have met before?" I ask.

"Chloe was your guardian, Tink. She did not leave your side from the time you were eight until you began your training on Olympus."

"I heard. She was my hidden angel, huh?"

"Prostáti can cloak themselves," Lana says. "They can become invisible."

"I know," I reply.

"Ari," Chloe says, "I can teach you and Davin how to cloak yourselves. Would you like to learn?"

"Maybe you could teach just me," I say. "Then I can sneak up on Davin and…"

Davin clears his throat. "She can teach both of us or neither of us."

I look at Davin and chuckle. "Yes, Chloe, we would be honored if you could teach us. Both of us."

"I would love to," Chloe says.

"Well, it's been a long day," I say, yawning. "If you don't mind, I am going to bed."

"Excellent idea," Davin agrees.

Davin and I bid the ladies goodnight, leaving them to catch up on old times.

Davin closes the bedroom door, wraps his arms around me, and pulls me close. "How do you feel?"

"Fine…until I think about Chloe's news. Then I feel distressed, apprehensive, frightened, and really angry. People aren't going to know what hit them. They may not even know who is on their side. Some may even think the apocalypse has come."

"We will not let that happen, Ari."

"But we don't know, Davin. We just don't know."

"We should defer judgment until we've completed training, met with your father, and established our strategy."

Suffering and destruction on a scale never before seen. The words resonate in my mind.

"I suppose. But could Chloe's tidings have been any worse? Davin, I…"

My eyes well up with tears and I begin to tremble.

He places his hands on my shoulders. "Whatever happens, I will be at your side. Always. We are partners. You will not face this alone."

"I know," I say, as tears begin to fall. "But…"

And then I'm hit with a tsunami of sadness, and I sob quietly, grieving for the souls I won't be able to save, knowing that once the battle begins, there will be no time for tears. No time for grieving.

Davin holds me close, letting me cry it out.

"Are you alright, Ari?" he asks, softly.

"Yes, I'm better. I had to get that out. The human part of me needs to cry sometimes. It's therapeutic."

"We're going to prevail, Love."

"I know, Darling."

"Are you very tired?" he asks.

"I can call up my energy reserves if the right opportunity presents itself. Did you have something in mind?"

He picks me up and carries me to our bed. "Well…there are other therapies that can be beneficial in times such as these."

"True," I say, as he lays me gently on the bed. "Very true."

The End of Book 1

Coming soon: Ariel Between Two Worlds, Episode 2: The Battle for Earth (sample chapter follows)

Sneak Peek
Book Two: The Battle for Earth
[PROLOGUE]

Standing barefoot in the surf, she stares out to sea. It's so beautiful. The kind of place normal people dream about. Under different circumstances, it might seem like Paradise. Instead, it's worse than hell.

In the distance, she can barely make out the speedboat as it darts toward Guam, forty miles away. "Goodbye Janus," she whispers. "Thank you so much for stealing my innocence, for making me understand there are things in this world worse than death."

Shoulders slumped, she turns slowly and walks along the beach. No one will come looking. The other angels are not a threat because she belongs to Janus—and Janus does not share his toys. "Angels," she muses to herself. They're not the lovely, protective creatures depicted in myth and literature. They're not very *angelic* at all. They're going to rule the world. That's what Janus said. They would fix things. Make things right. She believed him, too. Right up until the first time he raped her.

Turning left, she follows the steep slope up to the bluffs. Last year, she'd have been struggling for breath. But the angels made sure that their girls were in top condition. She had both a personal trainer and a stylist. If she could escape, she might be able to land a job as a model. She was *that* fit.

Reaching the crest of the hill, she pauses and gazes down at the surf, a hundred feet below. To her right, a dense patch of tropical vegetation covers the cave entrance—a hole in the ground, which she discovered several months ago, by falling into it. Fortunately, her injuries were not serious. Janus did not know.

The cave is her private place. A place where she dreams up elaborate escape plans. Plans that can never possibly work. But she does have one plan that *will* work.

Lowering herself through the opening, she drops to the cave floor and heads downhill, walking through a narrow corridor, inside a large rock formation that extends a hundred feet out into the ocean. At the end of the corridor is a large circular cavern with an opening to the sea along its far wall. During low tide, the opening is just a few feet above the water. At high tide, the cave is totally flooded.

Easing herself down, she sits against the hard, damp wall. Within an hour, the cave will begin to fill. She just has to sit there. The sea will do all the work, drawing her out and battering her against the sharp rocks below. She will not fight it. Death is her only hope for freedom. That is her plan. She closes her eyes, sighs, and waits.

Unseen and unheard, Calliope and Lycos fly low, circling the island, less than a hundred feet above the ground. They are Prostáti—the rarest and most deadly of all angels.

"Janus is not here," Lycos says, disappointment flavoring his voice.

"We knew he wouldn't be. Our mission will still succeed," Calliope answers. "Four of his most trusted generals are here. When we destroy them, Janus will have no choice but to regroup. It will set his plans back by months, giving Damian, Lana, and Chloe more time to prepare, more time to train Ariel and Davin."

"I would rather kill him now."

She sighed. "So would I. But you know we cannot."

"What of the humans, Callie? What will we do with them?"

The two angels counted twelve humans. Eleven are in the main house. The twelfth is near the beach, inside a cave, probably hiding.

"Let us deal with the Fallen first. Then we will assess the humans and determine our next step. Do you agree?"

"Yes. To the main house, then. After you, my love," he says with a grin.

Janus's four generals will not stand a chance.

The four fallen Serafeím—the generals—are gathered on a large terrace, overlooking the sea. Oblivious to the two invisible Prostáti approaching them, they sip drinks and chat.

Calliope and Lycos land on the terrace in complete silence, unsheathing their swords as they became visible.

Four chairs, and as many cocktails, go flying, as the generals leap to their feet, staggering backward.

"Surprise you?" Calliope asks calmly.

The generals are slack-jawed and speechless.

Lycos grins, waving his sword in greeting, as he points to each general. "Soros, Forin, Strok, and Belorik. We are pleased to see you."

The generals eye each other, looks of panic and confusion on their faces. Soros speaks. "I assume you are Prostáti?"

Lycos smiles at Calliope, then locks eyes with Soros. "Well, we're not leprechauns."

"Why are you here?" Soros demands.

"To kill you," Calliope says with a steely confidence.

"Serafeím were created to rule all angels. Including *you*," Belorik says.

"Then why do you not rule Janus? Why does he rule *you*, Serafeím?" Lycos asks with a smirk.

"Because he is one of us, idiot!" Belorik roars.

"Wrong," Calliope says.

Belorik shakes with rage, pointing a trembling finger toward Calliope. A pulse of energy pours into her torso, quickly dissipating with a loud pop.

She glares at him. "You cannot kill me, imbecile."

Calliope's sword moves impossibly fast, cutting cleanly through bone and cartilage as if through butter. Belorik's head tumbles from his shoulders, hitting the tile floor with a wet thwack.

She sighs and wipes the blade across the general's headless torso before sheathing it and turning to face Lycos. "Not the brightest star in the sky, was he?"

"Clearly not."

Calliope glares at Soros. "We sensed eleven humans in the house. Now there is only one. Why is that?"

"They are dead." Soros spits the words out as if he is describing vermin.

Forin cringes. "You did not have to kill them, Soros. They were children and they posed no threat to us or to our plans."

"They were pretty little monkeys, eh? I will get you another. Do not worry, my friend."

Calliope loses it. "You dreadful, despicable lump of excrement..."

Soros smirks and lunges at Calliope. "I will squash you like an insect..."

They are the last words he will ever speak. Calliope's sword moves faster than the general's brain can register, taking his head cleanly off. It lay on the terrace floor, smiling up at them.

"Impressive," Forin says, calmly. "What do you want from us."

Calliope walks closer and the two generals can smell her sweet breath as she whispers to Forin. "I want to know if you helped to kill the children. I will know if you lie to me."

"We did not know," Forin answers. "Soros and Belorik were...*deranged*."

Calliope grunts and backs up. "Where is Janus and what are his plans?"

"How will you kill us?" Strok asks.

Lycos points his sword at the bodies of the dead generals. "You understand that when you are killed with a Prostáti's sword, your soul is forfeit?"

"I do," Forin says.

"Tell us what you know," Calliope says, "and we will allow you to keep your souls. If not, you will taste my blade, and all that you are will cease to be. The choice is yours. And be forewarned. We *will* know if you lie."

Forin speaks first. "There are four trigger points: Beijing, Washington, Paris, and Damascus. We were to travel tomorrow. Janus is on his way to Beijing, where Soros would have met him."

"What do you mean by trigger points?" Lycos asks.

"We were to address regional government officials at each location," Forin explains. "Officials we have been *cultivating* for quite some time."

"Please get to the point," Calliope commands.

Strok takes the floor. "It's fairly simple. Beijing has been led to believe that the Americans and the Europeans are ready to institute excessive tariffs, which will undermine China's trade surplus. The Chinese will retaliate by launching a series of massive cyber-attacks. American and European intelligence operatives will *discover* the impending attacks, countering with a salvo of cruise missiles, dozens of them, designed to emit microwave bursts. As the missiles fly over major cities, they will generate electromagnetic pulses of sufficient magnitude to disable all electronic devices."

"Lights out?" Lycos mutters.

"Completely," Strok affirms. "Japan and South Korea will align with the Americans and Europeans, while Russia, Pakistan, and India will align with China. The entire civilized world will go dark within six days. Power grids will fail. Society will shut down."

"What about the Middle East?" Lycos asks.

"Utter devastation," Forin replies. "Syria and Iran will discover that Israel is planning a nuclear strike on Tehran. The Israelis will believe that Iran is planning a nuclear strike on Tel Aviv. The Middle East will be reduced to ashes."

"And when chaos reigns, the Fallen will strike?" Lycos asks.

"Yes," Forin replies.

"Is the Middle East the only region where nuclear weapons will be used?" Calliope asks.

"Yes," Forin answers. "Janus plans to use Los Angeles as his seat of power. It is essential that we keep North America from going toxic. We have been working with several human scientists to ensure that the fallout is contained."

"And can these plans go forward without you?" Calliope asks.

"Not according to the current schedule. Our teams need to be in place to coordinate the flow of false intelligence and the timing of each attack. Janus will need to replace us. The replacements will then need to establish the proper relationships. It will take a few months," Forin says.

"Interesting," Lycos comments. "While we have focused on protecting heads of state, you have been working with lower-level officials, whose leaders are clueless. Tell us more. Tell us everything."

And Florin and Strok do. They sing like birds.

"Janus is not Serafeím, is he?" Forin asks.

Calliope shakes her head. "He is Prostáti."

"I had my suspicions. Then you cannot stop him?"

"Oh, we could. But it is not our role."

Forin sighs deeply. "The prophecy? Damian's daughter?"

Calliope nods. "She and her Promise have a destiny. Janus is but a part of it, but yes…she will destroy him."

"When we first rebelled," Forin says, "I thought our cause was righteous. Once I realized how evil Janus was, I tried to reason with him."

"And how did he react?" Calliope asks.

"He tortured me. His Sages fashioned a collar, gilded with argosinio. It suppressed the absorption of the Essence. The first time…" Forin pauses and shudders, visibly. "He threw me in a cell and sliced off my arms and legs. Then he shared just enough energy with me to prevent me from bleeding out. And then he left me alone and isolated. I couldn't move. I lay on the ground, marinating in my own filth. The collar allowed me to absorb a small amount of energy. Enough so that I could heal. But it took months. I was broken. Lost."

"But you did not pray for forgiveness. Obviously, you recovered. But you continued to follow Janus."

"My parents were killed in the rebellion. So were Strok's. We were raised by Janus, and knew nothing of Paradise, except that they had abandoned us."

"Paradise abandons no one," Calliope says. "You must pay for your crimes, but your soul can still be redeemed."

"How?" Strok asks.

"Telling us about Janus's plans was a start. Look inside your hearts. The answers you both seek are there."

Forin gazes at Strok and nods, slowly. "We will try."

"In your opinion, is Janus rational enough to pull this off?" Lycos asks.

"He is obsessed, but rational. However, when he finds out we have been eliminated, that could change."

"Thank you," Lycos says. "Are you ready to die?"

Strok closes his eyes and nods.

"I am ready," Forin says with a slight bow of his head.

Beams of pure energy shoot from Calliope's hands into the heads of the two generals. It is the least painful, most merciful way to dispatch them. Once they are dead, Lycos incinerates the four bodies, turning them to fine white ash.

Calliope turns to Lycos. "If Janus acts rationally we will be able to stop him. But if he doesn't…"

Lycos nods slowly. "He has no idea what Ariel and Davin are capable of. He will not know that his generals betrayed his plan. If he acts impulsively, he will fail. He will take the time to ensure that his strategies are properly implemented. He has not come this far to allow emotion to dictate his actions."

"I sense a human," Lycos says, as he opens the glass doors that lead into the house.

A young girl emerges, looking utterly defeated. "You killed them?" she asks in a trembling voice.

"We did," Lycos says.

"They hurt us. They…"

"They will not hurt anyone again," Calliope says.

"Who are you?"

"I am Calliope and this is Lycos."

"I'm Sandy," the girl says. "You are angels? Good angels?"

"We are good angels," Calliope says with a warm smile. "You are safe now."

Sandy begins to sob. "They're all dead."

"The other girls?" Calliope asks.

"Yes."

"I am sorry we could not save the others," Calliope says. "How did you escape?"

"I hid outside. I'm sure that Soros would have found me eventually."

"There is someone hiding in a cave near the beach. Do you know who that might be?" Lycos asks.

Sandy gasps. "My God. Grace. Her angel left a few hours ago. I think she's going to kill herself."

"Lycos will stay with you while I go to Grace," Calliope says.

"Hurry, please. She must be terrified."

Calliope takes off running, not wanting to frighten Sandy. Once she is clear of the house, she leaps into the air, speeding toward the beach. Fortunately, it is not very far away.

Grace is easy to find, her emotions providing a clear and precise beacon. Calliope slips through the small opening into the cave. The girl is sitting against a rock wall, submerged in water up to her hips, sobbing uncontrollably. She does not look up.

"Grace, I am here to help you."

Grace looks up, startled to see a young woman dressed in a form-fitting white jumpsuit. *Or is it a uniform? Is she a soldier?* A sword hangs at her waist, but she does not look dangerous. "Are you an angel?"

The woman nods.

"I am Calliope and I was sent to stop the bad angels."

"Did you kill them?"

"Yes, child."

"How do I know I can trust you?" Grace asks.

"You don't. But if you allow me to help you up, I think you will see that I am trustworthy."

Calliope holds out her arms and smiles a smile that seems to show through to her soul. Grace reaches up, grasping the angel's hands, and is immediately overwhelmed by a sense of peace. Complete and utter peace. She allows Calliope to pull her into an embrace and it's the most wonderful thing she's ever felt.

"You are safe, child."

Grace shudders. "The other girls, did you save them?"

Calliope's heart sinks. "Only you and Sandy survive. I am sorry, but we were too late to save the others."

"They were my friends."

Calliope holds her tightly, protectively. "Sometimes bad things happen to good people. It is the price we pay for free will."

"Will you kill all of the bad angels?"

"Paradise has declared war on the fallen angels."

"I want to help. I want to fight with you."

Calliope smiles inwardly. "That is quite brave of you. How old are you, Grace?"

"Sixteen."

"You are a very beautiful young woman."

"Thank you. You're pretty beautiful, too."

Calliope grins. Even in her current disheveled state, the girl is quite lovely. Her golden hair and deep blue eyes are striking. She can see why Janus pursued her. "Are your parents alive?"

"I'm an orphan. I was living with a foster family. They hurt me, and so I ran away. That's when Janus found me. I thought he was…"

Grace's voice breaks and she sobs.

"You have no family then?"

"No one."

"Then I shall see to it that you are properly cared for. I can take you to a place where you will be safe and loved. Would you like that?"

"Heaven?"

Calliope suppresses a smile. "Not heaven, but someplace almost as nice. We'll need to fly. Would you like to fly with me?"

"You can carry me?"

"I am very strong for my size," Calliope says with a big smile.

"I'd like that…" Grace pauses, trying to remember the angel's name. "I'm sorry, what is your name again?"

"Calliope. But now that we are friends, you may call me Callie."

"That's such a pretty name. Does it have a special meaning?"

"It does. In the language of angels, I am one who inspires. I bring out the best in people."

"That's amazing, Callie. How would you say Grace in your language?"

Calliope locks eyes with the girl. There is something about her. Something old, something beautiful, something… "In my language you would be called Chari, which was the name of a very special angel."

"What was special about her?"

"She was like a princess. And I think you are very special, too."

"You do?"

Calliope smiles.

"Yes, child. I can feel your soul. It is strong and full of love."

"I would like to go with you, Callie."

"Excellent. Let's go to the house and see how Sandy is doing. She is with my husband, Lycos."

Grace gasps. Her opinion of angels is getting better by the moment. "Your husband?"

"Mm-hmm. Actually, the term we use is Promise."

"Is he as nice as you?"

Calliope chuckles. "He is much nicer than me."

Callie is the most beautiful woman Grace has ever seen. Black hair that shimmers like raven feathers, high cheekbones, a perfect nose, full lips, a model's figure, and gosh...her eyes. They're violet. The female angels who visit the island are very pretty, but in a cold, hard way. Callie, on the other hand, radiates goodness.

"Callie, can regular people ever become angels?"

"Now that is a very interesting question."

"Do you have an interesting answer?" Grace asks with a raised brow.

Calliope likes the girl. She has spirit. And she is smart, too. "It has happened twice."

Grace's eyes light up and she smiles. "So it can happen!"

Can it happen again? "It is very rare, and the circumstances were extraordinary. Let's take things one step at a time. All I can promise right now is that you will be safe and cared for. Okay?"

"Okay. Deal," Grace says. She won't allow herself to be sad any longer. And if she is going to be around Callie and the good angels, she will do everything in her power to become one of them. She's a survivor. And now she has a goal. A big one. "Are we going to fly to the house?"

"Hmm. It's not too far, and it is such a lovely day, and I so love the feel of the warm sand between my toes. Besides, I'd like to tell you a story, about a girl from Virginia. It's a really amazing story."

Calliope stands, arm in arm with Lycos, as Grace gawks. Calliope throws back her head and laughs. "Are you okay, Grace?"

Grace can't take her eyes off the angel couple. They're so gorgeous. "Huh?" Grace mumbles.

"It's alright, child. He has that effect on female angels, too."

Grace's face erupts in a wicked hot blush. "Oh, no. I mean, yes, he is very handsome. I just think you are both totally awesome. Please, I wasn't…"

"Grace, I am so glad you are safe," Sandy says, as she gathers her young friend in a big hug.

"Thanks," Grace whispers into Sandy's ear. "And thanks for saving me from making a complete fool of myself."

Sandy nods. "Did you hear about the other girls?"

"Callie told me. How were they…"

"Soros burned them, Grace. I'll never forget their screams, the smell, their expressions. Nothing is left of them except…ashes. They begged for mercy and Soros mocked them. The bastard mocked them!"

Grace cringes. Nothing can change what happened. Nothing can bring their friends back. "We're free now. You can go home."

"I know. Lycos is taking me. But I'm scared. My parents will never understand. They'll never believe me. They might even have me committed."

Sandy begins to cry and Lycos puts a protective arm around her shoulder. "I will make sure they believe you."

"They'll think I'm crazy…that we're both crazy."

"Lycos will make them understand. Trust me," Calliope says. "We are at war, Sandy. There are no more rules. If we are to succeed, we need as many people as possible to believe in us. No more secrets. It starts with you and Grace, and then with your parents. Do you understand?"

"Yes. But it's scary. And there are so many more things I *don't* understand."

"Lycos will help you to understand what's happening."

Sandy turns to face the handsome, golden-haired, violet-eyed angel. "You're really going to fly me to Michigan? Won't I freeze to death?"

Lycos smiles. "When we fly, we are encased inside a protective field. You won't be cold and it will be impossible for you to fall."

"Grace, where will you go?" Sandy asks.

"Callie is taking me to a safe place. I'm not sure…" She pauses and looks at Calliope. "Where are we going?"

Calliope smiles demurely. "Virginia. There is an angel base there."

Sandy looks a little surprised. "Are you sure, Grace? You're welcome to come home with me."

"I want to learn as much as I can. I want to help the good angels. I want to help us win," Grace says with a determination that makes Calliope and Lycos smile.

"We will," Lycos replies. "The Fallen will take months to recover from this. Can you imagine the look on Janus's face when he discovers his four top generals are missing?"

"I can," Calliope says. "But I'd rather imagine the look on his face when Ariel destroys him."

"The Fallen have no idea what awaits them," Lycos says.

"But neither do the humans," she counters, as she glances at Grace and Sandy.

"You have to let me help you, Callie. You just have to," Grace says.

Lycos grasps Calliope's hand. "The battle for Earth has begun. And it seems we have new allies."

Calliope puffs out her chest with pride and locks eyes with Grace. "Indeed we do."

The two angels soar into the sky, the sun at their backs, hope spreading out before them.

Calliope's arms are firmly wrapped around Grace—one arm along her chest and the other along her hips. She doesn't need to hold her. The Essence will keep her from falling. But she wants the girl to feel safe.

"Why aren't my legs dangling, Callie?"

"Ah, you noticed. Smart girl. There is an energy field around us. You and I are suspended inside. If I let you go, you will stay exactly where you are. Do you want to try?"

"Yes!"

Calliope releases her grip around Grace and holds her arms out straight in front of her.

Grace looks up and giggles. She doesn't fall. In fact, her back is still pressed against Callie's front. "You look like Superman. This is totally cool."

"I'm glad you are not frightened, Grace. Sandy looks a little scared."

Sandy and Lycos fly beside them, close enough for Grace to see their faces. Lycos smiles at her, but Sandy's eyes are tightly shut, her lips turned down. She looks terrified. "After the year I've had, I don't think anything can ever frighten me again. You knew I was trying to kill myself?"

"Yes."

"It was not for me. I wanted to die because I didn't want to serve him anymore. I know he liked being with me. I needed to take that away from him. It was all I had."

"You were remarkably brave, child. Would you like to talk about it?"

"I think so. It's a long story. Sure you want to hear it?"

"We're friends, Grace. Friends listen. Tell me all about it."

And she does. And Calliope cries as she hasn't in so many years because it all becomes so very clear. Lycos would say she was filled with righteous anger, but it's not anger driving her. It's love. And it's the one weapon she knows the Fallen can never wield.

About the Authors

When it comes to being a husband and wife (or wife and husband) writing team, there are advantages, or *benefits*. Chief among them is that you get to practice the love scenes. *He* writes, *she* steers, and...well, it's fun. *He* is a software designer and *she* is a doctor of education. AJ and CS Sparber live in the lovely town of Hudson, Ohio, with their son, their daughter, and an Aussie shepherd named Hunter. Woof.

www.ingramcontent.com/pod-product-compliance
Lightning Source LLC
Chambersburg PA
CBHW070641180626
46817CB00006B/2200